Second Night Stand

Second Night Stand

KARELIA & FAY STETZ-WATERS

FOREVER

New York Boston

Forever
Hachette Book Group
1290 Avenue of the Americas, New York, NY 10104
read-forever.com
@readforeverpub

First Edition: May 2024

Forever is an imprint of Grand Central Publishing. The Forever name and logo are registered trademarks of Hachette Book Group, Inc.

The publisher is not responsible for websites (or their content) that are not owned by the publisher.

Forever books may be purchased in bulk for business, educational, or promotional use. For information, please contact your local bookseller or the Hachette Book Group Special Markets Department at special.markets@hbgusa.com.

Library of Congress Cataloging-in-Publication Data

Names: Stetz-Waters, Karelia, author. | Stetz-Waters, Fay, author.
Title: Second night stand / Karelia Stetz-Waters and Fay Stetz-Waters.
Description: First edition. | New York : Forever, 2024.
Identifiers: LCCN 2023040926 | ISBN 9781538756119 (trade paperback) | ISBN 9781538756126 (ebook)
Subjects: LCGFT: Romance fiction. | Lesbian fiction. | Novels.
Classification: LCC PS3619.T47875 S43 2024 | DDC 813/.6—dc23/eng/20230908
LC record available at https://lccn.loc.gov/2023040926

ISBNs: 9781538756119 (trade paperback), 9781538756126 (ebook)

Printed in the United States of America

LSC-C

Printing 1, 2024

To courageous romantics everywhere.

Second Night Stand

chapter 1

Lillian Jackson sat in the corner of the Neptune Bar wearing a suit, contemplating the monoculture of iceberg salad and the Jägermeister shot before her, and wondering where she'd gone wrong. The endorphin high of her ballet audition ebbed into the aches and pains of being a professional dancer.

"Just come with us." Lillian's cousin Kia—provider of the shot—folded her elbows on the table. "Y'all just auditioned for *The Great American Talent Show.* Celebrate! We found this dope place that plays nineties hip-hop."

We.

Kia never quite got that the dancers of the Reed-Whitmer Ballet Company respected Lillian—their ballet master, lead dancer, and choreographer—but they didn't like her. They weren't supposed to. That wasn't her role.

Across the bar, the dancers of the Reed-Whitmer Company lingered by the door, obviously hoping Lillian would stay back, but too polite (or well trained) to leave without her.

"They'll have more fun without me," Lillian said. "Let 'em have tonight."

Because tomorrow or sometime when Lillian worked up the nerve, she'd have to tell them the truth: they weren't auditioning for the show because dance companies auditioned for things. They were auditioning because the company's financial sponsors, Thomas Reed and Charles Whitmer, had taken Lillian to a rooftop restaurant in LA, praised her dancers and her leadership, then told her the company wasn't making enough money and they were shutting it down. Then Whitmer had offered a lifeline. *We could get you an audition with* The Great American Talent Show. If they won, Thomas Reed and Charles Whitmer would keep them on the books.

She should have told the dancers. She hadn't.

"Don't worry. Y'all killed it!" Kia's Afro puffs bounced with her enthusiasm. She'd gotten into the performers-only auditions by printing herself a badge that read INFLUENCER because she was the kind of person who could get in places just by telling people she belonged there. "Plus you're all dressed to go out."

To a high-end charity fundraiser. Why had Lillian changed into a white linen suit immediately after the audition? Because a Black ballerina must be *professional beyond measure*; she heard her mother's voice in the back of her mind. The rest of the all-Black Reed-Whitmer Ballet Company hadn't gotten the memo and were sporting their streetwear. Kia wore overalls made out of a recycled billboard by an all-Black artist co-op because that was Kia. Who was impressed by a suit at the Neptune? No one.

Over Kia's shoulder, Lillian caught a woman in another booth watching her over the screen of a laptop. Okay. Maybe she'd impressed one person. The woman wore a blazer too, but hers was made of some shiny material, oversized with the cuffs rolled up, layered over a zippered hoodie and, beneath that, the hint of a red tank top. Or was it her bra? An elaborate lacework tattoo decorated her chest.

Their eyes met, and the woman swept a hand through her short hair and shot Lillian the cockiest smile she had seen outside of the melodramatic musicals her uncle occasionally dragged her to.

Kia turned around to stare. Then, to make it a little more obvious, she flipped up the lenses of her round, turquoise sunglasses, which she wore indoors for no reason except she was the kind of person who could get onto the set of a TV show by printing herself a badge.

"Oh, I get it." Kia turned back around. "Send me a pin so I know where you're going to spend your one night with her."

Lillian wasn't that predictable.

No. She was exactly that predictable. And it had been a while since she'd hooked up with a woman.

"I might just go back to the hotel."

"And get all up in her." Kia looked at the woman again. "She's cute. I like her for you." She flipped her blue lenses down again. "You gonna take that shot?"

Lillian shook her head. Kia took the shot with a satisfied smack of her lips.

"Don't forget that pin," she said and ambled toward the door.

chapter 2

Lillian's gaze drifted back to the woman with the laptop. The woman glared at the screen, muttering to it as though it had personally offended her, but when she felt Lillian watching her, the woman looked up and winked. *Actually* winked, but something about her expression said, *Can you believe I winked at you?* Lillian rolled her eyes, but she offered the woman a smile in return.

The woman closed the laptop, rose, and strolled over, her wide hips swaying in tight black jeans. Closer up, the hint of red underneath her sweatshirt appeared to be a corset, revealing the kind of generous cleavage that would make Lillian a lesbian if she hadn't already been one. Lillian also thought she made out the words COMIC-CON 2015 fading from the front of the sweatshirt. It was like the woman grabbed clothes from three different closets and somehow made them look hot. And cute.

Lillian didn't usually go for cute, but the outfit and the combination of over-the-top flirtation and her obvious frustration with the work on her laptop made Lillian smile inside. *You got a lot going on, girl.*

"Not going out with your friends?" the woman asked, trailing one finger along the edge of Lillian's table.

"No."

"Couldn't resist a night at the Neptune?"

The Neptune was very resistible. The woman, less so.

"I'm going to the bar," the woman said. "You need anything?"

"I'll have what you're having," Lillian said.

"Are you sure? It could be something bizarre," the woman purred.

"I think I can handle what the Neptune's serving."

The woman leaned against the bar while she waited, facing Lillian, one foot kicked up behind her, chin dipped down. Her gaze snaked its way through the room. She pursed her lips in a hint of a kiss, then shrugged and broke into a grin that said, *Did that work on you?*

Lillian shook her head.

And then that wink.

The woman held her palms up as if to say, *How about that one?* She returned a moment later with two lavender-colored martinis.

"Does that really work on women?" Lillian accepted the drink, smiling to let the woman know she was teasing.

"What?"

"Your act." Lillian winked with half her face.

"Oh. Yeah." The woman looked down, shuffling her foot. "It does." Then she looked up, and in a voice that was all sex and power and confidence and kisses running down a lover's neck, she whispered, "Does it work on you?"

Her voice made Lillian's body tingle.

"How can you be that sexy in a Comic-Con sweatshirt?" Lillian asked.

"Comic-Con is very sexy," the woman said with mock indignation.

"It's really not." Lillian patted the table across from her.

The woman sat.

"Thanks for the drink."

Up close, Lillian saw the lacework tattoo was made up of the zeros and ones of binary code and her dark hair wasn't black but navy blue.

"You a programmer?" Lillian asked. "Are you working?"

The woman glanced back at her laptop.

"I'm making an app that's supposed to mix your face with the faces of American presidents. It's for kids, but how is some ten-year-old going to tell the difference between Andrew Johnson and Herbert Hoover? And it's not even my project. I'm fixing it for someone who glitched it all up."

"Should I let you get back to it?"

"No. I can't take it anymore. It's so frustrating." On the word *frustrating*, the woman slipped from a normal tone to a sexy purr.

"You're too much."

The stress of the day felt farther away with this woman looking at her.

"Do you—" Lillian said at the same moment the woman said, "I haven't seen—"

Lillian tried again. "Do you come here often?"

"I haven't seen you around here," the woman said.

They both chuckled.

"You've done this before," Lillian said. "Now can you say that with a wink?"

The woman winked.

"I'm from LA." Lillian set the words out on the table like playing cards. "I'm leaving tomorrow."

And hopefully coming back for the show but probably not. The reality of it washed over her. Maybe she should have taken the Jäger shot.

"My kind of woman." The woman raised her glass.

They toasted and Lillian took a sip.

"Oh my God, it tastes like laundry soap."

"Crème de violette. You said you'd have what I was drinking."

"*Why* are you drinking it?"

"It's pretty." The woman held her purple drink up to the light. "It smells like flowers. And if you're seventeen and you and your girlfriend want to steal her parents' liquor and you don't want to get caught, drink the crème de violette. No one will miss it. Happy memories." The woman furrowed her brow. "Happy-ish." She held out her hand. "Blue Lenox."

Lillian raised an eyebrow. Blue Lenox? That was as stagey as the wink.

"I doubt that's your real name," Lillian said.

"My friends call me Blue."

"So even your friends don't know your real name?"

"Does it matter?"

Blue's eyes were so dark they were almost black, but Lillian still saw a shadow pass over them for a second, and she wished she hadn't said it.

"And who are you?" Blue asked.

"Lillian."

They stared at each other for a moment. Blue had a smear of glitter on her cheek.

"It's nice to meet you, Lillian." Blue tucked the tip of her tongue between her teeth, her smile opening around the pink tip. She winked again.

"Just to be clear," Lillian said, "your act doesn't work on me."

It kind of did. "But you're good at it, and it's hot when someone's good at something."

"Your act is working for me."

"I don't have an act."

She had so many, code switching so many times she didn't have a native language. It was almost a relief to be called on it.

Blue cocked her head.

"You are wearing a white linen suit to the Neptune. And it's after ten, and it's still ironed. That's a tour de force of staying on brand."

Blue touched the cuff of Lillian's jacket, rubbing the fabric between her fingers. Lillian felt a little shiver go through her as she stared too closely at the touch. She could almost feel Blue taking her delicately between two fingers and rubbing her the way she rubbed the fabric of the jacket.

"Linen-rayon blend." Blue made it sound sexy.

"You like textiles."

Blue nodded. "I sew. Impressed?"

The bartender interrupted, a glass of white wine in hand.

"That's for her." Blue nodded to Lillian.

"Sorry for the wait," the bartender said. "I had to run next door for wine. We don't serve a lot."

Next door was a store called Quikee Cigarette and Food Outlet, which didn't bode well for the wine, but it was actually good.

"I guessed you might not have a palate sophisticated enough to appreciate the violette," Blue said when the bartender had left. "Even though you're wearing white linen to a dive bar after ten o'clock. So you know I'm a programmer. Can I ask what you do?"

"Please don't."

That was what hookups were about. Not being anyone. Just a body intertwining with another body in a dance no one would ever see. She was good at that dance even if her last hookups had been lackluster. Truth: they'd left her with a dull sense of dissatisfaction. But it had been a while since she'd felt a woman's hands on her, and this woman could push the stress of the day to the back of Lillian's mind.

But before Lillian could speak, Blue said, "Just to be clear, we're doing this"—she gestured to the space between them—"because we're going to sleep together, right? And you're going back to LA, so no catching feelings?"

"I was going to be a little more subtle." Lillian laughed. "But yes."

Blue might like textiles, but she didn't do strings. She was perfect.

"Good." Blue folded her hands in front of her. "You want to hang out first? Not talk about what you do for work? Share fries? Dance?"

Blue motioned to the dance floor. The stereo blared a trending dance-challenge song that included the lines *Ride the pony. Next we zip, baby, zip.* The dancers were lining up and imitating zipping up jackets because that was a sexy dance move. Lillian watched the choreographic horror.

"*Zip, zip, zip me up and down?* That shred of self-respect people talk about? I still have it."

Blue looked a little hurt.

"I will dance. One song. Anything but the Zipper."

What was she doing? Lillian never danced for fun. Dancing for fun was inviting unnecessary injury, her mother, Eleanor, was probably thinking at this very moment. Breaking your body on a grand fouetté en tournant was the natural order. Tearing your ACL because you got knocked down by an errant twerker was unforgivably careless.

"To be denied the Zipper with a beautiful woman." Blue sighed. "If we're not going to dance yet, what will we talk about? You know I'm a programmer. But I'm not the least bit interested in what you do. Don't even tell me."

"Thank you."

Blue appraised her for a moment, then asked, "How do you feel about houseplants?"

Lillian made small talk with her lovers. It was crass to suck on a woman's vulva without first spending forty minutes discussing the weather and the best restaurants in town. (That was not one of her mother's edicts, although maybe she'd agree in the alternate universe where Lillian talked to Eleanor about anything besides ballet.) The trick to hookup chat was to be friendly without saying anything. No connection. No shared moment. Houseplants were as safe a topic of conversation as any.

"I kill plants." A dead ficus tree was waiting for her right now.

"Why would you do that?"

Because I travel all the time, and I'm never in LA, but when I am, there's always this moment when I imagine what it'd be like to come back to a home, not just a house. So I buy a plant. A plant says *home*. Okay, maybe plants weren't that safe a topic.

"I don't kill them on purpose." Lillian mimed giving Blue a playful swat.

"I have beautiful plants," Blue said. "It says a lot about me."

"What do your houseplants say about you?"

"Well." Blue sat back. "I have great style. I take care of things. I don't drop the ball." She winced. "Usually. I like the ones people think are plain. Everything is beautiful if you appreciate it."

"My mother collects hundred-dollar orchids."

"No wonder you're wearing ironed linen."

That was on point.

"If we knew each other," Lillian said, "I'd introduce you to my mother. If you suffered through hours of orchid talk, she'd give you one."

"That'd be nice," Blue said a little wistfully.

For no reason, that made Lillian ache. Those orchids were awful, all their delicate little needs and pollens and speckles that meant something if you cared about the difference between the dendrobiums and cymbidiums. If that made Blue happy, Lillian should ship her a crate of them.

After covering houseplants, Blue had a supply of odd but relatively innocuous small-talk questions. What was the weirdest billboard Lillian had ever seen? Which did she think was more interesting: praying mantises or dragonflies? Lillian had no opinion, but she gave Blue points for asking something no one had ever asked her about before.

"I like talking to people," Blue said, a hint of shyness hovering behind her sultry smile.

When Lillian checked her phone to see if they'd talked for the requisite forty minutes, it had been two hours.

The music in the bar had cut to a slow song with 6/8 timing.

"One dance before we go?" Blue asked.

Blue's hand was warm and strong as she pulled Lillian toward the dance floor. Before Lillian realized what was happening, Blue invited her into the first steps of a Viennese waltz. The other dancers cleared the floor. Lillian didn't dance ballroom, but you couldn't go through a lifetime of dance academies and not know the steps to a waltz. It probably wouldn't have mattered; Blue's grip was unwavering. Lillian felt warmth building as Blue guided Lillian's legs with her own, her leg almost slipping between

Lillian's, teasing her. When the waltz was first choreographed, people had been shocked by that sensual closeness. They said it was erotic. They weren't wrong.

"You know how to dance," Lillian said.

"You do too."

"You're just a good lead."

Blue trailed her fingers down Lillian's neck, sending a shiver of pleasure down Lillian's spine. As a turn of the waltz brought them close together, she brushed her lips over Lillian's. When the waltz brought them together again, Blue slowed their pace and kissed her.

It felt like their first kiss, which of course it was. But the women Lillian slept with blended into one so nothing felt new, but this did. She was just being sentimental. Tired and sad (if she'd admit it to herself). This was almost certainly the last trip she'd take with the Reed-Whitmer Ballet Company. That ending made everything feel heavier than it should. She pushed the feeling aside and returned Blue's kiss the next time the waltz swirled them together. She let her tongue ghost Blue's lips. Blue stumbled. Lillian caught her.

"You're strong," Blue whispered.

The song ended. Lillian closed her eyes, her cheek resting against Blue's hair. A hookup had to smell right. Blue's perfume smelled like cloves and cherry or expensive suede. It fit her perfectly.

"Let's go." Blue bit the last word off like toffee.

Lillian's hotel was a short walk away but she stopped at the door. She needed Blue's fingers inside her. She wanted to see Blue arch in pleasure. Who would Blue be in that moment? The programmer with philodendrons or the seductress? Finding out would be as satisfying as the orgasm Lillian's body yearned for.

Strange. Lillian liked to make a woman come because it was challenging with a stranger, and she liked to win. But she was rarely curious about the women themselves.

"Just to be clear, I hook up with women when I travel," Lillian said. "No strings. No phone numbers. No breakfast in the morning. I get a health check after every partner."

"I do too," Blue said.

A damp breeze wafted the smell of rain and concrete.

"I don't mean I think hookups are cheap." Lillian was taller than Blue. She gazed down at Blue's eyes, the same midnight-ocean blue as her hair. "I just mean, I'm looking for a shooting star. Not the moon. No scones in the morning. Are you good with just one night?" She had to be sure. She cared about her lovers enough not to want to hurt them, but Blue, with her silly wink and floral drink and love of plants and textiles—what was it with the textiles?—she really didn't want to hurt Blue.

"After we have sex," Lillian said, "I'm going to ask you to leave. I don't cuddle. I'm never going to buy a second bedside table. Not with anyone."

God, that hurt when she really thought about it. So she didn't.

"A second nightstand." Blue looked adorably pleased with her pun.

Lillian touched Blue's tattoo with her fingertips.

"I'm serious, Blue. Are you okay with never seeing each other again?"

"If I thought we'd have breakfast together…" Blue's smile was suggestive and gentle. "I would have told you my real name."

chapter 3

Lillian pushed open the door to her hotel room, admiring the curves of Blue's body. She looked strong and soft, her body feminine, her posture touched by a masculine energy, like the swagger of a young man who still thought the world would hand him everything. Sexier than the small, impossibly muscular dancers Lillian usually slept with.

A single table lamp cast the room in a soft glow. They paused in the center of the room. Blue stroked her fingers down the arm of Lillian's white suit jacket.

"Shooting stars," Blue said thoughtfully. "Like a sand painting. It's beautiful and then it's gone. Don't worry." Blue kissed her, nipping at her lip and sending exquisite shivers up Lillian's legs and between them. "You're gorgeous, but I'm not falling in love."

With that Lillian put her leg between Blue's and, holding Blue so she wouldn't trip, spun her around to push her against the wall.

Except she didn't push Blue against the wall.

At the same moment, Blue spun her around. Or tried. They collided in an awkward half turn, Blue's body soft against Lillian's. Her breath smelled pleasantly of cinnamon, like that old-fashioned gum trendy candy stores sold as retro. They laughed. Lillian brushed her lips against Blue's, then kissed Blue's neck, then ran the edge of her teeth along Blue's earlobe. She felt Blue's body tense and then relax.

"After tonight you'll—" Lillian whispered.

At the same moment Blue whispered, "I'm going to—"

Blue pulled back, her arms looped around Lillian's waist.

Lillian laughed. "How were you going to finish that sentence. *I'm going to…?*"

Blue studied her, pulling their hips closer together casually, as though the press of their bodies didn't make Lillian ache like a new flower pushing at the sepal that held it closed.

"Give you everything you've ever wanted?" Blue offered, in her sultry voice.

It did sound like her Sultry Voice, and it still turned Lillian on.

"How do you know you're not getting in too deep?" Lillian asked. "What if I want something bizarre?" Lillian gave Blue a quick peck on the lips to show that she was teasing.

Blue relaxed with a dramatic sigh.

"I can't say, *I'm going to give you the best semi-anonymous sex you can have with someone who doesn't know anything about your body.*"

"That does ruin the mood," Lillian said, pulling Blue's sweat-shirt off her shoulders.

"Does it really?" Blue asked, her voice rough.

"No."

"And how were you going to finish *after tonight you'll…?*" Blue asked.

"I don't know," Lillian murmured. "You'll be ruined for all others?"

"You wouldn't do that to me."

"I'll try."

Lillian gently bit Blue's jaw, just beneath her ear. Blue moaned. The sound made Lillian want to carry her to the bed and grind against her until the frustration of rehearsing with her dancers in a too-small hotel room, then parading themselves in front of the corporate judges, washed away. A dam breaking. She wanted Blue. How long had it been since she'd wanted a woman enough to be satisfied by sex? Really satisfied? She took lovers back to her hotel rooms, vaguely horny but never horny enough to find that shattering moment of relief. It would be different tonight. And if she could replace the cocky smile on Blue's lips with a face of ecstasy, Lillian would remember that instant for a long time.

Lillian trailed her fingers down Blue's chest, tracing the binary code tattoo.

"So who gets to lead this dance?" Blue murmured.

Lillian was always in control. In bed. Onstage.

"You did so well at the bar," Lillian said. "I'll *let* you lead."

A good lead knew how to be in charge without being controlling. Blue drew her to the wall and pressed her against it.

"You know that's my move," Lillian murmured.

"Is it really?" Blue shifted so her thigh was between her legs. The weight of Blue's body and hardness of the wall and the delicious pressure made Lillian groan.

Slowly Blue undid the first button of Lillian's blouse and then the next. Then Blue kissed her, forcefully but languidly, fondling Lillian's breast, rocking into Lillian, the rhythm burning like a spotlight off center, illuminating but not reaching the dancer.

It was extravagant and excruciating and wonderful.

Blue ran her hand between Lillian's legs, along the seam of Lillian's pants.

"Harder?"

Lillian pressed the back of her head against the wall, sinking her hips lower to chase Blue's touch.

"You tease," Lillian murmured.

"Harder?" Blue asked again.

Blue intensified the pressure of her fingers.

"Yes," Lillian growled.

Lillian countered Blue's touch, running her hand up Blue's thigh.

"Show me," Blue said.

Lillian felt like she was touching herself, because Blue copied her every movement, and she copied Blue's, and Blue groaned, and the sound undid Lillian. A moment later, Lillian was naked and Blue was naked except for a pair of silky boy shorts. Blue threw back the covers on the bed.

Blue fulfilled her promise. It was the best hookup sex Lillian had ever had. Blue eased her fingers into Lillian's body, asking, "More? Too much?" She filled Lillian to the point of erotic pain but not a second over into discomfort, like a dancer who knew just how far to reach without losing her balance. Just the way Lillian liked it. Lillian let herself go breathless, although, of course, she was a dancer. She could control every fiber of her body. Blue lifted her higher and higher. Then Blue held the flat of her fingers against Lillian's clit, drawing Lillian's hand to hers so Lillian could guide her and thrust against her. And Lillian was over the edge, her orgasm washing away the stress of worrying about the company and the frustration of wanting this intensity and never finding it with her lovers.

She let herself cry, "Oh God. Oh God."

Then she came back to herself. Blue grinned and then licked her own fingertips, then kissed Lillian. Was this Blue's cocky persona or the real woman with humor dancing behind her eyes? It didn't matter. That was the beauty of a single night. You didn't have to find out.

Blue pulled off her underwear and straddled Lillian's leg. Lillian urged Blue on with her hands on Blue's hips. A second later Blue shuddered, then collapsed. She lay on Lillian for just a moment, then rolled off, lying flat on her back.

Lillian propped herself up on one elbow and studied Blue. Except for her tattoo, she was as pale as the moon and their bodies looked beautiful together, pure cacao and sweet cream. Lillian reached to touch her, but Blue was already rolling away.

"No cuddling." Blue hopped up. She blew Lillian a flashy kiss, like a drag queen's adieu to her audience. "See you around, gorgeous."

That was it. That was exactly what Lillian had asked for. No cuddling. No scones. Blue dressed in a flash, took in Lillian's nakedness with a hungry look, and pushed the door open. Then she was gone.

Lillian rose, naked, her body still alive with Blue's touch, and dug through the packing cubes in her suitcase to find her sketchbook in which she'd drawn dancers in minute variations of every ballet position. If you could animate them somehow, compose choreography with images instead of Benesh Movement Notation, which most dancers found so hard to decipher. If she could put them together in an app. Ha! When and how would *she* make an app? Drawing was a useless hobby. When you were in professional ballet, all hobbies were useless. Her mother had taught her that. She took her sketchbook and sat down at the small table, still naked. An hour had passed before she looked up from her drawing of Blue's curvy body lying languid in messy sheets, very different from the lean, precise figures on the other pages. She couldn't get Blue right though. Blue hadn't lounged in Lillian's bed. She'd come and gone so quickly she could have been a dream.

chapter 4

Izzy Wells from Broken Bush, Oregon, stood on the stage of the dilapidated Roosevelt Theater, which she had bought because she was an idiot. No. She'd bought it to give Portland's diverse performers a place to share their talents without fear, a community space where people could throw off the shackles of society and...but she was still an idiot. A second mortgage on her house to pay the down payment? When had that been a good idea? And the repairs she was going to do because she was soooo handy? She could replace a set of steps. She could reupholster a seat. She could not abate black mold or fix the leaking roof.

She took a deep breath, trying not to breathe in the smell of impending financial ruin. She smiled down at a hundred-plus people in the yet-to-be-reupholstered seats. There were the members of her no-audition burlesque troupe, Velveteen Crush, their friends, family, and fans. There were her four closest friends, the founding members of the troupe, the most talented. Not that Izzy ranked people by talent, because Velveteen Crush was about expressing your true self, and if that meant reading poetry while writhing on the stage in a sleeping bag, then that was your truth.

But the founding members—Axel, Tock, Sarah, Arabella, and Izzy—were pretty effing amazing. These beautiful people were the reason she'd been an idiot. These people were why Izzy stood in front of the largest TV she'd been able to borrow. Behind her the two cheerful hosts of *The Great American Talent Show* bantered in front of a flashing column with the words STAR MAKER emblazoned on it. A clock mounted atop the column counted down like New Year's Eve.

"In just a few minutes, we're going to find out which ten teams made it to round two of *The Great American Talent Show*," one of the hosts exclaimed for the hundredth time.

In just a few minutes, Izzy would know. Would she and her four best friends drop everything, move into an apartment with all the other contestants, and show the TV-viewing world inclusivity and body positivity? Did she have a chance at prize money that would save the theater, her house, and her chance of ever buying anything on credit again? Or were they going to listen as the hosts read the list of winners, sit in deflated silence, and then say a bunch of upbeat stuff about how they didn't need a TV show to spread their message? There were ten teams and nine challenges between them and the prize. Long shot didn't begin to describe it. But if they didn't see their name on the screen tonight, Bank of America would reclaim a vintage theater with black mold, a leaking roof, possibly Izzy's house, and definitely Izzy's dreams.

"Speech, speech," someone called from the audience.

Oh yeah. That was why she was standing on the stage.

Izzy closed her eyes, trying to center herself, not spiral. When you spiraled, you were at the center? Yes, but it was the wrong center. It was just a metaphor. She took a deep breath. What was centering? The ocean? Those tabletop Zen gardens people put on their desks? Izzy's mind flashed back to the woman at the

Neptune. A few times since that night, Izzy had thought about the woman—Lillian—when she was panicking, and the thought had calmed her. That was odd. The woman was just a memory. Still, she was probably the most beautiful woman Izzy had ever slept with, so maybe it made sense that Lillian's memory could erase the Roosevelt Theater's mold problem. Izzy pictured her now. Her dark, luminescent skin set off by her halo of short, almost-shaved, platinum blond hair, like the essence of a dandelion puff without the extraneous fluff. And her clarity. *A shooting star. I don't cuddle.* Lillian was centered. And there was something else Izzy couldn't quite name. A feeling of safety? The fact that they hadn't just had sex, they'd had fun.

Izzy met her audience's eyes one by one.

"Hello, you beautiful wanderers." Izzy drawled her signature opening line, then raised her arms. "I want you to know how frickin' proud I am of you." Thoughts of black mold and Bank of America receded as Izzy slipped into her stage persona. She spread her arms. "We're going to be on TV, and that means reaching the trans kid in rural Oregon who doesn't know one other queer person. That means the girl who's been told she can't be sexy because she's fat is going to see a new vision of beauty." Izzy's breath rode high in her chest. "Our bodies aren't cogs in a system. We're going to turn people on and we're going to show them that our bodies are made for desire." Adrenaline pumped through Izzy's body.

The audience was hooting and whistling.

"There's no such thing as perfect." Izzy raised her arms higher.

Nervousness melted into the calm, hot, sensuous energy of performance. She was a mythical being with no past, no gender, no limits, no fears. (Well…there were murder hornets or getting stuck in a cave and, according to a survey she took in one of

Sarah's self-help books, the fear of abandonment, but basically no fears.) All Izzy had was the fierce, passionate love for the outcast and the stranger inside everyone.

"In our imperfection we are beautiful!"

The crowd cheered.

"But the most important thing isn't whether we get on the show or not," Izzy finished. "It's that we're all here. Together." She looked at the countdown on the screen. They were down to seconds. Izzy felt her stage persona slipping. She pulled her shoulders back. "We can!"

There was absolutely no way they could. No way an amateur burlesque group would get on a show that promised to find the best talent in the United States. Izzy had glimpsed the other performers auditioning for the first round. They had tour buses and matching outfits.

She stepped back so everyone could see the screen.

The group chanted, "Nine. Eight…"

Why had she started this troupe?

"Seven. Six…"

Why did she buy this theater?

"Five. Four. Three. Two. One."

Virtual confetti showered the screen. The group held its collective breath. A banner read WELCOME THE NEXT SEASON OF THE GREAT AMERICAN TALENT SHOW, and below that were names.

The first row of the audience rushed to the stage to read the small font scrolling up the screen. Izzy closed her eyes.

Sarah read the names out loud. "Retroactive Silence, modern dance. Dance Magic, magician dancer. What's that anyway? Mood of Motion, movement art. And what's that? BetaFlight, aerial performance. Spice Angels, step."

They would never make it.

"The Liam Ronan Irish Dance Company. The Reed-Whitmer Ballet Company. Effectz, hip-hop. Dream Team Marchers, dancing marching band. Oh! Holy shit!" Sarah squealed. "Velveteen Crush! We did it! We fucking did it!"

Suddenly everyone was crowding onto the stage. Someone turned Panic! at the Disco up to full volume. Champagne popped. Izzy considered passing out. Then she was lifted, crowd-surfing-style, by her friends and fans, everyone chanting her stage name.

"Blue Lenox! Blue Lenox!"

chapter 5

Kia pulled to a stop in the circular driveway in front of Lillian's parents' house.

"So are we going to eat in front of the TV to see if we're going to be on the show?" Kia asked.

"We?" Lillian shook her head.

Kia had decided that if the company got on the show, she was going to put her cooks in charge of her food truck and follow Lillian to Portland to be the Reed-Whitmer Ballet Company's official influencer, which probably meant hanging out with the dancers and trying to get Lillian to go dancing and take flaming shots.

Lillian got out of Kia's car. "Eleanor says we will have a civilized dinner." Lillian imitated her mother's arch tone.

"You and your mom aren't going to do that whole cold-staring thing are you?"

"Cold-staring is how Eleanor shows love," Lillian said, dropping her voice as they approached the wide steps leading into the formal entryway.

Kia knew not to say that Eleanor wasn't that bad. Lillian had made it clear she didn't want to hear it. Kia and her father, Lillian's uncle Carl, were like wild parrots to Eleanor: delightful, color-ful, occasionally annoying, always free to be themselves. Kia did not get to compare that experience of Eleanor Jackson with the woman who raised Lillian to dance Odette and Odile on the stage of the Palais Garnier.

"So are you excited?" Kia laced her arm through Lillian's.

About having dinner with her mother? Not really.

About the possibility of getting on *The Great American Talent Show*? Not really.

About the very real possibility that tomorrow she'd have to tell her dancers the truth: the Reed-Whitmer Ballet Company was done? That one broke her heart.

"It'll be fun." Kia squeezed her arm as they mounted the steps.

"Fun is where…" Lillian tried to remember Eleanor's opinion on fun.

Fun was the birthplace of mediocrity? Fun was laziness in disguise?

"Come on." Kia pulled her through the front door.

Lillian's parents and Uncle Carl were already seated in the dining room. Seven empty seats remained at the end of the table. There were probably deep-seated emotional reasons her parents furnished their house to look like an 1800s mansion, but it was a little extra.

Kia made her way around the table, hugging her father, Elea-nor, and Lillian's father, Erik, and then pulled up a seat. Lillian hesitated for a second. Should she hug her parents or just sit down? It seemed like something you should know. Not a difficult family decision.

"Well, have a seat, Lillian," Eleanor said.

"What's for dinner?" Kia unfurled her linen napkin. "You know I could've brought my new Cheetos-crusted hollandaise corn dogs."

"Oh, Kia," Eleanor said with a tolerant affection she never showed Lillian.

"I've been thinking of painting the *Serendipity* in the colors of Greece," Uncle Carl said. "I'll be sailing to Lesbos in the spring."

They'd obviously been in the middle of a conversation.

"Blue and white are good colors for a yacht if you have to live on a yacht," Eleanor said. "It'll be beautiful."

Carl was her favorite brother. He was also her only brother, but she loved him like a favorite. Her bright, yacht-sailing parrot.

"Not blue and white. Pink, red, and orange. The colors of Lesbos," Uncle Carl said. "The girls will love it."

The girls were his six or ten Cavalier King Charles spaniels.

"Oh Carl. Dogs are colorblind," Eleanor said.

Lillian checked her phone surreptitiously. Half an hour until the results of the second-round auditions. Half an hour until she found out whether the Reed-Whitmer Ballet Company went on the show or shut down. If it was shut down, her dancers would stay in touch with each other. They'd say they'd stay in touch with her, but they wouldn't.

The caterer Eleanor hired for any meal that wasn't protein and wheatgrass delivered a plate of fish to Lillian's place mat.

"Don't be nervous," Eleanor said.

"I'm not," Lillian said reflexively.

This was her life. Everything she'd worked for. Living up to her mother's legacy as the first Black dancer in the Julian Gienerva Ballet. Eleanor had made it a generation earlier. What excuse did Lillian have? If they'd rehearsed more? Had she been strict enough with the dancers? With herself? In minutes, the season's competitors (and her future) would be announced.

"It's not a tragedy if the company doesn't get on that television show." Eleanor pronounced *that television show* like she was talking about someone's mistress. "If you don't get on the show, I'll talk to Jean-Michel at the Studio de Danse. You know they've been wanting you for a visiting fellowship for years. You can teach."

Teach was the faithless relative of *that television show*.

"I teach," Eleanor added.

Eleanor taught after dancing leads until forty. Miraculously old for a ballerina. Kia shot Lillian a look that said, *Can we just enjoy our sustainably sourced sea bass?*

"Thanks, Mom," Lillian said. "I'm sure Jean-Michel is very nice."

"He's a monster. But the precision he demands out of his dancers..." Eleanor's voice was as smooth as polished mahogany. "He can watch twenty dancers at the same time and catch every flaw."

"If you don't get on the show, you and Kia can sail to Lesbos with me," Uncle Carl offered. "Lillian, you can find the perfect woman."

"I don't speak Greek."

"The language of love is universal," Uncle Carl said.

Lillian flashed back to Portland and the first-round auditions and the blue-haired woman with the fake name. Lillian usually didn't remember her hookups much after the fact, but she didn't laugh with them either. She'd laughed with the blue-haired woman. If that woman lived in LA, Lillian might break her no-second-night rule. Just this once. It'd feel good to laugh and then wash this night away with the best semi-anonymous sex she'd ever had. Blue would know her body even better this time. Lillian snapped her focus back to the table.

"What about my dancers?" Lillian had not meant to burst out.

"I'm not just doing this for myself. What about Imani, Pascale, Elijah, Jonathan, and Malik?"

All the days she ran them through eight hours of rehearsal, the hot LA sun blazing through the studio windows. They lived half their lives in hotels while they toured. Pascale was always in search of a new hairdresser to straighten her mushroom cap of processed hair. Elijah was always researching gay bars and then not going because, like Lillian, he had no time for a personal life. Lillian's personal life was burying a succession of houseplants and trying not to know the last names of the women she slept with. Her dancers had community with each other, but they'd given up the same things Lillian had.

"El, you need to let Lillian relax," Uncle Carl cut in.

"Relaxation is distraction, and distraction is the first step to failure," Eleanor said reflexively.

Lillian shot Kia a look that said, *See?*

Carl pressed a perfectly manicured hand to his chest. "How were we born of the same mother?" He turned to Lillian. "You need to swim free, my little puffin."

Kia grinned at Lillian. She was going to call Lillian little puffin for the next month.

"The point is," Eleanor said, "these shows are just corporate advertisements. Every week is sponsored by a different product. This week they'll flaunt themselves for Downy dryer sheets. Next week it's Washington Mutual. Lillian is too good for this. Lillian, darling, you're a star. You're a comet that comes once in a generation."

Lillian's phone alarm vibrated in her pocket. She took it out and set it on the table. She had the discipline to control her hands so they didn't shake.

"This show just wants people who'll cry on TV," Eleanor said.

Lillian touched her phone to wake up the screen.

"It's beneath you," Eleanor added.

Lillian held her breath and looked. She read the list twice. She expanded the screen to be sure she'd read correctly. She couldn't meet Eleanor's eyes.

"We made it."

chapter 6

Izzy sat in a chair in her best friend Sarah's salon, Root of the Matter, Sarah daubing her secret recipe onto Izzy's scalp in preparation for their first day on *The Great American Talent Show*. (Perfectly blue hair was as high maintenance as, say...the Large Hadron Collider.) Root of the Matter was peaceful even if Izzy's mind wasn't. The stylists Sarah rented to hadn't come in yet. Lassopryde played on the stereo. Outside, cars sloshed through the rain, but inside it was warm like a terrarium. Just the way Izzy liked it. Plants lined the windowsill and hung from the ceiling. Sarah's cat, Mr. Kitty, curled up in his basket nestled among pothos plants Izzy had started for Sarah.

"We're going to be on TV." Izzy stated the obvious. "It's happening."

"Nervous?" Sarah asked.

"Of course not."

Sarah glopped on more dye.

"It's normal to be nervous. We're all nervous," Sarah said meditatively. Her collection of self-help books kept her emotionally centered, and they would center Izzy too, if Izzy read them when

Sarah loaned them to her. Or so Sarah said. Izzy didn't know. She hadn't cracked a spine. Weren't the titles enough? *Say No to Dysfunction. You Are Worth Loving.*

"The show always starts with the signature challenge," Izzy said. "We need to show the world the beauty of gender diversity! Self-love!" She didn't need the books. "Body positivity! The chance to—"

Sarah put a hand on the shoulder of Izzy's plastic salon cape.

"I'm already on board, Blue. You don't have to give me the speech." Sarah pivoted. "You said you were looking into some stuff with the theater roof. How'd that go?"

Izzy saying *fine* would be lying to her friend. Telling Sarah the contractor had asked if it was supposed to be a green roof—it wasn't—would lead to a lecture Izzy didn't need about not making decisions that hurt her financial future even if she was trying to support the community.

Sarah wrapped a final strand of hair into foil to create a shimmer of lighter blue among the dark.

"Blue." Sarah drew Izzy's name out like a warning. "How's the roof?"

"The saddle flashing is up to code."

"Hmm." Sarah fitted a plastic cap over Izzy's head.

"Someone put in a lightweight seismic strap, which is good."

Thank God Sarah didn't know much about building. Izzy threw out some jargon that might have had something to do with roofing.

Sarah pulled off her gloves and spun Izzy's chair around. "Isn't that for earthquakes? What about the leaks?"

Okay, so Sarah wasn't impressed by the seismic strap.

"Fixing up the theater is expensive. I'd be worried except we're going to win *The Great American Talent Show.* Period." She put on her best Blue Lenox smile. "Tell me how gorgeous I'm going to look when you finish with me. Are they going to shut down the show on the first day? Just say, *Give Velveteen Crush the prize. They're too fabulous.*"

"You're using humor to deflect." Sarah had an associate's degree in psychology. That combined with being a hairstylist made her a therapist in her own mind.

But Izzy couldn't tell Sarah the truth. Not even Sarah. *I made a stupid mistake because I thought I could be the community's hero. I could lose everything. I'm terrified.* Even Sarah had met Izzy as Blue Lenox. Even Sarah chuckled when she saw Izzy's real name on a piece of mail. *Isadora Wells.* And of course, Sarah had a self-help book waiting for the moment Izzy wanted to talk about identity and vulnerability, but would Sarah really like the vulnerable, self-help-book Izzy? Blue Lenox enchanted every person she met; when you did that, you were safe in a way that banks couldn't touch.

"You know we can be the best and still not win, right?" Sarah said gently.

"We've already won by being who we are!"

Sarah sighed.

Izzy had to give her something. "Okay, I'm a little nervous."

"What are you doing for self-care?"

Izzy pictured Lillian, her body all muscle and angle. A Rodin sculpture cast out of bronze. Her light golden-brown eyes a mesmerizing contrast to her dark skin. How could someone be that striking? Izzy smiled at herself. She could picture the real Lillian looking mildly affronted. *I said no scones; certainly, don't use my body as some sort of centering prayer. What creepy self-help book did you get that out of?*

"What is it?" Sarah sat on the window ledge, studying Izzy.

Had Izzy been staring into space dreaming of Lillian?

"Did I tell you I hooked up with this woman a while back?"

"Narrow it down. What woman, when?"

Izzy shook her head. "Never mind. It was…nothing."

"No, tell me."

Izzy's phone rang. Hopefully it was one of the new company members with a crisis of confidence that demanded Izzy's attention. She couldn't possibly talk about her problems when someone needed saving. She pulled her phone out from beneath the plastic gown. The screen read *Megan Wells*. Her mother.

Don't answer. Easy. Just send it to voicemail. Izzy had too much to worry about without Megan calling to invite Izzy to California for her half sister Bella's birthday or a party in honor of Bella getting a promotion at work or whatever celebration Megan was having for the daughter she'd actually wanted. Every time it hurt. Every time Izzy ended up saying some polite version of *How about you get out of my life?* Every time Izzy ended up feeling like shit because (a) her mother never really loved her, Megan just wanted to seal the deal on her new life as the perfect suburban mom, and she couldn't do that without Izzy in the family Christmas card; and (b) Izzy was too old to still care about that shit. But Izzy hadn't read *Healing Your Inner Child*, and her inner child was stupid and vulnerable. Maybe she could heal her inner child if just *once* Megan put her first. If just once Megan wanted *her*, not for the Christmas card but just because Izzy mattered.

But Megan was not calling to say she was sorry about all the years of neglect and that she'd secretly adored Izzy that whole time, and even though she loved Bella and her husband, Rick, there was a hole in her heart that only Izzy could fill. Because Megan never called to say she was sorry, hole-in-her-heart etc. Which was why Izzy shouldn't let her inner child pick up.

Izzy touched accept.

"Honey," Megan cooed, "I'm so glad I caught you."

Time raced backward, the way it always did when her mother called. Izzy was scanning the high school auditorium for her mother. Megan was a singer. Of course she'd come to see Izzy starring in *Grease*. But she hadn't. The next memory was Izzy standing in front of their trailer watching her mother, stepfather, and Bella driving away, little Bella blowing kisses out of the back window.

"Megan," Izzy said.

Sarah's face read, *Really?* Sarah knew the history.

"It's Mom, honey."

Megan said it like she had never snuck Izzy into a bar and told Izzy to tell everyone that Megan was her older sister.

"I've been trying to message you on Instagram. I know you're busy. You probably haven't checked your messages. And Facebook is for people my age." Megan gave a nervous laugh. "So I'm glad you're there. I saw that you got on *The Great American Talent Show*. I'm praying for you to win," Megan said quickly. "Bella and Rick are too."

Did God want her to shimmy on national TV? If there was a God, he'd understand the importance of inclusivity and body positivity. But *The Great American Talent Show* was probably not at the top of his list of concerns. And who was this woman? *I'll pray for you?*

"I got a ticket to the studio audience." Megan's voice brightened hopefully. "I see you on Instagram. You're so talented! I know you'll make it through to the end." The rest came out in one breath. "I get to see my daughter up there."

Izzy's worthless inner child jumped up and down like she'd been handed a bouquet of balloons. *Mom wants to see me!*

But Megan had never come to Portland to see a performance. She hadn't even come when Izzy had toured the West Coast and performed an hour and a half away from Megan's home. Maybe Megan was still pining for the singing career she didn't have because she got pregnant at sixteen. Maybe she thought Izzy could introduce her to the judges and she'd get rediscovered. Maybe Izzy owed it to her.

"Um," Izzy said. "That's nice, but I won't be able to spend much time with you. The show's going to keep us busy."

"I know."

Right. Megan wasn't hoping for a weekend of mother-daughter time. Izzy should *not* care. A drop of blue dye slid down Izzy's cheek like a tear. Sarah wiped it away, her eyes still fixed on Izzy.

"I just want to support you. Cheer you on. That's my girl!"

"Um…Megan…Mom…" Why couldn't she get the words out? *Megan, this isn't your big break. I'm not going to introduce you to the producer. If you want to be on a reality TV show, audition yourself.* "That's…um…it's nice of you. You know it's fine if you just watch the show on TV. I don't need you to come up…" *If we're not even going to see each other.*

"We'll at least see each other backstage after the filming. You can introduce me to your friends. Goodness, I haven't performed for years. I love that backstage feeling."

"Never let your makeup slide."

That'd been Megan's favorite advice after *Don't burn the house down while I'm gone.*

Izzy, if you want the world to love you, never let your makeup slide.

"I did say that, didn't I?" Megan's voice rose nervously.

Sarah watched Izzy with her supportive-friend face on.

"You did. It's good advice. Speaking of…I'm getting my hair colored. It's time to rinse. Take care, Megan…Mom. Maybe I'll see you at the show when they bring the studio audience back-stage after filming."

"Wait, honey," Megan said. "If you think I want something from you, I don't. I promise. I just want to see you, honey. I'm so proud of you."

Izzy really had to read that book about the inner child.

"I could probably find time to hang out," Izzy said.

"Honey, I'd love that. Just you and me."

If Megan really didn't want to get on the show, that probably meant Megan would cancel the trip. Bella would win some award Megan had to celebrate. *Just you and me* would turn into *why don't you come down to California and come to Bella's honor society induction ceremony?* But maybe this once, it'd be different.

"Thanks. I'll see you." Izzy hung up and turned off the volume on her phone in one motion.

"You still got ten minutes on the dye." Sarah stood up and wiped a bit of dye off Izzy's forehead.

"Why do I fall for it?" Izzy asked.

"Would you like her to come support you?"

"She won't or she will and it'll be all about her. Nothing she's done has ever been about me."

Sarah walked around the back of the chair and put her arms around Izzy's shoulders.

"Well, you're going to have so many fans in the audience, and your friends...we're *all* about you, Blue Lenox."

So even your friends don't know your real name? For a second, the sympathy in Lillian's eyes had felt like a warm embrace. But the truth was, Blue Lenox was the best thing that had ever happened to Izzy Wells. And Blue Lenox did not need Megan Wells for anything.

chapter 7

On the first day of filming, a man assigned to be the company's runner collected Lillian and then Imani, Jonathan, Elijah, Pascale, and Malik from their rooms at the Lynnwood Terrace apartments, where they would stay for however long they stayed on the show. It seemed like a waste for the first team to get voted off. They'd just have moved in. Then the show would pack up their stuff and whisk them to the airport. You didn't get to stick around after the judges and the studio audience voted you off.

Lillian had negotiated her own studio apartment. A runner collected Lillian from her apartment then led her to the hallways where the other dancers shared two three-bedroom units. When Lillian and the runner arrived, the dancers were all together in the men's apartment. Elijah and Imani were watching performance videos, their heads bent together over a laptop like generals strategizing how they'd take down the opposition. Pascale was on the phone with her kids, looking teary like she always did when she talked to them. Jonathan stretched, as solid and as tall as a tree. Only Malik looked completely at peace, crocheting a sweater. His grandmother raised him, and this was one of her talents. They got up and followed the runner.

"We'll bus you to the venue," the runner said, leading them through the halls of the apartment. "Then it's a casual get-together with the other teams."

A few minutes later, they got out of the van. The show had staged the get-together in the grand ballroom of a vintage hotel. The wooden floor had a peculiar give to it, as though they were walking on a mattress, perhaps a 1920s sprung floor. Large windows looked down on the street.

The producer greeted them at the door. Lillian remembered him, Bryant Walker. He hadn't talked to them during the audition, but he'd been around checking his tablet and talking into a headset. The technology had looked odd on him since the rest of his outfit—cargo shorts, hiking boots, and a shirt with a vent in the back—said, *I'm going camping.* Maybe that was Oregon style.

"There'll be cameras, but we're just getting candid footage for the socials. We'll start getting that behind-the-scenes content up soon. It's the meta show. The show behind the show. If you can get them hooked on that, they'll all watch on prime time. See if you can build some rivalries, tensions." Bryant checked his tablet.

Some of the other contestants had already arrived. People milled around a bar at one end. The dancers in the Reed-Whitmer Ballet Company lined up beside Lillian, their hands at their sides: Jonathan, Malik, Elijah, Imani, Pascale. Each of them a hundred times more talented than *The Great American Talent Show* deserved. Pascale bounced nervously on her toes. Lillian shot her a look and she stopped. Kia finished up the line, allowed in with her magical influencer badge.

"Pretend we're not here," Bryant went on. "Just mingle. Have some food." He gestured to a long table by the two-story windows where caterers were setting up. "The bar is open. Fizz Bang soda is the official soft drink of the show, so the bartender will be serving everything in Fizz Bang cans. We have a carefully curated selection of fans. We want to see you interacting with the people. Get comfortable."

There were sofas and bistro tables set up in the front half of the large space. Men with cameras paced around checking angles and lighting. On the other side of the hall, another producer with a tablet was chatting to a group of Black men in matching streetwear.

"That's Effectz," Kia said. "Hip-hop dance. I was talking to one of the guys. Their stuff sounds dope."

"When were you talking to one of the guys? We haven't even met them."

Kia tucked her hands in the pockets of her colorful overalls.

"*You* haven't met them because you've been sitting in your apartment since we got here. Let's go have fun," she said to the dancers.

Jonathan and Malik looked at Lillian for permission. Pascale smoothed her hair although it was already straight and plastered to her head with gel. Elijah took Imani's hand and swung their arms.

"I've got this," Elijah said with a flick of his wrist. "Where are the boys? Wingman?" He looked at Imani.

"Always," she agreed.

Elijah never dated. As far as Lillian knew, he never even hooked up. The constant search for beautiful men was a joke. He was a dancer. Only a dancer. There was no room for distraction. Elijah and Imani bounded off. Lillian nodded to the other dancers to excuse them. Kia followed them, all of them laughing and talking at once.

Lillian wandered over to the windows and looked down on Portland's gay district. The street should have looked cheerful, but the rain drowned everything in gray. The rainbow crosswalks looked faded. A few determined smokers hung around outside the bar across the street.

Should she have told the dancers that this might be their last season together? It would add too much pressure. But dancers could handle pressure. She owed it to them. But now? If she was going to tell them, she should have told them the day Thomas Reed and Charles Whitmer talked to her. If they knew they'd be on their own soon though, they should be auditioning for other companies. Except the show contract forbade them from contacting any other companies or performance venues until after the first episode aired. So what was the point in stressing them out?

On the street, directly below the window, a group of people in colorful outfits and hair in a range of colors from bright orange to dark blue came into view. Even looking down on the tops of their heads, Lillian could tell they were having fun, jostling each other and high-fiving.

Blue hair.

Lillian's mind flashed back to the last time she was in Portland. Maybe she could find time to get back to the Neptune for a drink. She'd go during the day when the bar was empty. She'd dispel the magic of that night. She'd remove the Instagram filter that cast a glow on those memories and see the place for what it was. A dive bar where she'd met a nice hookup.

"Hey, girl." Kia's voice startled Lillian. "Why you staring out the window all '*Les Mis* dying in the attic'?"

Kia looked out the window.

"The guy from Effectz says there's someone downstairs signing women's breasts."

It was the colorful group Lillian had spotted coming down the street. And, yes, a woman was baring the top of her cleavage so the person with the blue hair could do something that looked very much like signing a name. Another woman queued up behind the first one, T-shirt pulled down.

"Please tell me that's not the competition."

"The burlesque group."

"We rehearsed for twelve hours yesterday," Lillian grumbled, more to the unfairness of the universe than to Kia. "And we're up against some dude who signs women's breasts."

"Chick."

"That doesn't make it better."

"It's not even staged. The guy from Effectz said a bunch of fans caught her on the street. I don't know why the show didn't stop her. Maybe the producers were all up here." Kia craned her neck. "Blue hair. Must be a Portland thing. That chick you hooked up with last time we were here, she had blue hair."

"I don't remember."

The breast signer disappeared from view. Lillian leaned her arms on the windowsill and rested her chin on her hands in a pose Eleanor would have called undignified and casual. The sound of voices got louder. Someone turned on music. She was vaguely aware of cameras moving past her, probably identifying her as the standoffish one.

"Aw shit, of course you remember," Kia said. "When I asked you how your night was, you said, *Nice*. Usually they're just *acceptable*."

"I've never said that." Had she?

"Girl," Kia strung the word out. "You told me you danced with her."

"I'm a dancer."

"Not like that. You liked her."

"Maybe you're right."

"I'm right." Kia bobbed her head back and forth, her Afro puffs bouncing. "I'm going to hit the bar. Try not to stress over here." She headed off, but she was back in a second, no drink in hand, her expression so smug it verged on evil.

"What?" Lillian asked.

"You don't even know. My dad is going to love this. Fate. Serendipity. Language of love. This is too good."

Whatever it was, it probably wasn't good.

"I'm dying to know." She wasn't.

"Take a look." Kia put her hands on Lillian's shoulders, turning her to face the party behind her.

Lillian looked.

"What?"

"Guess who's here."

"Who?"

"Blue hair over there."

"Yeah. You said she was one of the burlesque group."

The performer's back was turned toward them, but even from behind the woman exuded confidence. She wore a dark blue suit that matched her hair and glistened like an oil slick. Was she taking out a pen to sign another fan's breasts? Where were the producers to stop that tackiness? Maybe the show would cast her as the over-the-top one. They'd probably demand a rivalry between stuffy ballet and…whatever that display was.

Kia looked from Lillian to the performer and back. Her face said, *Gotcha*.

"I get it," Lillian said. "That's who we're up against. Thank you for reminding me."

Then the performer turned in their direction, and Lillian's life got so much more complicated.

chapter 8

How had Lillian not recognized the blue hair and that swagger? The sheer impossibility of it maybe.

"No." Lillian spun around so she was hidden behind Kia's Afro puffs. "Did you know?"

"Of course not." Kia was beaming like she'd bluffed her way into winning a poker tournament. "But I remember her."

Lillian felt her face heat up.

"Why is she here?" Lillian asked, although the answer was obvious.

The woman—Blue—was awful. She was the kind of self-absorbed, Instagram-famous performer who signed women's breasts. How had Lillian not noticed? Because she'd needed to get off and she'd needed another woman to help make it happen? Because Blue had recognized Lillian as the kind of person who wouldn't sleep with a douchebag and had adjusted her behavior accordingly?

"Maybe you two can hit it again," Kia said.

"Do you know how unprofessional it would look if I slept with one of the other contestants?" Lillian hissed. What would

Eleanor say? *A Black ballerina must be beyond reproach.* That's what she'd say.

"It's kind of romantic. You spent one night together and here you are."

"You sound like your dad."

Uncle Carl loved romance and stargazing and magical coincidences. He'd named his yacht *Serendipity*, for God's sake. And he liked lots and lots of spaniels. He didn't live in the same universe Lillian and Eleanor lived in.

"I have to talk to her," Lillian said.

"Mm-hmm," Kia hummed suggestively.

"Not. Like. That."

Had Blue seen her? Had Blue talked about her? Lillian hurried toward the crowd of people surrounding Blue.

"Excuse me," Lillian cut in.

Blue turned.

The oil slick suit was made out of some liquidy fabric that flowed over every curve of Blue's body, absorbing light and shining at the same time.

"You," Blue said, her voice almost inaudible beneath the sound of the party.

For a second, Lillian could have sworn she saw delight in Blue's eyes and the word *how?* form on Blue's lips. For a moment, Blue held Lillian's gaze, her eyes dark, as though she was remembering everything they'd done in a time-lapse sex scene.

Then she tipped her chin up.

"Sup?"

She managed to swagger without moving.

It looked good on her. The open front of her suit jacket revealed the swell of her large breasts, squeezed to their limits in a corset that looked like a bustier had mated with body armor. The whole outfit screamed, *I am going to ravage you in a steampunk version of* Cabaret.

"Do you like what you see?" Blue tongued the words, like she had just taken a bite off someone's edible panties. She trailed her fingers down the front of her corset.

Lillian was not speechless. She just couldn't quite find the right words for the moment. Blue had been sexy. But this incarnation…this was like the woman she'd met at the Neptune if the woman had gotten high on some of the synthetic fertilizers Eleanor refused to put on her orchids because they gave them an *unsustainable opulence.*

Before either of them could speak, a woman in a crew T-shirt rushed up to Blue.

"Oh my God, you're Blue Lenox. Your shows—" The woman drew a deep breath and held it as though Blue's performances were beyond expression. "Will you write *beautiful wanderer*?" She pulled a Sharpie out of her back pocket.

Blue eyed the Sharpie, then pulled a marker out of a secret compartment in her bustier.

"It's all vegetable ink." Blue held up the pen. "You could eat this."

The woman pulled the neck of her T-shirt down and closed her eyes. Blue deftly wrote *Hello, you beautiful wanderer. XOXO from Blue.* It was impressive that she got that much legible writing on a woman's chest.

Lillian felt Blue's attention focused on her even as Blue smiled at the woman. Lillian tried not to trace the lacework of binary tattoo on Blue's chest with her eyes, tried not to follow it down to the deep V of her cleavage.

"Oh my God, thank you. Thank you." The crew woman bounded away, hand pressed to her chest.

One of the camera operators called over, "Never, ever do that on camera."

Blue shrugged and turned away from him.

"Would you like me to sign your breast?" Blue dropped her voice to a velvet innuendo.

Lillian took the pen Blue was still holding and drew a line across the back of her hand. The ink disappeared on her dark skin.

"Sorry, your name wouldn't show up on my breasts." Lillian meant to sound curt, but it was such a ridiculous sentence to speak aloud it came out with a little chuckle.

"I'll buy a different marker," Blue said.

"Will it be made out of vegetable ink?"

"For you, it'll be made out of gold."

How did this act work on women? How were there people who actually wanted their breasts signed? In public. By a woman in a steampunk corset. Who was grinning like a cross between a wolf and a porn star. And why did part of Lillian whisper, *I totally get it.*

"I need to talk to you." Lillian pulled her eyes away from the swell of Blue's breasts. "Somewhere...else."

Lillian looked around for somewhere to escape. At the far side of the hall, a staircase led to a mezzanine. Lillian strode across the floor, not looking at Blue but feeling Blue behind her. Thank God no one had found the mezzanine yet. Upstairs, Lillian moved to the back of the mezzanine, where they'd be out of sight.

"You said you were a programmer," Lillian hissed. How was this woman here?!

"By day." Blue's expression said, *But I'm thinking about the night.* "And you are?"

"A dancer with the Reed-Whitmer Ballet Company."

"I'm dying to see you perform."

This was not a time to flirt.

"You don't know anything about me," Lillian hissed.

"How could I not be enchanted?"

"Could you please not be."

"Not be enchanted?" Blue leaned against the wall behind her. Her crossed arms managed to lift her breasts even more than the corset already had. Her eyes trailed down Lillian's body, not looking at her chest or her lips but following the outline of her right side, more suggestive in her discretion than leering at Lillian would have been.

"Could you drop the act?" Lillian gestured toward Blue's... everything. "I need to talk to you for two minutes, and then you can go back to graffitiing women's cleavage."

"Okay." Had Blue's light dimmed a little? "What do you want to talk about?"

What could Lillian say? *I'm somewhat horrified that I slept with you, could you please not tell anyone? Also I'm not attracted to you.* The way her eyes kept darting between Blue's handsome face and her gorgeous body made a liar of Lillian.

"There's a clause in the contract that says we have to disclose if we know anyone on the show or the crew." Lillian crossed her arms, mirroring Blue's posture, but coldly. "I presume you didn't know I'd be here. I didn't know you'd be here. Neither of us disclosed, and I think we should keep it that way."

"It's nice to see you."

"I just want to make sure we can keep our connection private," Lillian said. "It seems like that would be the most professional option."

"So I can't sign my name across your heart?" Blue sang a line of the Terence Trent D'Arby song, her voice dropping an octave, smoky and velvety.

"No." It came out like a sharp command she'd give her dancers the third time they'd made the same mistake.

"We can still have fun, right?" Blue's smile looked a little forced. "Maybe I can get you to dance the Zipper. Or the waltz?"

"I'm not here to have fun, and I'd prefer you treat me like a stranger. We haven't met. We certainly haven't slept together." Lillian checked behind her. Thank goodness, no one had come upstairs to eavesdrop.

"You consented to sleep with me." Blue dropped her arms to her sides, looking down. "You were lovely. Thank you. And you didn't consent to me telling the world. Or anyone. So I wouldn't. I promise."

Thank God, she hadn't totally misread Blue that night at the Neptune. Blue was respectful. She'd be discreet.

Just to be sure, Lillian added, "Do you know how many cameras are on us? Like a dozen more than you see. They take candids for the show's social media. People watch that feed as much as they watch the show. We don't need the show turning us into some queerbaiting are-they-or-aren't-they thing. We don't need them making something out of nothing."

"I get it." Blue looked hurt, like someone who'd offered up a gift only to have it cast away.

It made Lillian's heart ache, which almost made her point out that Blue was the one who'd run out of her hotel room like a woman picking up a latte on her way to work. Blue didn't get to be mournful when she'd been the one to say *no catching feelings*. But there were so many things in life that could make you mournful if you weren't careful to keep those feelings bottled up where they belonged.

"Hey, I didn't mean that that night was nothing." Lillian fumbled for the right words. "I just can't get distracted." Wait. Did that imply she'd thought about sleeping with Blue again and decided against it? The thought shouldn't even cross her mind.

Faster than the arc of a shooting star, Blue's sadness disappeared...or she hid it.

"No second nightstand?" Blue grinned.

"No. Never."

Except the moment Lillian had seen Blue, she'd thought about
it. Remembered. Wanted. She shoved the thought away.

"You honored me by sharing your body," Blue said seriously. "I
will absolutely respect your boundaries."

"Thank you."

"Let's start over," Blue said. "I'm Blue Lenox from Velveteen
Crush. We're a body-positive, LGBTQ-plus burlesque troupe,
tamed down for TV, of course. And we're going to crush you in
this competition, you pretentious, dance academy...something,
something, something." Blue cocked her head. "Isn't that how
we're supposed to talk to each other? Build up some rivalries?"

"You dreadfully woke, steampunk...something, something,"
Lillian said.

Blue's smile lit the dim mezzanine as though Lillian playing
along was the most delightful thing Blue had ever experienced.
They tossed a few over-the-top taunts back and forth and chat-
ted for a little while longer, then Blue said, "Come on. Let's get
back down there." When they were back downstairs, Blue added,
"Good luck. You'll need it."

Lillian watched Blue disappear into the crowd. Either of them
could get voted off tomorrow. The thought made Lillian's chest
tighten, but she released the muscles as quickly as they had closed
up. She heard her mother's words echo in her mind. *You can choose
dance or you can choose distraction.* There was no time for nerves,
and there was no time for distraction. She was in control of every
muscle in her body and every thought that crossed her mind.

chapter 9

Izzy and the four other competing members of Velveteen Crush—Sarah, Arabella, Tock, and Axel—stood in the foyer of the Lynnwood Terrace. A burgundy carpet and dim sconces gave the old apartment a speakeasy feel. They hadn't had a chance to move in. They'd been instructed to go straight to the basement underneath the soundstage for hair and makeup, then to the get-together with the other contestants. Now the producer stood in front of them, checking their names on his tablet like they were kids on a field trip. Izzy could barely follow. Lillian was *here*. On the show. A ballerina who didn't want to know Izzy except that after Lillian had clearly stated that fact, they'd fallen into an easy banter. Izzy tried to focus.

"Arabella," Bryant said.

If Velveteen Crush were a boy band, Arabella would be the Dangerous One. Vampire seductress of the dark web meets *none of us really knows what you do, and we like to keep it that way.*

Arabella raised one painted eyebrow. "Here."

"Tock," Bryant said.

"Yes," Tock said crisply, as though he were at work responding to the summons of a senator. He'd be the Preppy One.

"Sarah."

"Here." Sarah giggled, her Shirley Temple curls bouncing.

"Isadora."

"Blue," Izzy corrected.

"And Axel."

Axel gave an enthusiastic "Yes, sir," then added, "present because I am a gift." Axel shimmied his massive shoulders. He was a gift to the world, a drag performer by night, a physical trainer for assisted living facilities during the day, a true believer in "fitness is for everyone."

Arabella looked out from beneath tarantula-sized lashes.

"It's *Today is a gift. That's why we call it the present.*"

Ordinarily Izzy would tease Arabella for knowing the saying. Arabella's ethos said, *I've come to drag you to the land of the undead*, not *The present is a gift*. But Izzy's thoughts were pinging inside her brain like nervous Ping-Pong balls. Lillian was here!

"Well, I am a gift to the world," Axel said crossing his muscular arms.

"Welcome to *The Great American Talent Show*, where America's best performers compete for the prize of one million dollars. The Lynnwood Terrace will be your home away from home for the duration of the show," Bryant recited, heading down the hall and up a flight of stairs. "You can store your costumes and props for the Signature Act in the soundstage basement. After that, you'll be assigned costumers who will handle everything." He stopped in front of units 201 and 203. "You've been assigned one two-bedroom unit. Men." He pointed to unit 201. "And one three-bedroom. Women." He pointed to 203. "Don't trade rooms. It almost always works out better if we keep the men and women separate."

"No a priori justification for that," Tock said, like the legislative aide he was.

"Where do *I* go?" Axel asked.

"With Tock." Bryant looked confused. That was fair. Out of drag, Axel looked like he should win Sexiest Male Trainer.

From a messenger bag slung over one shoulder, Bryant took out five bulging envelopes. "Here's your welcome package. Keys. Here's my number if you need anything. And your forwarded mail." He handed around junk mail, discreetly looking away as he handed Izzy hers. The theater's electric bill with PAST DUE stamped on the front. Izzy tried to shove it into her back pocket, forgetting she was wearing a suit of shiny, skintight latex.

"Fan mail? Another woman throwing herself at your feet?" Arabella asked as they stepped into their apartment.

"Don't pretend *you* don't have fans," Izzy said.

"I'm a scion on the dark web." Arabella's dark bangs swept across her bloodred eyeliner. "I have supplicants."

"And we don't know if you're kidding," Izzy said.

Arabella went into one of the rooms, then exclaimed, with a momentary lack of macabre irony, "Ooh, look, it's got its own bathroom."

They all did, plus a common bathroom, kitchen, sitting room, and fully stocked fridge and bar. Izzy stood in the center of her room, staring at her suitcases, which some crew members had carried in. She wriggled out of her suit and dug around in her suitcase for sweatpants and her Comic-Con sweatshirt.

Outside her room, she heard someone open the apartment door, then Arabella called across the hallway, "*Bloodless Mingo* is playing on Burnside. It's about satanic dolls that kill miners in West Virginia. Who's in?"

A moment later, Izzy heard Tock say, "Rotten Tomatoes says it's a 'horror show you can't unsee.'" Tock wouldn't embark on anything without research. "I'm in!"

Not that doing research always led to good decisions.

Axel said, "Heck yeah!"

"Blue?" Arabella poked her head into Izzy's room. "Satanic horror show?"

"Trying to cut back."

"Sarah?" Arabella turned back to the living room.

"I'm going to stay here," Sarah said. "I'm going to practice my lash work for the salon."

Izzy walked to the bedroom window, half listening to her friends in the other room. Was Lillian across the courtyard in the room with the flicking television? Was she practicing a routine? No wonder she'd been so strong. Lillian had caught her when she stumbled. Why had that felt so good? It was nothing.

After her friends left for the movie, the apartment fell silent. Izzy stared at her reflection in the window. In her burlesque costumes she was divine. No one could deny it no matter what ordinary beauty standards might say. But in everyday clothes? At the end of a long day? Bone-structure-wise, she wasn't that pretty. Arabella was gorgeous (on the rare occasion anyone saw it beneath her goth makeup), and Sarah had a classic silent film star face. Izzy's face was a little too hard to be girl-next-door pretty and a little too round to be handsome. Lillian had met her in a jacked-up outfit: jeans she'd gained too much weight to wear gracefully, a blazer she'd bought as a prop for an *Addams Family*–themed show, a Comic-Con sweatshirt. Yeah, she'd had a corset under that, but only because she couldn't find a clean bra. Had Izzy even been wearing deodorant that night? It'd been a twelve-hour day, and she'd gone to the Neptune to finish working so she wouldn't give in to the temptation to fall asleep in front of the TV. Strange that Lillian had still noticed her. She must have exuded enough of Blue's confidence to make up for her outfit.

"Hey."

Izzy turned at the sound of Sarah's voice.

"Where are you, Blue?" Sarah stood in the doorway.

"What? Here."

"Who was that woman?"

"What woman?"

Sarah put her hands on her hips, giving Izzy a disbelieving look.

"The beautiful Black woman. In the white suit. Who pulled you into some dark corner because…? And you haven't said a word since then."

"I have."

"You've been a million miles away. You turned down satanic dolls at a movie theater that serves microbrew."

"You make that sound hard."

Izzy did like indie theaters, and Portland required that everyone in the city limits like microbrew.

"Come help me put eyelashes on Judy." In the kitchen, Sarah pulled her mannequin head out of its carrying case and plopped it on the table, but she didn't open the case of fake lashes. "What was up with that woman? She looked pissed."

Izzy remembered Lillian's perfume: warm, soft, sunny, like walking through a lemon orchard. (Not that Izzy had ever walked through a lemon orchard, but she had a lemon tree in a pot, and it smelled divine.) Lillian looked like she'd wear something sharp and expensive, a classic, like Chanel No. 5, but she smelled like sipping tea in a summer field.

"She's Lillian, of the Reed-Whitmer Ballet Company."

Sarah waited.

Lillian had asked Izzy not to mention their night together. Totally reasonable. It hadn't meant anything. Why had Lillian's demand still stung?

"Promise to keep it on the DL?" Izzy asked.

"Sure."

"I mean for real. It's a respect thing."

"Of course." Sarah looked curious and serious.

"You won't believe this. We hooked up a while back. It was the night of the first-round auditions. She must have been in Portland for those."

"You didn't tell me about her."

"I don't talk about my hookups. It's disrespectful."

"You don't give me a tour of their labia, but you tell me something. She doesn't seem like the kind of woman you forget in the morning."

No. She wasn't. Lillian had floated in and out of Izzy's mind since the night at the Neptune.

"I had no idea I'd see her again. And we were on the same page about hookups."

Just strangers coming together for one night, their bodies part of a human whole, their life stories their own secrets. That was what hookups were supposed to be.

"It was nothing. We just... don't want to make a big deal out of it because of the show."

"Are you interested in her?"

"No!" Izzy said too loudly. "We had fun though. We danced. She was easy to be around." It was important to tell Sarah something true about her feelings; Sarah would stay in therapist mode until Izzy did. "It was easy to be... real around her." She felt Lillian bumping into her as they both tried to kiss each other against the wall. She smiled at the memory.

"Your energy feels unfinished..." Sarah left the sentence open.

"Hmm." Izzy touched a finger to her lips in exaggerated contemplation. "Nope. It pretty much finished the way I wanted."

She could have stayed another hour. But the gold flecks sparkling in Lillian's eyes…a person could fall for that smart, sharp, friendly light.

"Are you downplaying your emotional experience?"

"Always." Denying it would inspire Sarah to ask more empathetic questions. Agreeing would also spawn an outpouring of empathy. Best to joke and agree. "Isn't that why you're always sending me links to therapists?"

Hopefully, Sarah wouldn't start in on the whole *there's nothing wrong with safe consensual hookups if that's really what you want, but you don't act like they make you happy anymore* lecture.

"There's nothing wrong with safe, consensual hookups if that's really what you want, but you don't act like they make you happy anymore," Sarah said.

"You know, there *was* unfinished business. She was wearing white. She had mud on her cuffs." Why had she noticed that while she was sliding the pants off a woman with the body of a Greek statue? "If she got those pants dry-cleaned, it would've set the stain. You have to use club soda first."

Sarah frowned.

"You care about her dry cleaning?"

"Not deeply, but linen is *so* temperamental."

"Izzy, are you sure you're in a good emotional place with this?"

"I'm not interested in her." How could anyone meet Lillian and not be interested? "Not like that. Not like relationship material. If I get in a relationship, it'll be with a nice social worker with two diabetic cats."

Izzy reached across the table and opened the lash kit. She turned Judy around and tweezed a single lash extension onto Judy's eyelid, skewering her in the eye instead. She didn't fall for modest women with diabetic cats. She fell for her mother in hot queer woman form every time. Charismatic? Check. A brilliant performer? Check. Likelihood of sticking around? Minus ten percent. Check.

Izzy tried to put another lash on Judy.

"A relationship could be a good thing for you," Sarah said. "But you said to tell you when I saw you going for *that* kind of woman again. You said, *Don't let me date unattainable women because I'm still chasing my mother's love.*"

"*You* said I was chasing my mother's love. I said it was hard to find the right balance between attractive and not an asshole."

But Sarah was right.

The opera singer from San Francisco. The injured WNBA player.

Sarah made sympathetic eye contact.

"Don't worry." Izzy stuck another eyelash in the vicinity of Judy's eye. "We're going to crush Lillian's company in the competition, and then we'll never see each other again." It felt like saying she'd never see the Milky Way again. "I'm not going to fall for her."

It'd been a couple of years since she threw herself at a brilliant, talented woman who eventually ended it with either *I need to focus on my career* or *I'm exploring my options.* The thing that hurt the most was her girlfriends' timing. The breakup always came after Izzy had gotten the flu or had to pull an all-nighter for work. She'd emerge from her office with greasy hair and dark circles under her eyes. There was always a moment when they looked at her and their eyes registered, *Oh, you're not Blue Lenox.*

chapter 10

Lillian stood in front of her dancers in the warehouse space the show had assigned them for rehearsals. The show occupied three distinct spaces: the soundstage, set up to look like a flashy theater; a labyrinth of basement greenrooms and makeup stations; and a warehouse with rehearsal spaces for every team. They'd been rehearsing for two days, from six a.m. until Lillian released them around eight, so that she could go back to her room and adjust the choreography. Lillian tried to fix the image of her dancers in her mind. If they lost—and they might lose tomorrow—she would never dance with them again or see them like this, all standing at attention.

There was Jonathan, their gentle giant, dreaming of one day returning home to dance for the Dance Theater of Harlem. Elijah, who swished his hips at every hot guy he passed and pursued none of them because his first love was dance. Malik, who called his grandmother every night. Pascale, with her mushroom cap of processed hair, who always gave ninety-nine percent and never a hundred and cried when a tour started because it meant more time away from her kids. And brilliant, insubordinate Imani. Lillian understood Eleanor when she watched Imani dance. How could you not push a talent like that to the breaking point? Once you saw Imani turn a grand fouetté en tournant, her soul spinning in the spotlight, her braids coiled up toward heaven, your life was complete. At least it felt that way for a second.

"How are you feeling about the choreography?" Lillian asked.

The dancers nodded.

"Good."

"Yes."

"Got it."

"Pascale? Questions? Problems? Issues?" Lillian asked.

Pascale straightened.

"No," Pascale said.

"Are you nervous?" Lillian asked, spreading her hands to include the whole company.

"Just excited to crush it." Elijah did an overly dramatic grand jeté.

The cameras would love him.

No one said anything else. They'd talk when Lillian was gone, just like Pascale cried when she thought Lillian couldn't see her. That was good. Lillian danced with the company, but they still needed a ballet master, the premier maître de ballet, someone who drove them to do better. Always. Someone to trust, fear, dislike, and revere at turns. Lillian had cultivated that persona. She committed, even when she was tired or nervous or uncertain about her choreography. A ballet master wasn't distracted by their own feelings. Had Eleanor said that? Or was that one hers?

"Fine. Go," Lillian said.

The dancers were out the door in seconds, their voices ringing out as soon as they were out of the space. Lillian walked slowly to her bag tossed in the corner. She pulled out her phone and glared at the screen. There was a perfectly punctuated text from Eleanor.

Eleanor: *When you're done with rehearsal, would you be so kind as to give me a call.*

Reluctantly, Lillian touched call.

"I know you're busy," Eleanor said by way of greeting. "If anyone can make that show see real talent, it's you. I'll be quick. I have something I'd like to discuss."

Just once she'd like Eleanor to greet her the way Uncle Carl greeted Kia when he called, usually jumping directly into conversation with something like *The Grand Hôtel Etienne is mixing a wheatgrass mimosa. What do you think? Genius or affront to humanity?*

"If it's the teaching fellowship in Paris, I'm not ready to commit." Lillian lowered her voice although the dancers were gone. It wasn't fair to the company for Lillian to have her own backup plan and nothing for them.

"If you're worried about the company, they'll be fine," Eleanor said, reading her mind. "Pascale can go parent her children."

Lillian shouldn't engage. She should find out what Eleanor wanted, get off the phone, and sleep as much as she could before call in the morning.

"There is nothing wrong with parenting her children," Lillian shot back instead.

"Of course not. Being a parent is a beautiful thing."

Eleanor tacked on a silent *for some people.*

Lillian relaxed the muscles in her throat and abdomen.

"What can I help you with, Mom?"

"Did you see the movie *Inevitable Comfort*? No?" Eleanor

answered for her. "You're too busy. Disciplined. The only way to win."

"I did see it. Kia made me."

"Did you like it?"

"I guess." She'd been more stressed about wasting time relaxing than she was focused on the movie, but every single person who cared about film said it was brilliant.

"The director, Ashlyn Stewart, she was a guest lecturer in your father's department last year. The Film Department loved her. And she's finishing up a documentary on dancers of color."

No. No. No.

It was obvious where Eleanor was going.

"The film is basically done. It'll be premiering in a few weeks, but I told Ashlyn she has to have your perspective. She said there's enough flexibility in the documentary format that she could splice in a few quotes from you."

Why can't the past be over?

"Our lawsuit was a landmark moment for the Lynn Bernau School," Eleanor said. "When we won, we changed ballet education."

Now everyone knows that saying, *The choreography calls for consistent complexion*, could get you sued.

"I know that was a difficult time for you," Eleanor said. "But this will be a paradigm-shifting documentary, and it won't be complete unless you're in it. You were at the center of that. Your talent made that lawsuit and everything that came after possible."

How much did Lillian want to relive, on camera, the most stressful time in her life, a time she still couldn't think about without getting nauseated? Not at all. She could still feel the bile rise in her throat as she waited backstage for a solo or audition. Before the lawsuit, Eleanor had pushed her to be her best, but as soon as

Eleanor put down the lawyer's retainer, sixteen-year-old Lillian had to be more than the best. If you sued one of America's premier dance schools because they weren't giving your talented daughter the parts she deserved, it better be obvious to every ballet master in the world that your daughter deserved them. It wasn't enough to be better than her peers; she had to be ten times as good. If she wasn't and they lost, Eleanor came off looking like a jealous dance mom. The case against the Lynn Bernau School set legal precedent for the idea that ballet companies couldn't pick their dancers based on race because choreography required *consistent coloring.*

After that, Lillian's friends didn't want to be associated with her. The school administration hated Lillian as she continued to study at the school while the lawsuit dragged on. *We must show them you belong there,* Eleanor had said when, in an uncharacteristic bout of tears, Lillian had begged Eleanor to let her change schools. Only her girlfriend kept texting and comforting her in the few moments they could steal together. But, according to Eleanor, *the girl was a distraction.* Lillian didn't know if she had been angrier at Eleanor for telling her to break up with her girlfriend or with herself for doing it. All she knew was that when she called it off, something inside her broke and something was reinforced with steel. Ballet was everything. You didn't get to be as good as Lillian was and fall in love too.

Wasn't it enough that she'd made that sacrifice? Did she really have to tell Ashlyn Stewart how great it was to give up a personal life to be the best? You couldn't be in a groundbreaking documentary and say, *I fought racism in dance, and I won, and sometimes when I'm having sex with a woman I'll never see again, I think,* I'd probably be happier if I'd lost. And why did Eleanor have to shove her in the spotlight again? Ashlyn was done with the film. She didn't need to fit Lillian in.

Could she get out of the interview? Maybe she could go sailing with Uncle Carl, get stranded on an island, live on coconuts...no. The Coast Guard would find her. She and Kia could move to...what country didn't have cell service or Wi-Fi? None. She had to say yes. Jacksons said yes. They didn't turn away from a chance to make a difference.

Lillian slid down the wall, until she sat on the cold concrete floor.

"You are an icon, Lillian. You truly are."

Lillian wanted to say, *You love Uncle Carl for having a yacht with a million spaniels. Why do I have to be a fucking icon?*

"Stewart's producer talked to one of *The Great American Talent Show* producers. You'll be filming a challenge in LA. Don't mention it. It's a huge surprise. It's reality TV, after all." Lillian could almost hear her mother roll her eyes. "He said the show wouldn't mind if you used your days off to do the interview. Generally, that's against contract, but having you on the show and in the documentary would be good publicity."

For a second, Lillian was back in the courtroom, sweating in a high-collared blouse, the eyes of every administrator at the Lynn Bernau School of Dance stabbing her from the gallery. Now she'd have to relive that so she could be an icon or a paradigm or a trailblazer or all the other hyperbolic things people had called her because when she was sixteen, her mother sued her dance school. Why couldn't Kia have been the dancer and Lillian have gotten the gay single father whose idea of activism was banning wheatgrass mimosas?

"Of course you don't have to," Eleanor said with uncharacteristic gentleness.

But Lillian did have to do it. Dancers knew how to move through pain.

"I'd be honored," Lillian said. She rushed through her goodbye and hung up.

Half of Lillian's mind was still in the courtroom as she stepped out of the rehearsal space into the hallway, swinging the door open and directly into...Blue. Blue dodged, then saw who it was.

"Oh," Blue gasped.

For a second, they stared at each other, Lillian taking in Blue's screamingly tangerine-colored suit and purple corset that lifted her breasts toward Lillian, the breasts she'd cupped for only a second. Lillian needed to learn the exact blend of caress and bite that made Blue—

No. She did not need to learn anything. Or look. Or think about. Especially because Blue was accompanied by what was probably her troupe: four of the most mismatched people Lillian had ever seen in one place. Lillian whirled away, but not before she felt a flash of delight at the sight of Blue, like she had when she was a teenager and saw a new post by one of her favorite dancers. She tamped it down and set her lips in a neutral line.

One of Blue's troupe, a woman with bright red curls, glared at Lillian and then walked on, followed by a trio that looked like a goth stripper, a businessman, and a quarterback.

"We'll be late, Blue," the redhead called over her shoulder.

"I'll be there." Blue turned back to Lillian. She looked like she was about to say something flirtatious, then stopped, her face resolving into a stranger's neutral politeness. "Sorry. After you." She gestured for Lillian to precede her.

Lillian should follow Blue's troupe, but suddenly the prospect of making conversation with the other performers exhausted her. She waited until Blue's troupe turned a corner.

Blue studied Lillian. "You okay?"

Totally. Absolutely. Always. She was in some windowless warehouse, in Portland, Oregon, a day away from letting a studio audience determine her fate, reliving the worst day of high school, an icon of Black ballet who wouldn't even consider saying no to her mother.

Lillian let out a long breath. "I just got off the phone with my mother."

"I know that feeling," Blue said ruefully.

"She is not a bad person. No. She's a good person. An excellent person. It's just..." Lillian hiked her bag higher on her shoulder. "I shouldn't complain."

"Do you want to talk about it?" Blue hesitated. "You don't have to, obviously, but sometimes it's easier to talk to a stranger."

"It's okay. You don't have to pretend we're strangers."

"Just that we haven't..." Blue spoke so quietly, Lillian wasn't sure she'd heard her behind the sound of the HVAC.

"Right," Lillian said. "But not because it wasn't...special."

Blue tucked her hands in the pockets of her traffic-cone-orange suit and bobbed from side to side as if trying to contain a little burst of happiness.

"So your mom?" Blue asked.

Lillian could not spill her feelings to Blue. Of all people! But suddenly Blue felt like just the person she wanted to talk to. Blue wouldn't rhapsodize about what an icon her mother was or tell her Eleanor wasn't as uptight as Lillian made out or call her a little puffin.

"You ever feel like you love everything that you do, but it's just too much, even if you love it?" Lillian let her bag slump to the floor.

"You just described my whole life. And is your mom one of those too-much things you love?"

"Yeah. She wants a favor. And it's not too much to ask, and it's important, and I said yes. It's just...I don't know."

"The last straw?"

"No. I'll do it. It's no big deal."

"But it is," Blue said sympathetically. "If it's a big deal to you, it is."

"I wonder what it's like to have a last straw, to have something that makes you fall apart or do the thing you never thought you'd do or give up or get on the next plane and go wherever it's going. That makes you go, *Oh, fuck this shit, I'm going to do whatever I want.*"

"I bet you never say *Fuck this shit*," Blue observed.

"Nope. You?"

"Look at me." Blue spread her arms, then gave her breasts a squeeze.

She clearly meant the gesture to say, *Obviously, I'm a fuck-this-shit kind of person.* But Lillian had seen Blue struggling over her president app. And Blue might sign women's breasts, but she cared about the toxicity of the pen she used. And Blue had been the most attentive lover Lillian had had in a long time, asking and listening and tuning in to Lillian's every movement.

"No." Lillian shook her head slowly. "I don't think you're like that."

Blue's eyes seemed to say, *Thank you.*

"If you have that last straw while we're on the show," Blue said, "you can come and find me if you want someone to talk to. My friend Sarah"—Blue gestured to the hallway where her people had gone—"she's not a therapist, but she thinks she is, so I get a lot of insight into...things. People. Feelings. She's loaned me a lot of self-help books."

"I've never had time to read a self-help book. Do they help?"

"I don't read them," Blue said, lightening her tone. "I don't want to deal with my deep emotional issues." She grinned. "Nah. I'm already perfect."

"You and me both."

They exhaled a collective sigh. Blue's grin faded to a real smile, tired and friendly. Depending on how the first challenge went, Lillian might never see that smile again. What a shame.

chapter 11

A huge television hung on one wall of the greenroom in the basement of the soundstage. Competitors could watch each other's performances on the TV...if they ever started. Izzy slouched on the sofa, staring at the blank screen. The greenroom was a comfortable purgatory. There were no windows, but there was nice furniture in shades of green, orange, and blue. Snacks filled a full-sized fridge. Another fridge held enough Fizz Bang soda to fill a bathtub.

Izzy had already sat on every piece of furniture and stared at every bit of wall. She was so nervous. Her stomach had tightened into a knot and hidden behind her other organs. She hadn't taken a breath in hours and she was hyperventilating. At the same time. She was so bored! How could you be this bored and still be having a heart attack? Apparently, it was possible. She tapped the binary code tattoo on her breastbone to calm herself. It didn't help. She stretched backward, her head hanging over the back of the sofa.

Behind her, Axel hovered in plank position, arms trembling. Tock paced back and forth, probably stressing more from the lack of Wi-Fi—which meant American politics was going on without him—than from the upcoming performance. Izzy sat up, seeing stars. Across from her, Sarah yanked at a snarl of yarn in her lap, ostensibly knitting a scarf although it looked more like she was trying to stab the wool into submission. Only Arabella was calm, lying on one of the sofas, hands crossed over her chest like a corpse.

They'd been up since six. They'd waited for Bryant to come to the greenroom and brief them. They'd waited for the costume department to check their costumes—they got to use their own for the Signature Act Challenge—for wardrobe-malfunction possibilities. Now they were waiting for...lunch? Makeup? Death? The first performers hadn't even gone on.

No. Izzy knew what she was waiting for.

First, she was waiting to perform because this was the first challenge standing between her and bankruptcy. No, no that wasn't what mattered. Velveteen Crush needed its own inclusive safe space. That mattered. Izzy's bankruptcy was just a possible side effect...an awful, very possible side effect. Given how dumb it was to buy the theater, it wasn't even a *side* effect. It was more like exactly the effect you'd expect if you poured everything you had and a lot of money you didn't have into buying an almost condemned theater.

She was definitely having a heart attack.

She closed her eyes and pictured Lillian's wry smile. But thoughts of Lillian didn't soothe the feeling that Izzy had drunk a hundred Red Bulls. Lillian was performing next. Lillian might lose. Izzy would never see her again. Of course, if Izzy was to save herself from financial ruin, Velveteen Crush would have to beat the Reed-Whitmer Ballet Company eventually, but it didn't have to be today. If she could see Lillian a few more times, maybe exchange numbers, and—no, no, no. On Izzy's list of bad ideas, Lillian appeared one line beneath the Roosevelt Theater.

But still, Lillian shouldn't get voted off in the first round.

The TV crackled to life. Arabella sat up. Tock stopped pacing. Axel turned up the volume on the TV.

The television screen flipped from one camera view to another. In one view, the judges sat on their dais. Another angle showed lights pulsing in the Star Maker, a twenty-foot column of pure LED. They'd seen the theater set empty and unlit. An assistant producer had spent an hour showing them how to enter the stage and where to stand when the judges critiqued them. But this was different.

Izzy tried to summon Blue's calm, but she needed to be onstage, performing. Then she could become the invincible Blue Lenox. Sitting here, chewing on her lip, sweating in her pre-costume T-shirt and jeans, she couldn't find Blue. If only they could have gone first.

The camera angles stopped cycling so quickly, eventually, settling on alternating shots of the judges and the stage. The judges faced forward. Sound came through the TV speakers, first a buzz of people talking on headsets or radios, then Bryant's voice.

"Quiet on set. Action in three."

The screen showed the view from a camera pointed at the stage. The hosts, Hallie and Harrison, ran down from the back of the soundstage, leapt onto the set, and started the speech that begun every season of *The Great American Talent Show*.

"We have ten teams all doing different performance styles," Harrison explained. "Each week, we're going to give them a special challenge, and they're going to compete to see which teams bring it and which team has to go home."

"We have three judges," Hallie said. "But we have four votes."

"Whaaaat?" Harrison exclaimed as though he had lost long-term memory.

"That's right. The fourth judge is you!" Hallie pointed at the audience and then at the neon thermometer on the side of the stage. The column flashed with a thousand lights. "The Star Maker! Everyone in the audience today will click for the performances they like best. In fact, we think your vote is so important, the first and last challenge will be determined entirely by the Star Maker."

"And what do our contestants win if they make it to the end?" Harrison asked, his memory of all previous seasons gone.

"One million dollars!" Hallie squealed.

"Now let's meet the judges!" Harrison said.

The live camera feed didn't look exactly like the show on television. The camera moved in too fast. Half of Harrison's face got lost off-screen for a second. Bryant called cut, and Hallie and Harrison performed their part again. But it was unmistakably the show. Later today, Velveteen Crush would be on that stage. They'd stand on the x's that marked where the contestants faced the judges and the Star Maker. They'd go on to the next round. They had to. Izzy closed her eyes and tried not to think about the bills piling up.

The camera switched to the judges. From somewhere off-screen, Bryant called action again. The camera stayed focused on the judges. Harrison's disembodied voice came over the speakers.

"Our first judge is Alejandro Pastega, founder of the performance art company Transformación Milán." Harrison drew out the A in Pastega for several beats.

The camera pulled in on Pastega, as slim and elegant as ever. He adjusted his heavy, black rectangular glasses and nodded at the camera. The next judge was new this season, a prima ballerina for the New York Ballet Company named Christina-Margarita Ebb Bessinger-Silas.

"That is a lot of names," Axel said without taking his eyes off the screen.

On-screen, Hallie said, "And finally, the reason some of the troupes are quaking in their boots."

"Or their pointe shoes," Harrison said.

Pastega and Many-Named Ballerina didn't matter. America watched the show for Paul Michael, aka the Prime Minister.

"Welcome," Hallie and Harrison said together, fluttering some jazz hands. "Prime Minister!"

The cameras zoomed in on the crown of the Prime Minister's head, his hair twisted in Bantu knots. When he looked up, he stared directly at the camera, impossibly handsome with his trademark smile that welcomed the audience like a secret handshake.

"Y'all ready to help me pick the next great American talent? We want to be wowed this season, don't we! No amateurs." He snapped his fingers and spoke into the camera. "Don't come lacking."

The studio audience cheered. Bryant called for another sound check.

"He's just as handsome on-screen as he is…on-screen," Axel said.

It made sense. This was for real.

"And our first performance of the season will be"—Harrison flung his arms open—"the Reed-Whitmer Ballet Company."

A knock on the door made them all look up. A young woman—a runner, the position was called—stood in the doorway.

"Blue Lenox. We're doing your first candid. Come with me," the runner said, oblivious to the emotional crisis Izzy was having in preparation for seeing the Reed-Whitmer Ballet Company perform as broadcast through a rotating series of cameras.

Izzy looked at Sarah.

"We'll tell you if she wins," Sarah said, sympathetic even though she'd recently given Izzy the you-told-me-not-to-let-you-fall-for-women-like-this speech.

"Who're you talking about?" Axel asked.

"No one," Izzy said, although Lillian was *not* no one.

"Ready?" the runner asked.

chapter 12

Blue followed the runner from the greenroom, down the hall, to another room, with a screen set up and a microphone hanging above it. A camera operator waved from her position behind a camera on an elaborate tripod. The woman who had led Izzy in indicated that she should sit on the stool in front of the screen. A man Izzy hadn't met yet hurried in a minute later.

"Blue. Right. Okay. I'm going to ask you a few questions. Just speak from the heart, and I'll let you know if we need you to adjust your content."

"Speak from the heart but you'll tell me if I get it wrong?"

"Exactly." The man didn't get the joke. He pointed to the camera operator. "Action. Blue Lenox, tell us about yourself."

What had she put in the initial personal history surveys? The more accurate she was, the sooner she could get back to the greenroom. Maybe one of the innumerable sound and light checks had delayed Lillian's performance.

"I grew up in a small town in eastern Oregon," she said. "My mom was a talented singer, and she inspired my love of performance. In high school I did theater, choir, dance team, even cheerleading."

Or maybe they wanted her to be spontaneous and dramatic. They'd keep her here until she cracked.

"My mother never came to my shows." That had pathos. And truth.

"How about, *I always wanted to follow in her footsteps*?" the man said.

"What?"

"Say, *I always wanted to follow in her footsteps.*"

Speak from the heart, but don't get it wrong. It was a joke, and it wasn't. Izzy repeated the line.

"When I went to college, I majored in dance and computer science," she went on.

"Say that again without computer science," the man said. "Let's keep it simple."

"When I went to college, I majored in dance, but I noticed there wasn't a lot of room in dance for diverse bodies, genders, and abilities."

"Cut *diverse* and say *different*," the man said. "And cut *genders.*"

"Different bodies and abilities."

How long was this going to go on?

"So I founded Velveteen Crush. It's a no-audition burlesque group. Everyone is welcome, no matter their skill level."

"How do you think you'll win *The Great American Talent Show* if you let everyone in?"

"Only five of us decided to go on the show, but we represent our whole troupe. We represent anyone who's wanted to dance or sing or juggle and has been told they couldn't."

The man gave a thumbs-up and went on with his questions.

Eventually, he checked his smartwatch, swore something about being behind schedule, and walked out.

"I'll walk you back to your greenroom," the woman who'd brought her said.

Would it be okay if she ran?

"Did Reed-Whitmer go on yet?"

"I don't think so."

Back in the greenroom, Izzy flung herself onto the sofa in front of the TV. The Reed-Whitmer Ballet Company had just emerged onstage. The show had enhanced—or detracted from—the performance with a stadium's worth of flashing lights. It must be dizzying to perform in that barrage of visual stimulation, but the dancers didn't miss a beat. The Star Maker shot up.

When the performance ended and the lights calmed down, a few of the dancers were panting, but Lillian looked as calm as if she had walked out of a café. Izzy wasn't supposed to notice the way Lillian's leotard cupped her body where Izzy had touched her and made her gasp with pleasure. Izzy wasn't supposed to find this sexy. Ballerinas were sexless, like a cross between angels and Barbie dolls. But Lillian's tights and leotard perfectly matched her dark skin. It looked like she was naked—and those legs! Izzy had ridden a fast orgasm on Lillian's thigh. Her body ached to do it again. She shifted in her seat. She was probably emitting pheromones that screamed, *I'm lusting after that woman.*

She had to be chill.

"I wonder if we've got any Fizz Bang soda." *Don't pay attention to me. I'm just thinking about drinking soda, not drinking the nectar of Lillian Jackson's body.*

"There's literally soda everywhere," Sarah said without taking her focus off the judges on the screen.

Alejandro said the company's technical precision was unparalleled.

Christina said the performance made her cry, although she didn't appear to be crying.

The Prime Minister steepled his fingers, considering.

"Very good, very good. Like Alejandro said, the level of skill..." He pressed a hand to his chest. "But a little advice for next time..."

The cameras zoomed in on Christina turning to the Prime Minister. "How could you have advice?! They were perfect."

"I want you to feel the dance, Ms. Jackson," the Prime Minister said.

"Damn, they're perfect," Izzy said.

"The perfect is the enemy of the good," Axel said.

Arabella sighed in his direction. "That's what you say when something isn't perfect, and you don't mind."

"No," Axel said. "They just crushed *good*. Good just went crying home to its mother."

"I wonder if they have to secure the rights to use that choreography," Tock said.

They all looked at him.

"They were amazing, and that's your takeaway?" Arabella asked.

Tock shrugged.

Izzy felt Sarah trying to read her. *Are you impressed by her dance, or are you developing a crush on yet another woman who's going to break your heart?*

"I think that's classic choreography. It's old enough they don't need to get the rights," Izzy said, not looking at Sarah so Sarah couldn't read anything in Izzy's eyes.

Tock muted the screen as the cameras once again broadcast shots of the empty stage and the judges drinking soda. Then

Velveteen Crush went back to waiting in purgatory. Izzy pretended to nap on one of the sofas, wishing she were alone so she could relieve the tension she felt remembering Lillian's hard thigh beneath her as she came and trying to get her mind around the fact that *she had slept with that woman.* That impossibly talented goddess who was longing for a last straw. They'd recognized something about each other in that moment. And she wanted to ask her, *How can you be so amazing and still be real?*

chapter 13

Around eleven p.m. a woman with a tablet appeared in the door to the Reed-Whitmer Ballet Company's greenroom. Lillian set down her sketchbook, where she'd been drawing on and off throughout the day. She'd been working on a sequence of drawings showing a relevé moving into an attitude turn. It would be so easy to "write" choreography with a series of animated videos. The choreographer could select different moves, transitions, and speeds and then share the sequence with her dancers. The app could save Lillian hours writing in Benesh and then translating the notes for her dancers. She'd never do anything with her app idea. She'd never have the time. But it was a good idea, and, just for once, she needed distraction.

She shouldn't be nervous. The modern dance troupe, Retroactive Silence, had come in several points lower than the Reed-Whitmer Ballet Company. They were safe. But Velveteen Crush was going last. The audience would vote them off even if they were good. Everyone knew the last interviewee never got the job, the last dancer never won the audition. There was research. Something about attention fatigue. And the studio audience looked beyond fatigued. One woman had passed out. They would hate the last act. God could descend onstage on a cloud, and they'd still be thinking, *When are we getting out of here?*

"You're free to go," the woman who'd appeared at the door said. "It's been a long day. Call is at six tomorrow for candids, team interactions, and anything we need to reshoot from last night. Costume got your outfits, yes?"

As soon as they'd finished their post-performance interviews, a trio of women had whisked their outfits away on a luggage cart, explaining that if they needed to reshoot anything, the outfits had to match yesterday exactly. *Sweat stains and all*, one woman had explained. *We photograph them and use water to re-create the stains if we need to reshoot.*

Lillian's eyes flew to the TV screen, which was broadcasting shots of the crew setting up for Velveteen Crush's act. The woman read her mind.

"We'll show you some clips if you need to talk about them in the candids, or Bryant can just give you the lines. We'd like you to say something like—" The woman scrolled through something on her tablet. "—*I appreciate their effort, but I don't know how an amateur group really thought they'd compete with professionals.* In your own words, of course. Going for snotty but not bitchy. And Bryant expects they'll get cut tonight, so we don't need to focus on them. So you guys can go."

Imani said, "We out."

Pascale said, "I need to call my kids."

Lillian opened her mouth to tell the dancers it was important to watch all the competitors. On the screen she caught a shot of Blue high-fiving some of the crew, her smile magnetic, her curves luscious. Lillian could watch Velveteen Crush's performance alone.

"Get some rest," Lillian said to her dancers.

She heard Elijah whisper, "Isn't rest where talent goes to die?" as he sashayed out of the room.

"You too," Lillian said to Kia, who had been happily working on her laptop, finalizing a marketing plan for a second food truck. She worked as hard as Lillian. At least she'd been as successful in the world of hipster street food as Lillian was in ballet. But Kia still had time for yachting with her father and taking weeks off to eavesdrop on the backstage workings of *The Great American Talent Show*.

Kia kissed the top of Lillian's head.

"I'll leave you alone to watch your burlesque babe."

"She's not my—"

Kia had already bounced out of the room.

And on the screen, Velveteen Crush was starting, and they were…not entirely awful.

The troupe did a kind of cancan with little cameos where each of the performers stepped forward and performed a solo. The drag queen sashayed. The man who'd looked like a presidential aide in his street clothes tap-danced while thrusting his hips and rubbing his chest. The red-haired woman made every part of her body jiggle. The lights in the Star Maker column plummeted. The center of the column flashed Velveteen Crush's dropping score. One point below Retroactive Silence. Now two points. Three.

And that was it; Velveteen Crush would come in dead last. Disappointment hit Lillian harder than she expected. She really wouldn't see Blue again. A hot, sad longing filled her body. She would never make Blue melt. And Lillian needed to. It wasn't just attraction. She wanted to tease Blue until she lost control and cried out in pleasure and Lillian saw the person behind the mask. She wanted to see Blue's cocky smile softened by the afterglow of a long, sensuous orgasm. She wanted to make Blue feel so good the hint of sadness left her eyes. And Lillian wouldn't, because the woman in the goth outfit was crawling around on the floor like a murderous, slow-motion cat. The Star Maker plunged.

That was for the best. This feeling was the kind of baseless crush she'd felt as a young teen when some girl caught her fancy and she'd dream up scenarios where they kissed and took road trips, and Eleanor would scold her for being distracted during rehearsals. She must be tired. It must be from sitting in a windowless room for twelve-plus hours waiting for nothing.

Except this.

Blue stepped forward. She wore the orange suit, but in the lights, it looked like fire, not fabric. She looked out at the audience as though she hadn't expected them to be there. Then she winked, and her wink said, *I know exactly what I'm doing, and I'm taking you with me.*

"Burlesque is a place in the margins." Blue must have been miked, because her voice resonated through the TV screen. "A place where we can explore what arouses us, what frightens us, a place where we can let go of shame."

The audience cheered with the mania of people who knew they could escape if they could just scream through one more act. Izzy pressed her fingertips to her lips and blew the audience a kiss. A tingle ran through Lillian's body. The Star Maker rose a point. A song Lillian didn't recognize played in the background.

"Have you ever felt as though you weren't enough?" Blue held her arms out. She timed her words to hang in the air when the song grew quiet. Then the song soared, and she raised her voice.

The Star Maker rose.

Blue slipped out of her jacket, carrying it casually over one shoulder.

"Not thin enough?" Her corset accented every sumptuous curve. "Not straight enough?" She blew a kiss to Sarah.

Jealousy stung Lillian like static electricity. Harmless. Fleeting. More an illusion than a feeling. Blue and Sarah weren't…were they? What was Lillian thinking? She didn't care.

"Not rich enough?" Blue strode across the stage, confident like she was strolling into a woman's bedroom. "You are enough. You fill the whole sky. The Milky Way is holding open its arms for you." She tossed her suit coat offstage and kept talking. Was it spoken word or a speech?

The applause died down because the audience was listening. The Star Maker hit eighty. How long was Blue's piece? Could she possibly pull up their score? The Reed-Whitmer Ballet Company had scored ninety-seven. The lowest score had been ninety-one, the highest ninety-nine.

The way Blue had smiled when Lillian had joked about the competitive things they were supposed to say to each other, so happy that Lillian was playing along, had been so charming. Not ruthlessly sexy like the woman onstage but cute, even a tiny bit shy. And tonight the Star Maker would destroy whatever dreams Blue had for the show, as it should. Velveteen Crush was the worst team, and mediocrity should fail. *But please*…a voice in the back of Lillian's mind whispered. *Give them one more week.*

Eighty-four.

Blue strode to the edge of the stage, turned her back, and slowly stroked her hands down her sides. The song's backbeat held her message in its heartbeat. She was going to take off her corset. No, the show wouldn't let her. Too risqué.

"It's okay to want things." Blue looked over her shoulder at the audience. "I want you."

She dropped her corset. The audience gasped. Somehow she wasn't topless but covered in a shimmering haze of fabric, as though she'd manifested a cloud of tulle.

"Did you think I'd give you the world?" Blue winked.

Velveteen Crush was bad, but Blue had taken charm to prima levels. The camera zoomed in on her face. The way her lips pulled up in a half smile, the way she commanded the camera's attention, it felt like she touched the deepest part of Lillian's heart, the rough, complicated chambers Lillian locked away, even from herself. Blue must be making the whole audience feel the same because the Star Maker edged up.

"We are here for one night. We. Are. Here. We breathe together." It was the kind of thing a yoga instructor said, but Blue said it like the words unlocked human connection. "And for everyone watching out there in America, you are my heart."

Eighty-seven.

"A gold thread ties us together."

Ninety-two.

Ninety-eight.

The song was ending.

Ninety-nine.

"So pure a gold." Blue's voice wasn't loud as much as it was huge. It melded with the last beat. She turned her back to the audience, swept her arms open, and everything she wore fell to the ground, replaced by a silky white robe. How did she do it? Someone must have turned on a fan, because it billowed around her, as large as a sail and as light as air. The song ended. The lights went off except for a single spotlight on Blue.

She was radiant.

"And Velveteen Crush comes in first with one hundred percent," Hallie sang out. "Congratulations, Velveteen Crush."

chapter 14

Izzy stood on the stage. The Star Maker flashed like the lights of Vegas. She was still vibrating with Blue Lenox's energy. She was glittering. She was a goddess. She was the spirit of burlesque. The nervous adrenaline that had been flowing through her body since they arrived at the apartment had turned into helium and electricity.

She barely heard the hosts until Harrison said, "We've got a big surprise for you."

The audience let out a dutiful *oooh*.

"I'm excited to announce the sponsor of the next challenge: USpin. With great video editing features and over a thousand appearance-enhancing filters, USpin is America's hippest new social media platform."

Fizz Bang soda was the official sponsor of the show, but every episode except the first one had an additional corporate sponsor. It was all part of the capitalist conspiracy, according to Arabella.

"Since Velveteen Crush came in first, you get to pick the dance for the next challenge based on one of USpin's viral dance challenges," Hallie said.

The audience cheered as though the cue card woman had a card reading *Cheer or we will make you stay here forever.*

Izzy caught her breath. The set felt huge. Even knowing it was a set, she felt like she was on TV with an audience of millions, a stage so high it disappeared from view until the cameras panned back.

"What'll it be?" Harrison prompted.

"I have to ask my troupe; we make all our decisions together." Izzy looked back at Tock, Axel, Arabella, and Sarah hugging each other and jumping up and down.

"No deliberation please," the Prime Minister announced from his place on the judges' dais. "Blue Lenox, choose!"

Behind her, Sarah said, "You got this."

Izzy stared into the lights. Was Lillian watching the performance on a TV screen in a windowless room underneath the stage? *I pick the waltz.* Of course not. That wasn't a USpin dance challenge. Izzy sought out the camera most likely to be focused on her face and winked.

"I think I know someone who'd love to dance the Zipper."

"You've done it at weddings and class reunions," Harrison said with wild enthusiasm. "The most popular USpin dance of all time. The Zipper!"

"And cut," Bryant called.

Velveteen Crush raced downstairs to their greenroom all talking over each other, high from the win.

"You saved our ass," Arabella said.

"*You're* the golden thread, Blue." Sarah threw her arms around Izzy.

"You crushed it!" Axel said.

"Should we go back to the apartment and debrief?" Tock asked.

Izzy needed a moment to think.

"I'll just be a minute," Izzy said. "Y'all go."

A moment later, Izzy was alone. She stood in the center of the room, turning slowly, every detail of the furniture, the black TV screen, the abandoned cans of Fizz Bang felt hyperreal, like an HD photo. They'd made it through the first challenge. The greenroom grew silent as her friends' voices faded from the hallway. Izzy shivered and put a sweatshirt over her costume. She should go, but she needed to process, just not with the team. She needed to take it all in. Her speech had worked. She'd reached the audience. When the show aired, she'd reach some kid in eastern Oregon who was like she'd been as a teen: young and scared and fierce. And she'd picked the Zipper to tease Lillian. Was that too much? Lillian wouldn't be mad, would she? She hadn't said anything that would break her promise to be discreet. She was just flirting. A little. On national TV.

Damn. What was she thinking? Her type was talented women with no interest in commitment who were bound to break her heart. In other words: Lillian. The archetypal talented, no-scones-in-the-morning woman. Why couldn't Izzy be hot for one of the Portland-based tech crew? There was that handsome woman whose job seemed to be rolling and unrolling cables. But no. She wanted Lillian's smile, blasé and incredulous at the same time. *Does that really work on women?*

Izzy shook her head to clear her thoughts. Time to go back to the Lynnwood Terrace. She grabbed her bag and stepped into the hall. How long had she been standing in the greenroom lost in her thoughts? The hall was eerily quiet, lit only by dim exit lights at either end of the hall. She paused.

The lights flickered.

Which way to the exit?

A second of darkness.

Shouldn't there be a runner to escort her?

Then... *What?!* Everything went black. Izzy froze. She thought the building had been silent, but there'd been an HVAC system humming. She hadn't noticed until it was gone. She held her hand in front of her face. She could see it. No. That was her mind filling in the silhouette.

Obviously, she wasn't afraid of the dark. God, if Sarah thought that, she would have an emotional-exploration intervention. But every dark room was the trailer Izzy grew up in, those nights when Megan went off to sing at one of the clubs in Bend or Portland, leaving seven-year-old Izzy hiding in her bedroom. Megan hadn't told her she had to keep the lights off when she was alone, but they'd lived in the middle of rangeland. Izzy had hated the dark, but turning the lights on felt like turning on a beacon. *Any creepy people or coyotes out there? I'm over here.* It hadn't *marked* her, despite what Sarah might think. But that kind of thing came back to you when you were alone in a labyrinthine basement in the pitch dark.

Instinctively she fumbled for her phone, but the show forbade cell phones on the soundstage and in the greenrooms.

Were those footsteps?

No.

She'd just trace her way along the wall. The security lights had to come back on. That was a fire code.

A rhythmic tap, tap, tap from somewhere down the hall?

"Hello?"

No one answered.

They should have let the contestants carry phones, the kind for kids with only two numbers programmed in. Then she'd have a flashlight.

That was definitely a footstep.

"Hello?" Izzy's voice echoed.

Why weren't they answering? A staff member would call out, *Power went out.* Another contestant would call, *Anyone else here?*

Her heart pounded at the top of her throat.

Someone who didn't answer didn't want Izzy to know they were there.

She took a step in what she hoped was the right direction. Maybe she had heard a voice? Her own voice bounced off the walls. Another footstep. It was like the Dark Room in the Halloween maze back in Broken Bush, Joe Barton jumping out at the people walking through. She'd screamed and clutched her girlfriend, like all the girls clutched their friends, but Amber-Lynn had shoved her away with an elbow to the ribs. *Not here.* And she'd needed Amber-Lynn to hold her because of all those nights in the trailer alone.

Bad things did happen to people in dark basements. Stalker fans. Serial killers. People reported sensing something wrong before an attack, except women were taught not to trust that intuition, so they walked into the apartment or got in the car. Izzy wasn't going to be that person. Better to overreact than to—

"Don't move," a calm voice said from somewhere behind her. "You'll trip."

And Izzy ran.

But the voice had bounced off the walls. It wasn't behind her. Izzy collided with someone. Powerful arms closed around her. Izzy screamed.

chapter 15

The voice said, "Blue, it's me." The arms held her tighter. "It's me. It's Lillian."

Izzy was hallucinating. She'd been seized by the serial killer, and in her last moments she was thinking about Lillian Jackson. A vision—well, not a vision, but a feeling—of comfort. Lillian's muscular body holding her.

A hand cupped the back of Izzy's head.

Izzy recognized a citrusy warm perfume.

"Say something." Lillian spoke quickly. "Are you okay?"

Of course she was okay. Izzy wasn't afraid of the dark. Izzy didn't have childhood issues, at least not in the presence of Lillian Jackson.

"Totally fine," Izzy said.

"I think they shut off some sort of generator." Lillian moved away, but she kept one hand on Izzy's hip. Izzy couldn't see anything, but they had to be close enough to kiss. "I didn't mean to scare you."

"A beautiful woman in the dark. When has that ever scared me?"

Lillian put her other hand on Izzy's breastbone, holding her lightly.

"You screamed." Lillian sounded worried.

There was no way Lillian didn't feel Izzy's heart pounding.

"You made me scream." Izzy steadied her breath and let the words out slowly, the way Blue Lenox would, putting a wink in every word. "It wasn't the first time."

"Are you flirting with me?"

Izzy could hear Lillian's bemused frown.

"Would you mind if I was?"

"You just thought someone was jumping you in a dark basement, and now you're flirting with me? And I did not make you scream before," Lillian added matter-of-factly. "You didn't give me a chance. What are you doing here in the dark?"

"I stayed back to...think." That was a little earnest. "To bask in my glory. I really was fabulous."

The fight-or-flight adrenaline in Izzy's body was changing— like water to wine—at the excitement of Lillian's touch.

"Blue Lenox." Lillian's hand found Izzy's cheek and she stroked it gently. "You are full of yourself."

Izzy trembled at Lillian's touch, but she kept her voice light.

"I saw your performance. I wish there hadn't been so many lights. I wanted to see more of you."

"The show was ridiculous with those lights. I felt like I was dancing in a lightning storm."

"Was it hard?"

"No."

Lillian said it without hesitation. Her confidence made Izzy's knees weak.

"Besides saving me, why didn't you go back to the Lynnwood?

Everyone's gone." Izzy's heart hung between the beat that said, *Maybe she stayed for you,* and the beat that said, *Of course not.*

"I was looking for you. To say I'm glad you made it through the round."

It was good Lillian couldn't see Izzy's smile. Too big. Too broad. Too representative of issues Sarah would love to process with her.

"I'm glad you did too," Izzy said.

"Wait. I'm supposed to say I came down here to crush your… overly woke, spoken word…" Lillian laughed as though she'd run out of ideas. "No. God, it was beautiful. To get an audience to love you when they'd been there for that long…"

"If they'd had phones, they would have been googling *false imprisonment.*"

With a whoosh of motors, the HVAC system resumed. The emergency lights flickered back on. Lillian stepped back. Izzy blinked as her eyes adjusted to the light, which seemed suddenly bright. The light caught in Lillian's almost shaved platinum blond hair. She'd changed into brown leather pants and a tan suit jacket. She looked like she should have a riding crop and a ten-thousand-dollar horse named Century. Opalescent gold lip gloss shone on her full lips, standing out against her skin like gold on onyx. Lillian stood with one hip cocked.

"Look at you." Lillian looked Izzy up and down. "In a…is that a Minecraft sweatshirt?" Lillian sounded pleased, not disappointed. "Come on. Let's get out of here."

Izzy followed Lillian down the hall to the staircase leading up to the soundstage and the exit to the street. Lillian stopped with her hand on the push bar that opened the door and hopefully didn't set off any alarms.

"I just want to be really clear," Lillian said.

Oh. This part. The butterflies in Izzy's stomach slowed their fluttering.

"Yeah?"

"Just to be clear, I'm not going to sleep with you again."

"I didn't ask."

Lillian touched Izzy's jaw, just the lightest touch with two fingers. "But now, unless you say no, I'm going to kiss you one more time because you are…" Lillian seemed to lose her train of thought. "Because you're you."

Izzy gasped.

"Is that a yes?"

Izzy could only nod.

Then Lillian's lips were on hers, forceful and commanding. But the way she ran her hand up Izzy's neck and into her hair, cradling her head…it was so tender. Lillian nipped Izzy's lip, just enough to make Izzy gasp again, then she kissed the same spot. The blend of sensations lit the hallway with stars. Lillian circled Izzy's waist, pulling them together. Izzy moaned as Lillian moved her leg between Izzy's, the pressure making Izzy's hips undulate, matching the rhythm of Lillian's. Lillian wanted her. Izzy could feel it in the push-pull of tenderness and strength. Every thrust of Lillian's hips was a fight between rushing and holding back. And oh God, Izzy could break her no-second-nights rule. A sensible voice in the back of her head said, *No.* Everything else in her said, *Yes.* Then she felt Lillian stiffen as though she had mustered the resolve to resist something she desperately needed. And just as quickly as Lillian had kissed her, she released her.

"Good night, Blue." With that, Lillian pushed open the door, held it long enough for Izzy to exit, trailed her fingertips across Izzy's back, and then, with the speed of a track star and the grace of a model, Lillian strode away.

chapter 16

Kia was in Lillian's studio apartment when Lillian got back, her laptop open to whatever marketing plan or over-the-top street food trend she was researching.

"It's one o'clock," Lillian said. "What are you doing here? You have your own place."

Kia had rented a tiny home in a tiny-home village on the other side of the river.

"Waiting for you," Kia said. "I wanted to see how it went with your burlesque babe."

"Nothing happened with her," Lillian said quickly.

Kia turned from her computer, giving Lillian her full attention.

"She wasn't the last performance? Didn't go onstage? I'm not waiting to hear if they made it?"

Oh. Yeah. That's what Kia was talking about.

"They made it. Retroactive Silence lost."

Lillian dropped her bag on the floor. Her sketchbook and a water bottle fell out. She flopped onto the bed without picking them up. (Eleanor would have called the movement *indecorous*.) Lillian draped her arm across her eyes.

"I cannot mess this up."

"Mess what up?"

"Everything. The company. This stupid show. Imani is so close to being discovered. Jonathan and Malik have spent their whole career dancing together. They're like two halves of one person. And Pascale. What do I tell her? That she missed out on her kids' childhood to dance, and now I ruined it because I couldn't get my shit together and focus?"

"Whoa. I know y'all made it through the challenge," Kia said. "Your burlesque babe did too. What's all the angst?"

Lillian sat up again.

"She's not *my* anything."

"So you say."

"I can't be distracted. I need to be one hundred percent here. On the stage. In rehearsal. Focused."

Lillian stood up and paced across the small studio.

"You're always focused."

Lillian whirled around. She pressed her fingertips to her forehead.

"Okay, fine. I kissed Blue."

Why had she done it?

"I would never have guessed," Kia said.

"I know. I can't believe it either."

"Irony," Kia said, eyebrows raising above her glasses. "I could totally have guessed."

"How?"

Kia's eyebrows said, *I'm not even going to answer that.*

"Are you going to sleep with her again?"

"I don't want to sleep with her." Yes, she did. "I don't want to…" *Take her to the height of pleasure until she explodes into a galaxy of stars.* "I mean, if we weren't on the show and she wasn't a distraction and we hadn't had sex once, I could hit that. But no. No!"

"Is that my lil' puffin throwing herself on the bed like a swooning maiden?" Uncle Carl's voice came from Kia's laptop.

Why hadn't Kia warned her! Kia wasn't researching whipped cream sandwiches. She was talking to her father.

"You did not tell me you were Zooming with your dad," Lillian protested. "Uncle Carl, you didn't..."

"Heard everything, my dear. Don't worry. When you're my age, you don't faint at tales of Sapphic love. Kia said you met someone special."

"She's not—" Lillian was going to finish the sentence with *special.*

But Lillian could see exactly how Blue would look if Blue heard her. *She's not special.* Blue's cocky smile would go brittle for a second, and then she'd be right back to flirting outrageously, but it wouldn't be quite the same.

"And her troupe made it on the show. What a beautiful coincidence." On the blurry screen, Uncle Carl pressed a hand to his heart. "Fate can be a loving goddess."

Kia looked at Lillian, grinning, as she said, "Lillian told me they spent a diverting night together."

"I never said *diverting.*"

"Oh, that's right. Was it funny and hot as fuck?"

"Kia! My uncle does *not* want to hear about my sex life."

"Your uncle most certainly does want to hear about your *love* life," Uncle Carl said. "I love the part about love." He sounded like the spoken interlude between two songs in a musical.

"There is no love part. There is no part at all. This show is work, and I'm working."

"Oh, my lil' puffin. You are your mother's daughter. I'm going to log off and let you two young people discuss this mysterious woman that our lil' puffin has kissed twice. But remember, my dear, even Eleanor married the man of her dreams."

"I'm not—" Uncle Carl left the Zoom call in the middle of Lillian's sentence. "—going to get married," Lillian finished to the blank screen.

"Talk." Kia sat down cross-legged on the bed and motioned for Lillian to sit beside her. "What did you do?"

"I stuck around to congratulate her. There was a power outage, just for a minute." Lillian skipped the part where Blue had screamed and then melted into her arms, how it made her feel protective and strong and turned-on. Or how seeing Blue in a sweatshirt felt oddly like seeing Blue naked, a part of her true self revealed. Or how hot that was. She could almost see Blue smiling in the darkness because she'd memorized the way one corner of Blue's lip raised as though Blue was trying not to smile but not trying hard.

"Then we walked out and before we left, I just…"

"Grabbed her, shoved her against a wall, and kissed her?"

"Yeah."

"For real?!"

"I told her we'd never do it again." Lillian winced. "I asked her not to tell anyone on the show that we've been together."

"And then you shoved her up against a wall and kissed her."

"With consent."

"I love you, coz, but you're giving the girl some messed-up mixed messages."

Kia was right. Lillian squeezed her eyes closed. Beneath her facade Blue was sensitive, not broken, not weak, but sensitive. Someone who deserved to be handled carefully.

"I won't do it again." Lillian looked around the small apartment. "I can't get off track, and I don't want to hurt her. I want her to lose. I want all of them to lose." She stared at the landscape print on the wall. "We have to win. I'm just going to…" *Try not to speak to her again. Avoid her. Tell Blue this time I mean it: never again.*

"Or," Kia said, "you could do something totally crazy?"

"What?"

"You could…" Kia drew the words out. "Stop sending her mixed messages, take her out to dinner. You know, be nice to her and then kiss her."

It was a lovely picture. Blue would like it. Lillian could almost see the happy surprise on Blue's face if Lillian asked her out. And Lillian ached at the impossibility of it.

"I didn't work this hard to throw it away on a…relationship. And I'm not interested. Seriously."

Kia leaned off the bed, stretching to reach Lillian's sketchbook lying on the floor. She held the book open against her chest.

"You're really not interested?"

"No."

Kia lowered the sketchbook.

Oh.

It had fallen open to the sketch of Blue naked.

"That's not—" Lillian had colored Blue's hair with blue ballpoint pen. "Give it here." She never drew in color. "You weren't supposed to see that." Lillian snatched the sketchbook out of Kia's hand.

Blue had promised not to tell people they slept together. And now Kia had seen Lillian's sketch of Blue naked. Lillian really was messing up.

"It's good," Kia said. "It's even better than your other ones."

"She's a striking model. That's all." Lillian turned down the corner of the page so she could find it easily when Kia wasn't looking.

"Damn, girl," Kia said. "You are so hooked."

chapter 17

Sarah was in her bedroom by the time Izzy got back to their apartment. Arabella sat on the sofa reading a hardcover book with an all-black cover. Presumably she slept, but no one had witnessed it.

"Where were you?" Arabella asked.

"The power went off in the basement. Pitch black. I got lost."

"Nice." Arabella turned back to her book, then looked up again. "You were fucking amazing today. I see why you're the great Blue Lenox."

"Thanks."

Izzy wandered into her bedroom.

She kissed me. Her body was alive. It usually took more to get her aroused. First she decided she wanted to sleep with a woman; her body woke up as they touched. It took a while. Lillian set her on fire with one kiss. And her heart raced with a giddy feeling that made her want to throw handfuls of glitter in the air. Lillian kissed her! And yes, Lillian said that was all. They were not going to do it again, and Izzy always respected boundaries. But maybe if Lillian didn't want to sleep with her (or didn't *want* to want to sleep with her), they could talk. It had been so easy to talk to Lillian at the Neptune. For those few moments, Izzy's worries had receded into the background. Lillian saw through Blue Lenox. Izzy tried to keep up the act—it worked on women—but Lillian's eyes had sparkled with amusement, and her smile seemed to say, *You're cute.* And Lillian hadn't laughed when Izzy screamed in the darkness. Lillian had held her.

Sarah knocked on her door. Izzy was still standing in the middle of her room.

"Arabella said you got stuck in the soundstage basement. You okay?"

"I'm fine." Her voice sounded like a balloon whisking upward in a breeze.

Sarah bounded over to Izzy and gave her a hug.

"We did it! We made it through the first challenge, Blue."

Oh yes, that.

Sarah pulled back. "There's something else. Your energy is swirling."

"Lillian kissed me. She was in the basement, and she was looking for me."

Sarah sat on Izzy's bed and motioned for her to sit, but Izzy was too awake. She paced the room. "Then the lights went out." Izzy recounted the story. "And I screamed, and she held me."

Sarah's expression stopped Izzy before she added, *And I felt so safe, and I like that she cared about me, and I just wanted to stay in her arms forever.*

"Blue." Sarah caught Izzy's hand as Izzy paced by. "Sit." Sarah took Izzy's other hand. "She's a professional ballerina who lives in LA and is competing with us on a TV show, and she said she doesn't want anything from you. You told me to tell you not to chase women like that. Ambitious, driven women who don't put relationships first." Sarah put her counselor face on, making strong eye contact. "I just don't want you to get hurt. You're wonderful, and any woman would be lucky to have you, but that doesn't mean Lillian…"

Izzy could feel Lillian's kiss, Lillian's hand on her back, Lillian cupping her head. *Say something… are you okay?*

"What if she's different?"

Sarah drew her into a hug.

"I don't know her," Sarah said in a tone that said, *I totally know her.* "But you might be on your way to getting your heart broken again, and I think you need to win this competition more than you let on. And I think if Lillian hurts you, Arabella's going to drag her into the dark web, and no one is ever going to see her again."

"My found family." Izzy let her head rest on Sarah's shoulders. "I love y'all."

"Speaking of family," Sarah said slowly. "Your mom sent you a package."

"Can you write *return to sender* on it?"

"I'll leave it on the counter."

Izzy lay in bed for a long time staring at a print on the wall, a picture of a green field dotted with wildflowers. Even back home in the dry rangeland, they had wildflowers. And even though Izzy knew—absolutely and totally knew—Sarah was right, she kept replaying how sweet Lillian had been and how passionately Lillian had kissed her, and it felt like Sarah must have been talking about someone else.

Two days later, Izzy was standing on a wooden platform wearing a white wedding dress while one of the costumers pinned the hem. She tried to push aside memories of Lillian's kiss. Every time she thought about it her body surged to life with eager longing. She'd remember Lillian clutching her back, and suddenly she'd be aware of her clitoris in a way she thought only horny teenagers felt. It was inconvenient to be consumed with longing. Like now. She absolutely should not be thinking about Lillian. And it wasn't just sex that distracted her. What was Lillian doing right now? Was she having fun? Was she stressed? Had the kiss lit her body and heart the way it lit Izzy's? Izzy rubbed a fold of tulle between her fingers. *Focus. Focus. Focus.*

The dress would feature in a future challenge. Bryant and his staff were using the time between the first and second rounds to prepare for things that were supposed to look spontaneous when they happened, like when Izzy pulled this dress out of a box and exclaimed in surprise like she'd never seen it before. Velveteen Crush would hit the gay-marriage note hard to keep the Allure Bridal Collection challenge on Velveteen Crush's brand. They were not going to reinforce some out-of-date man-and-wife, honor-and-obey business.

But it was hard to stay focused on subverting the patriarchy. She hadn't seen Lillian for two days. She'd looked for Lillian every time she came out of the greenroom, lingered at every exit in case Lillian was walking out at the same time, but their paths didn't cross. Was Lillian avoiding her? Or just hung up in rehearsals interrupted every two minutes by someone rushing in and demanding one of them do a profile video?

Izzy fidgeted.

"You make your own costumes when you're not on the show, right?" the costumer asked, taking a pin out from between his lips and tucking it into the fabric. "Those are some dope outfits.

I know you could fix these hems up, but lucky, you got me. Hems are boring."

Izzy could use a hem to sew and keep her mind off Lillian. She ran Velveteen Crush's Zipper routine through her mind. They'd choreographed a synchronized homage to classic burlesque, zipping their zippered outfits up and down, teasing the audience with the promise of skin but never showing it. It was sexy and modest at the same time. It was hard to do burlesque as a unified act. They were used to each doing their own acts, but they'd all worked together on one act for Zipper Redux, adding a little of Tock's staccato energy, Arabella's darkness, Sarah's playful sexiness, Axel in a dress. This was their world. They'd make it through. They had to.

Lillian had to.

Izzy had to see her.

No. She had to think about the Roosevelt Theater disintegrating while she stood on the costumer's platform. Mold was spreading. Newts had probably invaded the drainpipes.

Bryant burst into the room, interrupting the newts clogging the Roosevelt's drains.

"We're going to pair up groups for some conflict scenes. Come on."

A moment later, Izzy and the rest of Velveteen Crush were standing in one of the rehearsal spaces. The other groups were positioned around the room. Izzy looked for Lillian, but Lillian was talking to one of her dancers, her back to the room.

"We need some fight footage," Bryant said. "Who's got a beef with one of the other groups?"

The Great American Talent Show had failed to cast for repressed anger. The groups looked around at each other. No one spoke.

"We're going to have you rehearse in the same space. Get in each other's way. Fight. Battle. Floss. Whatever drama you got. It's good if we can make this as real as possible. Who's going to step on your turf?"

Izzy froze at the sound of Lillian's voice. It didn't seem like Lillian was even paying attention, but she whirled around.

"Velveteen Crush."

Was that because they had beef? Or was that because...she wanted to spend the afternoon play fighting with each other? Finally, Lillian looked at her, giving a little shrug and dipping her chin almost coyly. And the ceiling of the room lifted and the blue sky shone through.

chapter 18

An hour later Velveteen Crush was dressed to rehearse. Bryant led them to another rehearsal warehouse nearby. Classical music played through the wall.

"I want you to run in. Get all in their way. The music's going to change. Tell them to get out of your space. The cameras are already set up. Blue, I want you to really play this up." He pushed the door open and mouthed, *Run*.

Izzy didn't need an invitation to run toward Lillian, but when she saw Lillian, she stopped. Lillian stood in the center of the room, on pointe, one leg raised straight up like human anatomy didn't apply to her. Then she moved out of the pose and, with a running start, leapt in a series of five-forty barrel turns. Izzy remembered the term from class because the professor had called it the move that separated dancers from gods.

"Like that," she said to one of her dancers.

"With a five-forty?" he asked.

"Not with a five-forty," Lillian said, as though that were painfully obvious. She turned and looked directly at Izzy. "I was just showing off."

Izzy's professor had been right. Lillian was a goddess. Izzy closed her mouth, which was hanging open.

"Try that again," Bryant said. "Blue, you look like a Taylor Swift fangirl. You hate Lillian, remember?"

Izzy felt a blush creeping up her neck, but she put on her best Blue Lenox smile.

They tried their entrance again. Bryant gave Izzy a thumbs-up as she got in Lillian's face. Lillian was even more beautiful than Izzy remembered. Her lips were full and soft and commanding, glistening with a pale iridescent gloss that echoed the platinum of her almost shaved hair. And her eyes. It was the amusement in her eyes that took Izzy's words away.

"Step off, you queenpin." Lillian made it sound like an endearment and also like she was speaking to the queen of England...or she was the queen of England. Queen of England adjacent.

Izzy was supposed to insult her, but all she could manage was, "That was amazing."

To hear Lillian's feet on the floor. To feel the air displace as she passed. To watch every muscle of her body in complete control, so incredibly strong. And she'd touched that body. And Lillian had kissed her. "It's like Mount Everest. You've seen calendar pages and those documentaries about people who climb up there, but you don't know what the mountain *really* looks like. You could watch all the documentaries and still not know what it would feel like to be there."

"Is that an insult? Are you comparing me to a frigid mountain where climbers get sucked into ice crevasses?"

Lillian pronounced *crevasse* the British way, which was sexy.

"No, I mean seeing you in real life...you're even more amazing than you are on-screen."

"For fuck's sake, you look like you're in love with each other," Bryant called out.

Lillian cleared her throat and touched the cuff of Izzy's suit. The show had asked her to wear one of her signature suits, this one green corduroy with orange collars, cuffs, and racing stripes on the pants. Beneath it she wore a gold corset she'd made out of a lampshade.

"The sixties wants its suit back," Lillian said. She turned her head so the cameras couldn't see her. "You look hot," she whispered.

Then louder she added, "It looks like you hunted a sofa and harvested its pelt."

Izzy burst out laughing.

"Cut! Let's try a different pair: Sarah, Imani." Bryant pointed.

Sarah and Imani certainly looked like opposites, if not like enemies. Sarah's red curls bounced as she sprang toward Imani like a sexy boxer. Imani planted her hands on her hips, everything from the pose of her feet to the coil of braids on her head exuding melodramatic disdain.

"Blue. Lillian. Try to find something you hate about each other. You're the leads, and I *will* have a ballet-versus-burlesque queenpin throw down."

Lillian trailed the tips of her fingers across Izzy's lower back as she moved out of the way so Imani and Sarah could fight over nothing. Izzy almost melted into a pool of longing. She followed Lillian to the sidelines to watch.

"My cousin Kia says I'm sending you terribly mixed messages," Lillian said without taking her eyes off Imani and Sarah. "I'm sorry." She sounded sincere. "Do you hate me?"

"No. Sarah says I have unresolved issues from childhood and need to read books with *empowerment* in the title. Do you hate *me*?"

"You can't hate someone for that. It's not their fault."

Izzy swallowed away the tightness she suddenly felt in her throat. They were just playing, but the words felt like a warm sweater on a cold day.

"Did you make your suit?" Lillian asked.

"I did. Burlesque is all about costuming. You can buy costumes, but it doesn't feel real to me."

"I'm impressed."

"I do all sorts of impressive things. Build computers. Change spark plugs." Izzy cocked her hip out and let her suit jacket fall open. "That work for you?"

"I need…" Lillian purred.

Then she stopped, took a deep breath, and closed her eyes. Izzy could feel Lillian compose herself. Sarah would say that Lillian had a big aura. Now she'd sucked it into the outline of her body.

In a conversational tone she said, "How long have you lived in Portland?"

"You're trying not to send me mixed messages by making small talk?"

Oddly, it wasn't hard to call Lillian on the shift in tone. It was like they were in it together, being real, while all around them people were pretending. Izzy pressed her shoulder against Lillian's for a second.

"Is it working?" Lillian asked.

"No."

"Damn."

They were both still watching the lack of drama unfolding between Imani and Sarah, but out of the corner of her eye, Izzy could see Lillian purse her lips to hold back a smile.

"I've got to try harder," Lillian said.

"At what?"

"Not being attracted to you when I absolutely cannot get distracted." The purr was back in Lillian's voice.

"That's not a mixed message at all."

"I'm trying. It's hard to resist a woman in a nineteen sixties couch."

Bryant's voice cut through the space.

"Imani could you *please* call Sarah a bitch."

Sarah and Imani were looking at each other like new employees who hadn't been given instructions.

Axel jumped in. "You can't use the female as a pejorative."

"Pick a fight with *each other*." Bryant threw up his hands. "Not me." The plaid of Bryant's vented hiking shirt vibrated with frustration. "If someone doesn't fight, I will make you all live in a yurt together until you eat each other. I will cut off your water supply. Wait. I've got it. Get over here." He gathered the group around him. "This whole thing is about classy prep school dancers clashing with sexy burlesque. You." He pointed to Velveteen Crush. "You tell them they'd get kicked out of the club they're so boring."

"What club?" Axel asked.

"Any club. Ballet, you tell them it doesn't take any skill to do what they do. Velveteen Crush, you come back with *Bet you can't...* What can you do that they can't?"

"Twerk?" Izzy grinned at Lillian.

"You challenge them to a twerkathon," Bryant said. "Work that ass."

One of the ballet dancers, a petite light-skinned man, demonstrated for his colleagues.

Imani said, "Twerking actually has interesting roots in traditional African dance."

"No." Lillian glared at Izzy, then at Bryant, her expression cold and impenetrable. She stepped forward, putting a hand on Bryant's elbow. "Come with me."

Izzy had never seen something so commanding. Bryant followed her as though she were the producer and he was the contestant who'd signed a hundred contracts saying he'd do anything she asked. She moved Bryant toward the far corner of the room. Lillian's body language said *she* would lock Bryant in a yurt.

The ballet dancers looked at each other. Axel shrugged.

"Hi, I'm Axel. We didn't really get to introduce ourselves."

The groups shook hands. There was small talk. Izzy watched Lillian. Sarah watched Izzy.

"I should see what's up," Izzy said to Sarah, ignoring Sarah's look that said, *I am locking you in a yurt until you read some books on not making the same bad choices over and over again.*

Izzy walked toward Lillian and Bryant. A camera followed her.

When Izzy got close, she heard Bryant saying, "Contract line twenty-three point four. You are required to let us film other footage as needed."

"This is not needed." Lillian's back was to Izzy. "My dancers are professionals. We are not a burlesque group. I will not have them twerking like some cheap strip show."

Izzy felt like a vase of flowers unceremoniously swept to the floor and shattered.

Bryant stepped away from Lillian. She turned to follow him and caught sight of Izzy. In the camera's eye, it would look like Lillian was talking to Izzy.

"That's it!" Bryant said enthusiastically. "You won't have your dancers twerking like some cheap strip show. Blue, what are you going to say to that?" Bryant beckoned the camera operator closer.

How could Lillian have praised her performance, then call

Velveteen Crush a cheap strip show? Izzy tried to find the answer in Lillian's face, but all she saw was chagrin. Lillian was embarrassed, not because she thought it, but because she'd gotten caught saying it. Another powerful, successful, charismatic woman who knew she was too good for Izzy. No, not knew, thought. Sarah would remind her to make that distinction.

"Nothing"—Blue Lenox's fire rose in Izzy's chest—"I have ever done has been cheap."

With that, Izzy whirled on her heel and walked out. Behind her, she heard Bryant yell, "Cut. Now that's the kind of drama I want."

chapter 19

Lillian saw hurt fill Blue's face, and then it was gone. Like trading out a stage set, the sweet, blushing woman who'd rambled about Mount Everest was gone, and in her place was a blue fire, a woman who could entrance an exhausted audience, a woman who carried a pen so she could sign women's bodies because women wanted her to mark them.

Lillian reeled on the camera operator.

"You will *not* put that in the show."

Lillian hadn't meant it. Or maybe she had. Sort of. But with sociocultural context. The oversexualizing of the Black body. The expectation that Black dancers find their African roots no matter how many generations of their family lived in LA. Everything her mother had fought for, that she'd fought for, that she'd sacrificed *everything* for was on the line. And Lillian had messed up and spit out words that were near the truth but not the truth.

"Erase it," Lillian hissed.

Blue's pain was not for Middle America to enjoy over a Hungry-Man dinner. The camera operator's weary expression said Lillian would never win on that front.

Sarah, the red-haired woman who was supposed to fight with Imani, glared at Lillian. Blue didn't return. Lillian longed to say, *I didn't mean it like that. Tell her I didn't.* But Sarah's expression said Lillian would do as well with her as with the camera operator. The rest of the afternoon dragged on, one artificial conflict after another. Lillian messed up the choreography and forgot to spot and got dizzy in a simple pirouette.

Finally, Imani pulled her aside.

"Are you okay?"

Lillian barked, "Yes," then "no, I'm not," and then "your cabriole is stiff."

Talk about mixed messages.

And distraction. Lillian couldn't have this. She was messing up because she had inadvertently hurt the feelings of a woman who was eavesdropping on an argument Lillian had to win. Pascale would have had to explain twerking to her children. Someone would make a GIF of Imani's ass. And Lillian would have to face Eleanor, who'd lecture her about not letting the media control the narrative. Eleanor would be too classy to state the thesis out loud. *You were in charge and you didn't protect them.* And the fact that Blue wanted to make that about herself and her troupe was not Lillian's fault.

Except it kind of was.

After the show released them, Lillian went back to her apartment. Kia was out. Lillian lay on top of the covers on her bed. Not her fault. They barely knew each other. Blue shouldn't care what Lillian thought. Except it wasn't about fault. Lillian wasn't the defendant in a court case. She just needed Blue to feel better. And she needed to focus, and Blue would be less of a distraction if Lillian could erase the flash of hurt she'd seen in her midnight-blue eyes before Blue stepped back into character. Lillian would apologize, not for caring about her dancers' reputations but for phrasing it so crassly. She should have summoned Eleanor's cool authority and given Bryant a lecture on the legacy of racism in modern film and television. Then she could have told him about the *Brassavola* orchid until he locked himself in a yurt to escape.

Lillian sat up. What was she doing lying on her bed? This was not an unsurmountable problem. She'd find Blue. Explain. And it'd be fine. If Blue stayed pissed, that was on her. Actually, that'd be for the best. She and Blue would stay away from each other. Except not right now, because right now she needed to find her.

Lillian rose, put on a white blazer over the T-shirt and jeans she'd changed into when she returned to her apartment. The only pair of jeans she'd brought…no, the only pair she owned. Did she own another T-shirt too? Of course she did. Somewhere. She should change into a suit. She heard Eleanor in the back of her mind. *A Black ballerina's standards must be higher than anyone else's in the room.* Whatever. She put on the sneakers she wore to work out.

The halls of the Lynnwood Terrace were empty, but Lillian could hear voices coming from the apartments. A blast of hip-hop music suggested she was walking past Effectz's rooms. There was laughter coming from inside the apartment assigned to Imani and Pascale. She paused at the door before knocking. Their laughter died down as soon as Imani opened the door.

"Quick question." Lillian gestured to Imani to follow her into the hall.

Imani looked curious as she followed Lillian.

"Do you know which apartments are Velveteen Crush's?" Lillian asked as matter-of-factly as she could.

"I think they're above us." Imani cocked her head. "Why? Is this about rehearsal?" Imani took in Lillian's sneakers and jeans. "You sure you're okay?"

"Why wouldn't I be?" Lillian snapped.

"You're wearing sneakers."

"You've seen me in sneakers three hundred days out of the year."

She should have worn a suit.

"Yeah, but not in public." Imani looked genuinely concerned, as if Lillian had shown up drenched.

And suddenly it felt like a lot of work to find something curt to say to remind Imani that Imani didn't have to be concerned about her. That wasn't Imani's responsibility, and Lillian's life was not her business. Lillian sighed.

"I pissed off Blue Lenox."

"I guessed. Weren't you supposed to?"

"Not like that."

"Like how?"

"It doesn't matter." Lillian turned to go.

"Did you hurt her feelings?" Imani said, as though it was hard to process the idea of Lillian caring about someone's feelings.

"Yes."

Imani shouldn't look that surprised. Lillian wasn't a monster.

"Are you going to go apologize?" Imani asked.

"Yes," Lillian snapped. *As unbelievable as that is, I'm going to apologize.*

"Cool." Imani's expression settled somewhere between surprise and approval. She pushed open the door to the apartment and called in. "Hey, Axel, where'd you say Blue was?"

Her dancers were hanging out with Axel from Velveteen Crush. Lillian peeked in. The man who dressed like he was perpetually ready to give legislative testimony—see, wearing a suit wasn't that odd—was there too. And the woman with the dark eye makeup.

"She was bummed out about something," Axel said. "She went to get dinner alone. Try the Neptune."

chapter 20

Lillian found Blue at the same booth she'd been in when they met. Blue's laptop was open to some incomprehensible interface of characters and numbers. An untouched sandwich sat at the end of the table. But Blue wasn't looking at her computer. She was staring at a small gift box open in front of her, fingering a swatch of fabric.

Lillian hesitated. Blue's shoulders slumped. She tossed the swatch of fabric back in the box, leaned her head back against the vinyl booth, and sighed.

"Blue," Lillian said.

Blue jumped. She didn't look happy, but she didn't look like she was going to tell Lillian to go away.

"Can I talk to you?"

"Sure." There was no ire in her voice, just wariness.

"I'm sorry."

Blue didn't say anything.

"I don't think what you do is cheap."

"First, I hit you with the Zipper, then Bryant wants you to twerk. You have a brand. I get it. If someone told me to advertise diet pills, I'd tell them to fuck off. You have to commit, or your brand is all over the place." Blue pushed the box away and pulled her laptop closer. "It's nice of you to apologize."

That was it. Blue was dismissing her. Lillian hovered at the end of the table.

"Can I buy you one of those horrible purple drinks?" Lillian blurted. "I'll get one too, and I'll drink it, and I'll pretend that it doesn't taste like dryer sheets."

Blue's brow furrowed. "Crème de violette is the nectar of the gods."

"I'm not sure you can prove that empirically."

Please let Blue smile.

Blue pondered for a moment. "Ask them to put a skewer of lychees in it."

There was that hint of a smile.

The Neptune didn't seem like the kind of place that would have lychees, but, as it turned out, it did.

"For Blue Lenox," the bartender said and tucked the skewer in the drink. "For you too?"

"Sure."

When she returned, Blue motioned for Lillian to sit. Lillian handed her a drink.

"You were amazing onstage," Lillian said. "My uncle and Kia love burlesque. They're always trying to get me to go. It's a beautiful art form. I didn't mean to disparage it."

Blue sucked a lychee off her skewer, managing to look sexy and glum at the same time.

"You wouldn't be the first."

"I shouldn't have said what I said. The thing is it's so hard for a Black dancer not to be sexualized. They can be so talented, but no one notices until they do ballet in stilettos."

"Not an unattractive picture," Blue said.

Lillian was about to say, *But it's not who we are.*

"But if that's not who you are…" Blue said. "If Bryant tries that again, I'll run interference. I'll tell him my mother died twerking and it's too triggering."

Blue looked so somber. Her mother couldn't really have died twerking?

"She didn't," Blue added.

Lillian couldn't tell if it was amusement or irritation in Blue's expression.

"I stripped for a while." Blue set the words out like a challenge. "I'm not ashamed of that."

"You shouldn't be."

"I double majored in computer science and dance. There was no way I could've done school if I'd had a regular job."

"Did you like it?" Lillian asked.

"School or stripping?"

"Either. Both."

"School, absolutely. Stripping was okay. The places I worked at were safe enough."

There was so much Lillian didn't know about Blue. Questions she had no right to ask, questions she never asked women. *What was your childhood like? How did you become this mesmerizing blend of persona and realness?*

Was Kia right? Was she hooked?

"I bet you've always had your shit together," Blue said.

"Can I tell you something?" Lillian said.

"Of course." Blue's voice softened. "What's up?"

Lillian shouldn't tell Blue about Reed and Whitmer's ultimatum, not when her dancers were still in the dark, but suddenly she needed to lay that burden on the table between them. She needed that emotional release the same way she'd needed Blue's hands on her in her hotel room, and not just because she needed someone, but because Blue made her feel like life didn't have to be so heavy.

"No." Lillian stopped herself. "I can't." She rubbed her temples. "I don't have my shit together. I just wear the hell out of a suit."

"If you want to tell me something in confidence," Blue said, "I can keep it private."

"That's not fair to you. And it wasn't fair to ask you not to talk about us. That's your story too. You get to talk about whatever you like. I don't want to tell you what you can and can't do."

"But you don't?"

"What?"

"You said you can't talk about it, and you're worried. It's hard to have secrets. Trust me. I get it."

"Truth?" Lillian gripped the stem of her martini glass with both hands, a wave of guilt crashing over her for what she hadn't told her dancers. "A lot of ballet companies don't make a big profit. We're backed by donors who believe in the art. For us, it's Charles Whitmer and Thomas Reed. They believe in diversifying ballet. But they've lost too much money on us, even for patrons of the arts. If we don't win, they're dropping their sponsorship. If we lose, we split up."

"Oh, Lillian." Blue put her hand over Lillian's, easing Lillian's hand off the stem of her glass.

Blue's touch relaxed a bit of the stress tightening Lillian's body.

"If there's footage of my dancers twerking, that's going to be the first thing companies see when they research them before an audition. One viral video of Elijah twerking could ruin his career. What classical ballet company wants their audiences to see that when they google their favorite dancer? And it's hard enough for Pascale to convince people she has kids and she's serious about

her career, but a twerking mom? No way. And Imani's phenom-
enal. If we can showcase her in another season or two with the
Reed-Whitmer Ballet Company, she'll be able to audition for the
best companies in the world, but if we split up, she might end up
with a mediocre company or a dance master who doesn't want
her in the spotlight. Everything will be hard for them if we don't
win, but at least if we stay on brand, like you said...if the only
thing we put out there is our top performances...I have to protect
them. It's not that I don't respect what you do. It really isn't."

"Those videos would hurt you too." Blue kept her hand on
Lillian's.

"No. I am so. Incredibly. Good." She hadn't meant it to sound
bitter. "None of that stuff will touch me. Plus my mother is
famous. I'm the best, and she was the best before me. I'm an *icon*."
Lillian sipped her drink. Dryer sheets went well with privileged
bitterness. Crème de violette should use that in its marketing. "I
want to lift my dancers up."

"You really love them."

"Don't tell them."

"Why not? Everyone wants to be loved."

"It's not my role in the company."

"That's sad," Blue said, but not in a mean way. "You love them
and they don't know?"

"Maybe I don't love them enough. I haven't told them. They
think we're having fun on a TV show. They're all friends. They
love working together. I was going to tell them. Then I was worried it'd throw them off their game, but maybe we'll lose, and I'll
think, *If only I'd have told them. They would've worked harder.*"

Why was she talking so much?

"That's a lot to carry." Blue coaxed Lillian's other hand off her
martini glass, then released Lillian's hands.

"What if I'm letting them down?"

"You did your best and you love them."

"But what if my best is wrong?"

"Your love isn't wrong."

"Are you always this nice?"

"I think so. I like people. I want them to be happy."

Are you happy? Lillian almost spoke the words out loud.

chapter 21

They were quiet for a moment. She could tell Blue was leaving space for her to say more, but speaking that much truth left Lillian more exhausted than an hour onstage.

"Can I ask what made you do the show?" Lillian asked.

"We want to show the world that beauty comes in all shapes and sizes. Everyone deserves the spotlight if they want it." Blue launched into an inspirational speech. When she finished she added, "I bought an old theater so my troupe can have a...home." She interjected a bit more about inclusivity and safe space, but she seemed to run out of steam. "It's going to be fabulous, but it is old, as in no-ADA-bathrooms, what's-wrong-with-lead-paint old. Ugh. I can't talk to one more contractor. I don't even want to think about it. Can we pretend all I have on my plate is winning *The Great American Talent Show?*"

"We won't talk about it then." What pleasant direction could Lillian take the conversation? "Did you get a present?" She nodded to the box.

The way Blue said no told Lillian she had not found a pleasant topic of conversation.

"We don't have to talk about that either," Lillian said.

"Sarah says I'm not supposed to bottle everything up."

"Do you?"

"Of course," Blue said the same way someone might say, *Of course I shower.* A little humor returned to Blue's eyes. "Okay. Can I tell you something?"

After she'd poured her heart out to Blue? Yeah, she could tell her something.

"Of course."

Blue pushed the box in Lillian's direction.

On top was a wedding invitation. Bella and Ace requested the pleasure of your presence at their wedding. A handwritten note at the bottom read, *There's still room for another bridesmaid. Bella and I hope you'll say yes. Love, Mom.* There were also fabric samples, a photo of a hideous bridesmaid's dress, and paint chips. Apparently the wedding colors were Terra-cotta Rose, Compassionate Pink, and Gilded Sunset.

Lillian held up the photo of the dress, gauging Blue's feelings. Her face did not read, *How romantic.*

"It looks like a meringue mated with a mermaid?" Lillian posed it as a question.

Blue's laugh was half sigh, half chuckle. "I could wear it ironically if I could strip out of it."

"Not an unattractive picture." Was that too much?

"Watch out, I'll invite you."

"Something tells me you're not excited about this," Lillian said.

"I barely know my sister. I'm sure she's nice, but she's way younger than me. She's my half sister, not that that would make her less of a sister if I knew her, but I was out of the house before she was ten." Sadness crossed Blue's dark eyes. "No. They were out of the house before Bella was ten. I was still in the house." Blue ran a hand through her hair and leaned back in the booth. "People go to weddings for people they don't know all the time."

Now it was Lillian who touched Blue's hand, feeling Blue flinch and then relax as Lillian stroked the top of Blue's hand with her thumb. Blue's skin was soft. The touch felt as intimate as everything they'd done in Lillian's hotel room. Lillian stopped.

"Do you want to go to the wedding?" Lillian asked.

Blue's vibe definitely didn't say, *I'm looking forward to this celebration of everlasting love.*

"I have to. It's one day. Bella never did anything to me."

Had her parents done something? That was too personal. Lillian just left that open silence for Blue to say whatever she wanted, but Blue shook off her sadness.

"I'll buy her an Instant Pot and hook up with one of the bridesmaids, which I will not be one of. I could peel a woman out of this meringue."

Lillian felt a tinge of jealousy.

"You're going to hook up with a bridesmaid when you took *me* to the wedding?"

Blue's smile made Lillian's heart light up.

"So you *are* going to come with me? I'm guessing it's going to be religious and all dance-around-the-Maypole Pagan and hip. Basically whoever you are, you're gonna be uncomfortable."

"As long as I'm wearing Gilded Compassionate Terra-cotta."

"We'll have to match."

"I feel like you already have a coral-colored suit."

Blue cocked her head in thought. "No, but do I have time to make one?"

"Can you hunt down a pink sofa?" To let Blue know she was teasing, she added, "You know you looked fantastic, right?"

"I did." Blue's persona glistened beneath her messy hair and baggy sweatshirt. "And I made that out of curtains, not a sofa. So you'll come?" She folded her arms on the table as though finishing a business deal.

"Yes, but you have to take the hit and listen to my mother's orchid lectures."

"Deal." Blue held out her hand to shake Lillian's. "Awkward wedding with semi-estranged family for interesting information about houseplants. I'm getting the better end of this deal."

What was Lillian doing joking about going to a wedding? She didn't even eat breakfast with the women she slept with. And she could ruin so many things if she didn't stay focused. Eleanor said discipline bred discipline. But maybe discipline was a finite resource. And after a lifetime of twelve-hour rehearsals, did Lillian have enough discipline left to resist Blue's playful smile?

chapter 22

Izzy and Lillian walked back to the Lynnwood in silence. Izzy could still feel the place where Lillian had stroked her hand, the touch both soothing and erotic. Without discussion, they passed by the main entrance to the apartment complex. In the back of the building was a small alcove sheltered beneath a brick arch, pots of wisteria climbing trellises on either side. In the alcove Lillian and Izzy were invisible to the street. The doors to the apartment were made of opaque, rippled glass. Lillian stood a few paces away, her white blazer shining in the dim light, her face in shadows.

"So," Izzy said.

"So."

"You said you didn't want to do this." Izzy forced herself not to fiddle with the key chain in her pocket.

Izzy didn't have to say what *this* was.

"I have to stay focused." Lillian leaned against the wall—a dangerous proposition for a white blazer—and let out a groan. "We have to rehearse the Zipper. We're getting costumed for some bridal challenge we don't even have a brief on yet." Nothing in her posture or her voice was a rejection.

Their desire filled the alcove. It winked in the darkness like a thousand shooting stars. Izzy's body felt alive like it did right before she stepped out onstage and languid as though she'd just stepped out of a bath.

"Sarah says you'd be bad for me." Izzy hesitated. "It's not personal. You know, childhood issues."

Right now, she didn't have issues with anything except not kissing Lillian against the wall of the alcove. (You could wash a white blazer.)

"I wouldn't want to hurt you."

The sincerity in Lillian's voice changed the electric tension in the air, making it softer, a deeper frequency. Lillian took a step toward her. She was taller than Izzy. Izzy hadn't noticed before.

"And I have to think about my dancers." Lillian's voice held the same affection. "I have to win. I have to best you."

The way she said *best you* sounded like a promise that had nothing to do with the show.

"So do I." Need pulsed between Izzy's legs, and affection pulsed in her heart.

"We shouldn't."

The last part of Izzy's brain not flooded with endorphins reminded her that, actually, they really *shouldn't.*

"So what are we going to do?" Lillian asked.

"Well." Izzy touched Lillian's hip. "What I want is to take you right here. But I think"—she ran her hand down Lillian's leg—"what we're going to do is resist each other until the show ends. The sexual tension will get so hot we can't bear it. Then we'll both get to the finale. Velveteen Crush against Reed-Whitmer. Of course, one of us will lose, which is terrible. But we almost won't notice because we'll fall on each other. We'll be so desperate. I will do everything you have ever wanted."

"I will ruin you for all others."

"We won't have to worry about scones in the morning because in the morning we'll still be making—" No, not making love. "Having the best not-anonymous sex we've ever had."

"I'll ravage you." Lillian touched Izzy's cheek, then glided her fingertips over Izzy's ear.

Izzy almost crumpled at the touch.

"I will destroy you with pleasure," Izzy breathed.

"Our second-night stand."

"Yes."

"I can't wait."

"Waiting will make it even better." Izzy knew. This was what burlesque was all about: The tease. Anticipation. Promise. Hope.

"And then what will happen?" Lillian asked.

Izzy closed her eyes, longing for Lillian's kiss. Sarah was wrong. Being with Lillian wouldn't bring up childhood issues. Lillian would dispel them. How could Izzy care that Megan hadn't come to her school play when Izzy had touched Lillian Jackson and lost her? To be that close to a star and then watch her disappear into the darkness, Izzy would never recover.

"Then," Izzy whispered, "you'll leave."

Lillian ghosted her lips over Izzy's. Izzy considered fainting.

"How foolish," Lillian said as she turned toward the door to let herself into the Lynnwood, once again leaving Izzy trembling in the wake of her kiss.

chapter 23

〰

All the members of Velveteen Crush sat on the green-room sofa except Izzy, who sat on the back of an armchair, her feet on the seat. On the screen, the judges were critiquing the last performance. Christina thought it was delightful. The Prime Minister wanted to see more energy. Next, the aerial performers, BetaFlight, did a routine while a projector projected a series of zipper images on the screen behind them. The Prime Minister said the act was like being inside the mind of a baggage handler on psilocybin. Effectz did a mind-blowing hip-hop routine wearing multicolored pants covered in zippers.

Then a runner poked her head in the door to let Velveteen Crush know they were on next, which meant in an hour, after they'd been miked and unmiked and powdered and adjusted. Finally, they got their ten-minute warning. The assistant led them to the waiting area behind the stage. A camera followed them. Izzy tried to give a pep talk, but she got lost somewhere between *the Zipper is an important cultural phenomenon* and *this is our chance to show America that...something...pride...* Her friends looked at her. She had to pull it together. She had to get nervous about the performance they were about to do, not worry that Lillian and the Reed-Whitmer dancers would do something conservative, and the Prime Minister would vote them off for not *dancing with authenticity*.

"You're all amazing, and I love you," Izzy finished.

She held her breath as the lights backstage went dark. She could hear Hallie and Harrison introduce them. Then a man with an enormous glowing smartwatch counted to three on his fingers and motioned them out, like a police officer directing traffic.

Izzy barely remembered the performance, but she heard the crowd cheering when they finished. The Star Maker flashed, bathing her friends' faces with light. She pulled up the zipper on the front of her corset, the one she had promised to unzip throughout the performance but never did. She winked at the crowd, and they cheered again.

Harrison and Hallie asked about their inspiration for the performance.

Izzy said, "It's about being vulnerable, being exactly who you are in your beautiful entirety."

"Hard to imagine how you could accomplish that with a dance dedicated to the zipper," the Prime Minister said, "but I think you did it."

Back in the greenroom, Sarah pulled Izzy aside.

"You were great out there, but your energy is very…loose. Is it because of—" Sarah mouthed, *Lillian*.

Lillian had so much at stake. And Izzy did too, and so did the LGBTQ+ community that needed the Roosevelt Theater to be their safe space. She'd gotten calls from three roofing contractors, each bidding higher than the last. Izzy should be poring over their emails. Instead she was melting with desire for Lillian Jackson. She'd dreamed about kissing Lillian in the alcove and woken up aroused in a way she couldn't resolve with her own touch. Eventually she and Lillian would sleep together. Then Lillian would leave. Izzy would cry. Sarah would loan Izzy more books on functional relationships that Izzy would feel dysfunctional for not reading. She knew all that, but she didn't feel it. Lillian wanted her, tenderly and lustfully. Izzy felt that with every cell of her body. Lillian didn't just want to have sex with Blue Lenox, she liked Izzy Wells.

"No," Izzy said quickly.

Axel looked up from where he was doing Russian twists on the floor.

"The lead for the Reed-Whitmer Ballet Company?" he asked as though Sarah had spoken out loud.

"No," Izzy said.

"She's cool." Axel sat up as though Izzy had not just denied that Lillian was the topic of conversation.

"You haven't crushed on anyone for a long time," Arabella said without looking up from whatever dark web espionage she was conducting on the phone she was not supposed to have in the greenroom. "It's very Hallmark-y, but I'll allow it."

"I checked the contract," Tock said. "You can date other contestants, but any footage they take of you is fair game for the show."

"Sarah!" Izzy protested.

The troupe was close, but that didn't mean Sarah got to tell them about Izzy's feelings without her permission.

"She didn't tell us," Arabella added.

Sarah looked miffed. "I wouldn't."

"Keep the friends who hear you when you never said a word," Axel said.

Arabella looked over at him. "That one actually works. Good job."

Tock said, "I wanted to warn you if you two were going to get in any legal trouble, so I looked it up in the contract. You're fine."

"But I didn't say anything. I didn't…Lillian and I didn't…"

Izzy had kept her anxiety and her excitement under wraps. There was no way anyone could guess what was going through her mind, not even her friends. Well, maybe Sarah, but not Tock, who filled his brain with statutes. Arabella was too busy possibly hacking SpaceX. (It was better not to ask.) Axel had been texting his clients every chance he got.

She was Blue Lenox. No one saw the messy person inside Blue Lenox. That's why everyone adored her.

"How?" Izzy asked.

Axel went back to Russian twisting, the tap of his medicine ball punctuating his sentences.

"You fought with her in rehearsal." Tap.

"Not really, I mean…" *Yes.*

"You ran off." Tap. "You were all bummed and went out to eat shitty bar food alone."

"The Neptune isn't that bad."

"And probably drink those purple drinks." Tap. "Imani said that something was up with Lillian." Tap. "Then Lillian came looking for you?"

She did?

"Then today you're all calm and happy."

Calm was overstating it.

"The evidence is circumstantial," Tock said, "but there's a strong correlation."

"She could get voted off today." The thought made Izzy's stomach knot up.

"Don't worry," Axel added. "I talked to some of the people from Dream Team Marchers, and they said they saw Mood of Motion practicing and they were a bag full of terrible, *and* Spice Angels didn't include a zipper at all. They're totally off brief. There's no way Reed-Whitmer won't make it through this round. I'm glad you have a crush." Axel stood up and put his enormous arm around Izzy. "That's great."

No. It was an emotional train wreck happening in slow motion, but it felt good hanging out with her friends and getting teased about liking a woman.

Reed-Whitmer did make it. Watching Lillian on-screen, Izzy felt like a teenager watching their favorite celebrity crush on TV. The Star Maker liked Lillian's company more than Mood of Motion. Izzy held her breath while Alejandro advised the company to add more energy to the slow parts and Christina said she felt like the performance opened something up for her. The Prime Minister said, "This performance told a story." He steepled his fingers. "I don't think it's your story, but it's *a* story. What I'm looking for this season is authenticity. I see a glimmer of realness. You better spark that glimmer, because you're going on to the next round." In the end, BetaFlight's zippers were the fail of the day, and they went home. When all the groups had performed, the hosts announced the next round, a beach trip in honor of their next corporate sponsor, Lie in Wait Outdoor Wear.

chapter 24

Retroactive Silence and BetaFlight were gone. The Reed-Whitmer Ballet Company had made it to the third challenge. Lillian stood in a beachfront parking lot sheltering from the wind behind one of *The Great American Talent Show* tour buses. It was cold on the Oregon coast, the sky blue but with a bank of dark clouds in the distance. The rest of the performers had hurried out to grab muffins from the windblown craft services table and retreated to the warmth of the buses. They were early. The call sheet read, *8:15 a.m. meet with fans, then joyful frolic on the beach wearing Lie in Wait Outdoor Wear—Where Style Meets Survival.* The buses had pulled in around seven. But Lillian couldn't sit on the bus with the eyes of her dancers on her as she tried to choreograph something that showcased their skills and said neon survival wear. Imani would ask if she wanted help. Pascale would ask if she wanted them to stretch or run through some basic formations. Did she? Maybe? Probably?

Getting to the beach had meant a five a.m. wake-up. Lillian wasn't tired, even though she'd been up all night replaying her moment with Blue in the alcove, her mind drifting over Blue's body, between her legs…what Lillian would do for her. The questions she would ask to learn about Blue's body. Now Lillian was taut with unspent energy. She was distracted. There was no denying it. She hadn't masturbated. She should have. Maybe she wouldn't feel as restless as the wind whipping around the bus if she'd released the tension in her body. But how could she look at Blue after she'd clutched her vibrator to her clit thinking about sucking Blue's nipples? How could she—

"Hey."

Lillian let out a startled gasp. Blue stood beside her, coffees in hand.

"I thought you might want one."

Lillian had conjured Blue with her illicit thoughts. She fumbled for words.

"Or not," Blue said.

If only it were coffee that left Lillian speechless.

"Thank you." Lillian quickly took the proffered coffee and hid her nerves behind its steam.

"Should I…go?" Blue motioned toward Velveteen Crush's bus.

"No. No." Yes, she probably should. "No." Lillian never got nervous around women. Who was she?

Blue leaned back against the bus, sipping her coffee along with some of her hair. The wind wouldn't leave it alone, and it whipped around her like a storm.

"Not long enough for a ponytail." She pulled a lock out of her mouth and shook her head. "Too long to not do *that*."

Would anyone see them if she held Blue's hair out of her eyes and kissed her?

"Is this awkward?" Blue asked cheerfully as though they were in it together, not separated by a gulf of innuendo and conflicting intentions.

"Yeah?"

"I thought so." Blue took another sip of her coffee, watching the crew unpack gear and a few contestants get off the buses and then rethink their decision. "Do we mind?" she asked after a beat.

How could a moment be awkward and good? Somehow it was.

"I don't."

"Me neither." Blue spread open her arms and did a slow circle. "Like my outfit?"

She sported full Lie in Wait Outdoor Wear. Lillian did too, but she'd hidden hers beneath her white boiled-wool coat. Out of sight. The only appropriate place for it.

"You know that saying *No one ever lost money underestimating the taste of the American public*?" Lillian said. "I think this is the exception."

"It'll sell when they see me in it." Blue put a hand on her hip, exhibiting her neon-pink one-piece. "The Lie in Wait rep said neon scares omnivores because it looks like poisonous fruit. And the coat scares away puffer fish."

Blue had pulled the front zipper low enough to reveal the tops of her breasts in a tight black tank top. Over the one-piece, she wore a puffer coat. Lillian put her hand on Blue's shoulder and turned her around again, even though Lillian had seen the back of the coat, which was painted with the face of a giant puffer fish. Mostly she just wanted to touch Blue's shoulder.

Blue managed to make the ensemble look good.

"When are you going to wear a ski jacket and need to be protected from puffer fish?" Lillian asked.

"Better safe than sorry. I have an exciting life. What have you got on under that coat?"

"I'm hoping we'll break into groups and you'll never have to see it."

"Come on," Blue said, pretending to pull on Lillian's coat. "How could you not look gorgeous?"

Lillian had been assigned a pair of the cougar-deflecting jeans, baggy, urban-wear jeans with giant eyes painted on the thighs and, regrettably, on the ass (to protect from stealth attacks).

Lillian pretended to pull away. "I think they gave us the worst ones because we're the *uptight ballet company*." Every season had one. "I will wear this outfit for *exactly* as long as I have to and not one minute more."

Had she just told Blue she was planning to strip the second they finished filming?

Blue smiled, catching the tip of her tongue between her teeth. Adorable. Devastatingly sexy. What was Lillian doing? Staying focused wasn't just about not having sex. It probably included not hiding out beside the bus and flirting when she should be in the bus giving her dancers a lecture about...something.

On the other side of the parking lot, Bryant lifted a bullhorn to his mouth, calling the contestants and cameras to him.

"I'm safe from puffer fish, but what does your white boiled-wool coat protect you from?" Blue asked as they headed toward the gathering spot.

"Mermaids."

Blue chuckled. "You know what happens when you hear the sirens."

You crash onto the rocks.

"They seduce you." Blue hurried toward Bryant. It seemed like she only walked ahead so she could look back over her shoulder, her smile saying, *Run away with me.*

A tiny voice in the back of Lillian's mind said, *Yes.*

"Thank you to our corporate sponsor. I know when I go out in the wild, I feel safer wearing Lie in Wait." Bryant was geared up in colorful outdoor wear as well. "We have kites for all team members," Bryant went on, "for your frolicking."

Production assistants were starting to hand out individually packaged kites.

"We're looking for the spontaneous fun you get to have when you're wearing Lie in Wait." Static screeched on Bryant's bullhorn. "Today we want you to show America your playful side. You're not just fierce competitors fighting to make it to the quarterfinals, you're human beings who take time to relax occasionally. And of course, we can use friendships you make now to generate conflict later on. Be thinking about alliances and rivalries. Please sign all consent waivers. Then down to the beach, everyone. The cameras are waiting."

"The puffer fish waits for no one," Blue said, heading toward her troupe.

Lillian watched her. She jumped when Kia—allowed on the bus because she had a badge—threw an arm around her shoulder. Kia tsked, raised the flip-up shades of her turquoise glasses, and then flipped them back down emphatically.

"What?" Lillian demanded.

"Hooked." Kia's eyes followed Blue.

Down on the beach, the dancers set about flying kites. It was harder than it looked. Jonathan unfurled his kite and chased Pascale with it, holding its flapping wings. Malik ran after them, the crocheted scarf he'd added to his outfit flapping behind him. Elijah skipped, swishing his hips. The dancers scattered as the kite nosedived. Imani swore she'd do better. Her authoritative tone reminded Lillian of herself. Imani got tangled in the strings before she'd gotten her kite off the ground. Then she and Pascale carefully detangled it only to crash it into the surf. None of the contestants were doing any better. Their squeals and laughter carried over the sound of the wind and waves, interspersed with "Watch out!" and "It's going down!"

"Get in the shot," one of the camera operators instructed Lillian.

"Come on," Imani commanded. "It's fun."

Reluctantly, Lillian removed her coat and handed it to an assistant. She got in the shot and followed the camera operator's instructions to wave a kite over her head. She held her kite up for the required amount of time, then wrestled it back to the ground and handed it to Imani, who'd lost hers in the water. The camera operator moved to the next group, but the dancers kept playing, chasing each other and crashing their kites. Lillian stood on the sidelines. If the company disbanded—and, face it, how would they beat Effectz?—she'd only have memories of these people she'd worked so hard beside. She wanted to fix the moment in her memory. The dancers had so few opportunities to be these people. Playful. Carefree. And part of Lillian longed to run into their midst, but they weren't her friends. They were her dancers. Her job was to make them stars.

Imani waved to Lillian.

"Look." Imani pointed.

Blue was walking toward them.

"I get to see your outfit after all," Blue called out.

"Doesn't she look dope," Imani said as Blue approached. "How do you do that?"

"What?" Blue asked innocently.

Imani's eyes traveled upward. The bank of charcoal-colored clouds was rolling in, turning the day into twilight.

"There." Imani pointed to the sky.

Lillian looked up then back at Blue's hands. She was holding the spool of a kite as casually as she'd held her coffee. And up in the sky, like a seagull riding the currents, soared her kite.

It was like turning a perfect grand allegro contretemps on the stage of the Palais Garnier. One second of immortality.

"Oh, that?" Blue's hair blew back, the same color as the sea. "I'm just showing off."

Suddenly, Imani was busy asking Malik what kind of yarn he'd used for his scarf.

"Do you want to fly it?" Blue held out the spool.

"I'll crash it."

"You won't. It's too high up to go down without a fight. When you're getting up there, you have to edge it up and back." Blue swayed as though dancing to a slow song. "I like edging."

"Does that really work on women?" Lillian gave Blue a gentle shove, just to feel Blue's arm beneath her puffer coat.

"Edging? Of course. Oh, Lillian, you have heard of it, haven't you?" Blue opened her eyes in mock distress. "It works on lots of women. Do you want me to explain?"

If Blue had said, *Do you want to fuck on the sand?* Lillian might just have said yes.

"No. I do not need you to explain," Lillian hissed, glancing at Imani and Malik. "I meant talking dirty about your kite. Does that work on women?"

"I only talk dirty about my kite"—Blue nipped the word *kite* with her teeth—"to you."

Lillian blessed her dark complexion, which hid her blush. She could feel heat flush up and down her body.

"You'll feel the string get *tight.*" Blue sighed the word.

Lillian was a breath away from dying of lust. *Famous ballerina drops dead on beach. Cause of death unknown.*

"You don't think you can go any higher, but that's when you can really fly. I got it up there for you. Do you want it?" Blue asked with shy pride.

Blue looked beautiful and rakish and vulnerable as she held out the spool.

Of course Lillian wanted it.

Blue kept her hands around Lillian's until Lillian's grip tightened on the spool. It was exhilarating, the tension in the string connecting her to the soaring kite, like a part of her soul was flying. She wasn't up in the sky, but in another way she was right there.

It was a lot like making love to a woman.

chapter 25

The sound of Bryant's bullhorn fought its way through the wind.

"Back to the buses. There's a storm coming."

Izzy didn't move. Lillian was mesmerizing, staring up at the kite with a delighted smile.

"I get why people do this," she said. "You'd think, *What's fun about getting a piece of nylon up in the sky on the end of a string?* But it's...it's like part of us is up there." She looked over, her eyes full of amazement.

What would it be like if Lillian said *us* and didn't just mean *us flying a kite*?

"The buses!" Bryant managed to convey irritation through the bullhorn.

Around them contestants were wrestling kites back into bags, an almost impossible feat with the wind blowing. The schedule for the day said they'd be staying at some place called the Kite Sand Resort, a minor sponsor who wouldn't make it onto the show but might get some play in *The Great American Talent Show* socials.

"When we get back to the hotel, do you want to go for a walk on the beach?" Izzy asked.

"Isn't there a storm?"

"Exactly."

On the horizon, streaks of gold and pink light cut through the black clouds. The wind whipped up the surf.

"You'll love it," Izzy said. "We'll ditch the cameras and everyone and get out in the storm. It'll call to your soul!" She flung her arms wide to make the statement melodramatic, not dreadfully earnest. On an afternoon like this, with the clouds gathering, you could stand on the beach and not see one other person. It was just you and the vastness of the ocean. Something about Lillian was vast and beautiful and strong and fierce like that.

"What about the puffer fish? They're dangerous this time of year." Lillian handed the spool back to Izzy. Izzy cupped Lillian's hands as she took it, and Lillian let her fingertips trace Izzy's palm. She held Izzy's eyes as she did, and just as the string held the kite to the spool, Lillian's gaze held them together.

"It's the sirens you have to look out for." Izzy couldn't look away from Lillian's golden-brown eyes. Had the waves stopped breaking? Had the wind stilled? Were they the only people who'd ever stood on this beach?

Lillian broke the moment with a little laugh. "I'll come find you when we get to the hotel." With that, Lillian followed her dancers. Looking over her shoulder, she shot Izzy an ostentatious wink.

"Hey, that's my trick," Izzy called, surprised that she could still form words.

Lillian winked again. "It works on women, doesn't it?"

Yes. Yes, it did.

"And by the way, if anyone can rock Lie in Wait, it's you," Lillian added, turning to walk backward, her arms spread wide.

Izzy thought she might never stop grinning.

Sarah and the rest of Velveteen Crush caught Izzy up in their midst as they hurried toward the buses.

"I like her," Arabella said. "She's strong. She could take a man down in a fight."

"Lillian could not—" Izzy began. Actually, Lillian could probably take a man down in a fight.

"She seems sweet," Axel said.

Sarah fell into stride beside Izzy.

"I know. I know," Izzy said. "Tell me she's going to break my heart."

Sarah shook her head and, proving that her amateur therapist skills needed some work, said, "Maybe it won't be a train wreck this time."

The buses deposited them at the Kite Sand Resort, a midcentury-modern hotel set on a bluff. Lillian caught up with Izzy as runners handed out keys to the contestants.

"Meet me behind the hotel in ten?"

Lillian said, "In ten," and a little golden windstorm kicked up in Izzy's heart.

Izzy ran her bag up to her room faster than running onstage, but she paused when she came back down. Lillian was waiting for her on a patch of sandy grass behind the hotel, gazing at the ocean, her white coat flying out behind her, like a heroine on the cover of a novel. Izzy approached her slowly, taking in every detail. Lillian's turtleneck sweater and, surely a concession to the coast, her sneakers. When Lillian turned, her smile warmed the cold wind.

"I won't take you out far," Izzy said. "We'll be back before it starts to rain."

On the beach, the receding tide had revealed a field of craggy, black boulders. Pushed by the wind, a piece of kelp flopped along the beach. Izzy's hair blew in her eyes and caught in the corners of her mouth. Lillian, with her short platinum hair, looked as composed as always.

"You said this would speak to my soul?" Lillian looked pensive.

"We can go back in."

"I don't want to go back in." Lillian stepped close enough that anyone who had seen their silhouettes from the hotel would think they were kissing.

Izzy's body thrummed with her nearness. Lillian tucked a length of Izzy's hair behind her ear, and the touch of her cool fingers made Izzy's knees weak.

"I want to go out in it," Lillian said. "It does speak to me. And even if it didn't, if you want to show it to me, I want to see it."

Izzy's hair escaped again, and her heart escaped her chest and went dancing along the beach.

"So how do you know how to fly kites when the rest of us almost put an eye out?" Lillian asked, beginning to walk down the beach.

"I started coming here in college. It was my place to go when I'd gotten dumped by some heartless girl," Izzy said ruefully.

"Dumb girl." Lillian looped her arm through Izzy's as they began to walk.

"I was a lost cause in college. I wanted to date every girl who'd leave because they were passionate about something that wasn't me. I had a crush on this girl who was a legit model. I didn't care that she was beautiful. She was just so intense about what she did. She was premed. She'd study all morning, exercise, then fly to New York for photo shoots. And she liked rugby players, so I joined the team."

"Rugby? I bet you were hot. Did you have a striped shirt?"

"All of it, but I was terrified. I lied to the coach, said I'd played in high school. I watched a bunch of YouTube videos about rugby. And despite what people think, the College of YouTube cannot teach you everything you need to know."

"I could see how that could go wrong," Lillian said sympathetically.

"I ran away from the ball because I knew if I caught it, a dozen women would pile on top of me, which wouldn't be a bad thing except they were all covered in mud and trying to break me in half."

Lillian laughed, but it seemed like she was laughing at life, not at Izzy's young self.

"Finally, I smoked pot in the locker room so I'd get kicked off the team."

"Why not just quit?"

"I wanted the girl to think I was a badass."

"Did she?"

"For a few nights. For a few nights, I thought we were in love. Then she started dating a daughter of a senator, and it broke my heart. Then there was a soccer player from the Seattle Reign. Rachel from the WNBA."

"You like athletes?"

"I liked their intensity."

"I met Rachel when she'd torn her ACL. She broke up with me the day she got cleared to play again. And the opera singer. God, I was so bad at it all." But Izzy didn't feel sad. It was kind of funny how over-the-top she'd been with her dating choices.

"You didn't always want shooting stars?" Lillian asked.

"I was a twentysomething lesbian whose mother left her to fend for herself at eighteen. Of course I wanted someone to love me."

"Your mom wasn't there for you?"

"Nah."

"Is it something you talk about?"

"You don't want to hear my poor sad child story."

"I do, if you want to tell it." Lillian still had her arm looped through Izzy's, and she pulled Izzy closer.

And Izzy did want to tell her.

"Well," Izzy began. "Megan—my mom—got pregnant really young, but she was already a great singer. She opened for some artists up in Portland. *She* could have been on *The Great American Talent Show.* I thought she was so amazing. Beautiful. Funny.

"When I was with Megan…my mom, it felt like magic. Like we were fairy princesses. She'd take me to the Dollar Tree, and we'd spend hours looking at whatever little vases or glass beads they had. She'd start singing, and everyone would stop and listen."

Strange, the memory was still sweet even though Izzy knew what came next.

"And my mom wanted that but in a bigger way."

"Did she go on to sing?"

"She performed a lot, so I was alone a lot."

"Like as a teenager?"

Despite their heavy coats, Izzy could feel the warmth of Lillian's body beside her.

"Like seven or eight. She'd leave for a weekend. She made sure there was food and TV for me."

"She left a seven-year-old alone for weekends?"

"Yeah."

All those dark nights in the trailer listening to every sound.

"That's child neglect!"

A reflexive protectiveness flared in Izzy's heart. Megan wasn't a bad mom. Izzy had been mature. She didn't need a babysitter.

The flame died as quickly as it rose. Megan *was* a bad mom. Not the worst by a long shot, but she wasn't winning any PTA awards.

"I survived. I got all into school stuff. Plays. Choir. Dance team. We didn't have great extracurriculars in Broken Bush, but there was always someone like my mom who'd never gotten to live their dreams, so they helped teens do bad versions of *Brigadoon*, and in the land of bad *Brigadoon*, I was a star."

"And then?"

"She met a man, Rick. He's a good guy. They planned to have a baby. Painted a room. Had a baby shower. Then when I turned eighteen, they left. Like I was a foster kid, and I'd aged out. Rick got a transfer to California. We still owned a trailer. Megan said I could live there. She gave me a hundred dollars cash and told me to call anytime. But what was I supposed to call about?"

"Their baby was Bella, the one who's getting married?"

"Yeah. The other day Megan called me saying how proud she was that I made it on the show." Too little, too late. "She says she has a ticket to the studio audience to an upcoming show."

"Are you…happy about that?"

"She probably just wants to be on TV, but if she came just to see *me*…" Izzy had barely admitted it to herself. "I did a lot of school plays, and she never came. Sarah says my inner child wants her to show up."

Megan was coming to Portland to see her. Coming to one show didn't make up for leaving her in so many different ways, but it was everything her teenage self had wanted. To see Megan in the audience as she took the stage on opening night of the school play. To run into Megan's arms backstage as all the parents crowded around to hug their kids. To go out to dinner at Applebee's afterward. It'd be a little taste of that life. Maybe Megan would get her a bouquet of flowers. Maybe Izzy would dry them. Maybe a little taste was enough.

"When she comes to the show…then when I go to Bella's wedding, maybe I'll feel like part of their family. I don't know. Probably not."

The wind kicked up, but not so much that it blew sand in their eyes. The clouds were heavy but not raining.

"Maybe that's why I bought the theater. It's a place for my found family to be safe. At least for now."

"For now?"

"If the bank doesn't take it. That thing is a money pit."

"Is that why you need the prize money?"

"No." *Yes.* "It'd help but…" To win, they had to beat Reed-Whitmer. She didn't want to think about that now. She wanted to enjoy this moment. "I want to make it beautiful so I can bring gorgeous women there and seduce them."

Izzy flashed Blue's smile. Lillian shook her head with what looked like indulgent affection. Then Lillian stopped, turned toward Izzy, and wrapped her arms around her, deflating the puffer fish coat and holding her close. The hug was so unexpected, Izzy stiffened for a second, but Lillian didn't let go, and Izzy melted. Lillian nestled Izzy's head against her shoulder, stroking Izzy's tangled hair.

"I really am fine," Izzy murmured. Lillian's coat smelled of her sunlight-warm perfume. Memories of Broken Bush whisked away on the wind.

"I know," Lillian said. "But that doesn't make it easy."

Izzy could have stood there through the storm and never gotten cold.

When Izzy finally broke their embrace because they really

couldn't stand there forever even though she longed to, Lillian took her by the shoulders, studying her, her gaze indescribably tender. Lillian adjusted the collar of Izzy's puffer coat and patted the shoulders to fluff it up.

"You," Lillian said slowly, "really are the *only* person who can make this stuff look good."

Izzy felt as light as her kite as they began walking again.

"What about you? What were you like in high school?" Izzy asked after a little while.

Lillian pressed her hand to Izzy's back for a moment, then began with a caution Izzy recognized. *Which piece of the story should I tell?*

"The family is me, my parents, Kia, and her dad, my uncle Carl. My parents live in this house that looks like a Jane Austen mansion, except it's new construction, and I'm sure that has something to do with their inner children. And Uncle Carl lives on a yacht and owns a million spaniels." Lillian launched into a story about her uncle taking her sailing. It sounded like Lillian lived in a fairy tale. But Lillian left things out. Izzy heard it in her pauses. Izzy wanted to ask, but she didn't know how to stop Lillian and say, *You can tell me the rest of it if you want.*

The sky spit a few drops of rain. They kept walking. The story about the yacht led into a list of strange recipes Kia had cooked in her food truck. Izzy laughed and launched into stories of failed performances. Izzy could walk forever talking to Lillian. But a few drops would be a downpour in twenty minutes.

"We should go back," Izzy said reluctantly. "I want you to love it out here, not get hypothermia."

"Can we go a little farther?" Lillian turned to the ocean and the black sky slashed with gold. "How did you know I would love it out here?"

"It's you. Intense. Beautiful." That sounded too romantic. "I mean dangerous. Siren-ous. You'll lure me to my ruin."

As if to illustrate her words, the rain let loose.

"You're the siren," Lillian called over the sound of the wind.

"Sirens are just misunderstood mermaids."

"Come on, mermaid. We should go back."

They turned. The shoreline of tall, sandy bluffs disappeared into the fog and the gathering darkness with no hotel in sight. How had they walked so far? It had felt like mere minutes. A walk back in this rain? They really would get hypothermia. And what if the tide was coming in? Izzy assessed the water. It looked closer than it had before. This was king tide season when waves crashed over Highway 101 in Depoe Bay, the ocean nipped kayaks out of people's backyards, and at least one beachfront property slid into the water. If they walked back, they'd have to scramble over rocks, the waves lapping their heels. They'd make it, but it'd be scary. What if Lillian slipped? Cut her hands? Twisted an ankle? The walk would certainly wreck her coat. And she'd be scared. Izzy couldn't let anything happen to her.

A cluster of lights shone on top of a nearby bluff.

"There's something up there," Izzy said. "Maybe we can dry off and call someone to get us."

chapter 26

Lillian didn't need to catch her breath as they neared the top of the wooden staircase that led from the beach to the lights, which turned out to be cottages on the bluff. Blue paused for a moment, looking back at the stairs.

"That was a climb," she said.

Lillian resisted the urge to put her hand on Blue's back. Blue did not need Lillian to steady her. Blue was a little out of breath, not gasping. No, Lillian wanted to put her hand on Blue's back because of the faraway look in Blue's eyes when she talked about her childhood. She hadn't even noticed Lillian staring at her as they walked. Or staring at her now. Blue's cheeks were flushed, her blue hair windblown. The faraway look was gone now, and her smile made her eyes into sweet half-moons.

Lillian forced herself to look away from Blue and at the cottages, a cluster of rentals half-hidden behind a wall of buoys, anchors, and other flotsam. A wooden sign identified the place as Barnacle Bob's Vacation Cottages. A MANAGER sign hung on the first cottage.

"Let's check it out," Blue said and headed for the manager's cottage.

Inside, a man with a long white beard and a tie-dyed T-shirt sat at a desk made out of driftwood.

"Well, hello, friends!" he greeted them.

"We just walked from Galeton." Blue caught her breath. "Do you mind if we dry off while I call someone to pick us up?"

"Of course you can warm up here. There's a fire in the grand lodge."

Nothing about Barnacle Bob's said *grand* or *lodge*.

"But your ride will have a hard time getting here from Galeton," he said apologetically. "There's a landslide on 101. Internet says they won't have it cleared 'til tomorrow."

The desire to walk on the beach forever dissipated. Lillian needed to finish the choreography for their Lie in Wait dance and start rehearsing her dancers. They were performing tomorrow. Her dancers' careers rested in her hands, but *she'd* gone walking with the woman she liked. She'd asked, *Can we go a little farther?* She'd forgotten all about incorporating Lie in Wait Outdoor Wear into a ballet performance that the judges would think was emotive or real or whatever they were looking for.

"Can we go around?"

"There's a slide on Highway 20 too," the man said.

"Is that bad?"

"Pretty much means you can't get back to Galeton right now."

Eleanor had warned her: Black dancers couldn't make this kind of mistake. Not getting hemmed in by landslides, exactly, but dropping the ball. Poor judgment. Lateness. A handsome, white, male lead was quirky if he was distracted; a Black woman was a liability.

"Don't worry. I've got one cabin left." The man surveyed a set of cubby holes on the wall behind him. "You want it? It's the Captain Cozy's Cottage. We serve dinner family-style in the lodge. We've got a group of retirees and some kids from the Netherlands staying here. Lovely people. You'll have a wonderful time."

Lillian could not spend the night in Captain Cozy's Cottage when she should be working with her dancers.

"And DOT always gets these things cleared up. You can be out of here by ten tomorrow. Better than camping on the beach," the man added.

It'd be okay. That would give her enough time to work with her dancers. She could work on the choreography tonight on her phone. A thought struck her like a wave but not a cold, Oregon wave full of killer puffer fish. She wasn't just spending the night in a cottage. She was spending the night in a cottage with Blue. Lillian looked at Blue. Blue looked at her. The air between them vibrated. The frequency pulsed between Lillian's legs. Blue licked her lips in a gesture both nervous and sexual. And all the discipline of a prima ballerina cracked. Lillian turned back to the man.

"We'd love to stay in Captain Cozy's Cottage."

Lillian stepped outside and called Bryant while Blue collected the keys. Bryant conceded that a natural disaster was the *only* excuse for being off set.

"Get back here ASAP," he grumbled.

"DOT always gets these things cleared up by morning," Lillian said, although she had no idea what the Oregon Department of Transportation did or did not do.

Blue emerged from the manager's office, keys in hand, and motioned that she was heading to the cabin. Lillian gave her an *I'll be there in a sec* gesture. Lillian sheltered under the eaves of the manager's cottage, ended her call with Bryant, and checked her texts.

Kia: I'm drinking chardonnay with Imani. Where are you?

Lillian: Tell her not to drink.

Kia texted back immediately.

Kia: Too late. Where are you?

At Barnacle Bob's Vacation Cottages getting ready to share Captain Cozy's Cottage with a woman I don't get to sleep with until one of us gets voted off the show.

Lillian: went for a walk

Kia: With Blue?

Why would you say that? Of course I didn't go for a walk with *Blue*. I have professional boundaries and make decisions that further the best interests of my company.

Lillian: I'm fine but I can't get back until tomorrow.

Kia: Hell yeah! 😁

Lillian: Not like that. There was a landslide. Can't get back. We rented a place on the other side.

Kia: A "landslide" 😂

Lillian: Yes. A landslide.

Kia: How'd a "landslide" happen?

Lillian: The way landslides happen.

Kia: Are you going to eat Blue's scones?

Lillian: No!

They were not having scones. She was not going to gaze into Blue's mysterious eyes. Lillian could feel Kia's smirk through the phone screen.

Lillian: Probably not

Lillian: 50/50

Kia: don't angst about it, just 🥐🍩🥨🥄

Blue had turned on the lights in their cottage. Now she popped her head out and beckoned for Lillian, silhouetted by the light from inside. Behind the cottage, the sky was a luminous navy blue. The same shade as Blue's hair. Lillian lifted her phone and took a picture. This was one of those moments. Everything hung in the air midleap. Would she make the landing? Could she do the grand jeté? Would she land one centimeter off balance and end everything?

Lillian: *I don't know what to do.*

The truth in six words.

She texted the photo to Kia.

Kia: *Say yes*

Nothing was that simple, but Lillian pocketed her phone and walked down the cracking cement path that led to their cottage. The open living room and kitchenette were paneled in knotty pine. Sea-themed knickknacks decorated end tables. A book called *Rogan: A Seafaring Journey to Manhood* took pride of place on the mantel of a woodburning fireplace. Lillian's eyes strayed to the open bedroom door. One room. One bed. No sofa that anyone could pretend to sleep on.

"Not what you're used to," Blue said apologetically.

"I like it. It reminds me of my uncle's yacht. I have happy memories of knotty pine." Lillian picked up a ceramic figurine of a sea captain sitting in an outhouse. "I miss the spaniels though."

Blue knelt beside the fireplace, took some sticks out of a basket, and propped them up in the hearth.

"Did you call your people?" Lillian asked.

"Yeah." Blue stood up.

Lillian took a step toward Blue at the same moment Blue moved toward her. They stopped. They were standing so close, she could feel Blue's breath on her face. She caught a hint of Blue's sophisticated cherry perfume. Without makeup Blue looked older than she did onstage, and sexier. Maybe that was the *realness* the Prime Minister was always talking about.

"Are we going to make good life choices?" Lillian asked.

"Of course." Blue's eyes said no. She reached past Lillian. The movement brought her even closer. But she didn't touch her. Instead she plucked *Rogan: A Seafaring Journey to Manhood* off the shelf.

"When I'm lying in bed," Blue said, "trying not to go crazy with you *right* there, I'll read this. I'll be like a teenage boy trying to think about baseball."

The thought of Blue being frustrated and reading about seafaring made Lillian want to pull Blue to her and grind her hip between Blue's legs. Everything else fled Lillian's mind. What ballet? What competition?

"Will it work?" Lillian asked.

Blue took a step back and opened the book. *"Even as a lad my elders saw something of the adventuring world in me."*

Lillian ran her fingertips along the spine of the book, touching the back while Blue held its edges. Blue's breath caught as she read on. The sound almost undid Lillian.

"Untold men had gone before me, but I bore a mark of inherent excellence."

"Do you think if I kissed you one more time, it would help? Satisfy you? Relieve you"—Lillian hung on the word *relieve* because the image of Blue stirring with untouched desire was too delicious—"of the need to read about Rogan?"

"I'm sure it would," Blue whispered. Her eyes were wide. Her lips parted. "Obviously one kiss would be enough to put that all behind me."

"I wouldn't want you to suffer." Lillian put her hand on Blue's waist, savoring her softness, and pulled Blue to her. "Just once more," she murmured against Blue's lips.

Blue's kiss was drinking water in the desert. Blue held the back of Lillian's head as she pressed her lips hard and frantic against Lillian's. Lillian slowed their kiss as if to stop. Blue stifled a moan of protest. Lillian pulled away just long enough to press Blue against the wall beside the fireplace.

"I'm the one who's supposed to—"

Blue gasped as Lillian pressed her leg between Blue's, holding her with her hips. Because Lillian had control of every muscle in her body and because she'd been with enough women to read Blue's gasps, she moved her hips in exactly the right way. Or the wrong way if she'd been trying to free Blue's mind of distraction. Blue almost sobbed. She clutched Lillian's hips. And Lillian kissed her. *Just one more kiss.* Who was Lillian kidding? The only question was how long before Lillian laid Blue on Captain Cozy's Cottage's bed and ravished her. Lillian pulled away a second before the urge to come against Blue's leg became irresistible.

Lillian returned her breath and her heartbeat to an even rhythm.

"Is that better?" Lillian asked.

Blue was flushed, one hand pressed against the wall behind her.

"You know it's not." She looked like she might collapse.

"I won't do it again then." Lillian grinned. "Let's go get dinner at the lodge."

"You're killing me."

"You have to wait until the end of the show."

"I'm going to explode." Blue leaned her head back against the wall. "Lillian. You...I..."

Confident, charismatic Blue Lenox at a loss for words. That was as satisfying as landing a perfect jeté on the Walroux Fousse Center stage. No, it felt better.

"You're not going to leave me like this?"

If Blue had been any other woman, Lillian would have stripped them both down, come against Blue's leg, and been at the lodge before the diners had seconds. But this was Blue.

"Are you asking me to compromise my principles?" Lillian asked.

"Please, Lillian. Yes."

"Well, if I'm going to compromise my principles, *our* principles, I want to take my time, and dinner at Barnacle Bob's waits for no one."

Lillian picked up her key, smiled at Blue, and headed for the door, her body begging her to reconsider.

The *grand lodge* was a larger cabin with a wall of windows facing the ocean. Dinner was spaghetti brought to the table in a giant pot and set on a trivet in the shape of an octopus. The manager sat down with the guests. The other guests were split between two groups, some from an over-fifty community in Idaho and six young people from the Netherlands who'd come to have the *authentic American experience.*

"We've rented pickup trucks," one of the tourists from the Netherlands said in barely accented English.

Why had Lillian decided to make Blue wait? Maybe she should grab Blue's hand and drag her away. *I need you now.* But on a totally practical level, there weren't other food options at Barnacle Bob's, and Blue would need her strength. Lillian smiled to herself.

Blue sparkled, instantly the center of attention, but as soon as the group's attention landed on her, she shared it. She was like a kaleidoscope of mirrors reflecting the sweetest, funniest things about the other guests. A retiree who looked older than God told a story about stealing a golf cart when he was a teenager. Blue listened, rapt, laughing at all the right places. Then she riffed off the story until it became something special they all shared. She suggested hideous Americana the group from the Netherlands could visit on their trip: a taxidermied-alligator-petting museum, the world's largest ball of gum.

Despite the fierce need to ride Blue and come against her flesh, Lillian could have watched her forever. Blue made a community out of strangers eating spaghetti in a rustic cabin. She was kind. She made everyone belong. It wasn't hard to see how she'd gathered a burlesque troupe around her, how Portland loved her. Lillian could even see why women thrust their breasts at Blue for a signature so they could take a little of her magic with them. And she could see how Blue was so much more than flash and sex appeal. And as Blue charmed the guests, she kept looking at Lillian imploringly. Lillian wanted to give Blue anything and everything Blue wanted.

Eventually dinner was finished. The other guests excused themselves. Lillian looked at Blue.

"Shall we?" she asked.

Outside in the rain, Blue leaned against Lillian. "You did that to tease me."

"You need to eat. You need your strength." Lillian grinned. "And I want this to last. I want to take my time. You're worth it."

"That's the nicest thing a lover's said to me," Blue said.

"I hope that's not true."

But if it was, Lillian wanted to be the one to say it.

Lillian was in so much trouble.

Blue followed her into the cottage. Lillian meant to control their kiss, to tease Blue, and to break her with pleasure. But as soon as they were inside, Blue pressed her against the wall where Lillian had pinned Blue earlier. Blue leaned her whole body against Lillian's, every inch of her softness touching Lillian. Lillian clutched Blue so fervently she felt all of Blue all at once, her hands pulling

Blue closer, her mouth open for Blue's kiss. She needed Blue. She'd waited too long. She needed to give in now.

Blue ran the side of her thumb down Lillian's belly and lower, tracing the zipper of Lillian's pants.

"What would you like me to do to you?" she asked.

"What do *you* want?" Lillian gasped.

"To make you sing."

Blue kissed down the side of Lillian's neck, pushing her coat off and tossing it across a chair. She bit the juncture of Lillian's shoulder and her neck. She caught Lillian's nipple between her fingers, pinching her through her sweater. The spark of pain made everything feel clearer, sharper, better.

When Blue finally pulled away, her eyes were dreamy and desperate.

"Can I go down on you?" she asked.

Lillian nodded. She wanted to taste Blue too, wanted to explore the delicate minutiae of her body, but she was too turned on to refuse. A moment later they were in the bedroom. Blue turned up the baseboard heater and cast the cover off the bed. She stripped Lillian quickly, kissing her the whole time, then gave her a soft shove toward the bed. Lillian lay down. Blue followed her, kissing quickly down her belly. Lillian's hips bucked. It was still too slow. She tried to formulate the words. *I appreciate the foreplay, and maybe afterward, but could you please, now!*

Blue settled herself between Lillian's legs, her cheek resting on Lillian's thigh, suddenly calm, looking up at Lillian like they were lying on a picnic blanket discussing whether they'd go swimming later.

"Are you going to just—" Lillian protested. *I need you.*

"*You* made me go to dinner." Lillian could feel Blue chuckle. "Do you know how long it takes for people to eat spaghetti?"

Blue trailed her fingers lazily over Lillian's vulva.

"I…" For once Lillian's ballet training was not enough to slow her heartbeat.

"They have to roll every noodle onto their fork," Blue said slowly. "Is there anything I should know?" Blue asked, more serious. "Things you like? Don't like?"

"I'll tell you if anything doesn't feel right." *Please. Now. Kiss me.* Lillian's hips bucked.

Blue slid between Lillian's legs, kissing Lillian's inner thighs, then drifted her lips across Lillian's hair.

"You smell good." Blue touched the tip of her tongue to Lillian's opening. "And taste good."

Lillian almost screamed at the insufficient pleasure. Blue licked her again. And again. And again. Nowhere near her clit. Lillian squirmed and moaned. She felt Blue's hands tighten on her hips, was vaguely aware of Blue thrusting her own hips into the bed. She dug her hands into Blue's hair.

"Oh, Blue, please."

She never called women's names during sex. In some ways, names didn't matter when it was just a one-night hookup. But now she needed Blue, not just someone.

She pressed her hips toward Blue's lips. "This is what I want."

And Blue gave her what she wanted, kissing and sucking her clit. She massaged Lillian's mons and pressed her fingers inside Lillian. The whole world distilled down to those sensations, the spotlight getting brighter and smaller, the pirouette getting faster, until Lillian spun out of control and came with a silent cry.

When she came back to her senses, she realized that Blue had rolled away from her. Blue was touching herself with both hands, three fingers pushing inside herself, while her other hand rubbed at her clit with hard, jerky movements. Without looking at her, Blue reached for Lillian's hand and guided it to her opening.

"Touch me," Blue gasped.

There was nothing Lillian wanted to do more. Blue moved her hand so Lillian could touch her and Blue could capture her labia and her clit in her hands. Blue was wet. Hot. Swollen. Lillian rubbed Blue's opening, then slipped two fingers inside her. Blue clutched at herself so awkwardly it was hard to imagine she could come from that chaotic rubbing and yanking.

"Oh. I'm going to..." Blue's eyes squeezed shut. "I need it so much I'm going to cry."

Blue ground the heel of her hand against herself, squeezing her eyes so tightly closed a tear did slide down her cheek. Lillian saw it in the light coming from beneath the curtains.

"I need to... yes! Yes. Yes!"

Blue's back arched and her body spasmed.

When her orgasm subsided, she rolled onto her belly, her face pressed to the pillow. She lay motionless.

Lillian put a hand on her back. "Are you okay?"

Blue nodded into the pillow. Then she rolled over, seemed to regret it, and rolled back onto her belly.

"It's supposed to be artful," Blue said into the pillow.

"What?"

"Me."

"It's not a performance." Lillian stroked Blue's back, feeling a rush of tenderness.

When Blue finally rolled over and looked her in the eyes, Lillian could see the truth they both knew: Everything in life was performance. And a woman like Blue shouldn't come like that. It was too real. Too vulnerable. Sexy but too desperate to be on brand. If you were going to hook up with strangers, you should keep your *I need it so much I'm going to cry* to yourself. But they weren't strangers.

Lillian leaned on one elbow, gazing down at Blue and stroking the pattern of zeros and ones on her chest.

"If I wasn't already a lesbian, you'd make me gay."

"Don't you want a dancer with rock-hard thighs?"

"I want you, Blue." There it was. A truth that was too big to fit in the cottage or the tour bus or her studio apartment in the Lynn-wood Terrace. "I want you, Isadora Wells from Broken Bush."

"My real name." Blue's face lit with delight.

"Did you think this whole time I didn't google you? Does anyone call you Isadora?"

"It's Izzy."

It was an unpretentious name. The kind of name that made you think of pigtails and flowery dresses. The kind of life neither of them had lived.

"Do you like Izzy?" Lillian asked.

"Yeah." Blue turned her head, not hiding her face but not meeting Lillian's eyes. "All my friends used to call me Izzy. I don't know when Blue became everything I was."

"It's not."

"Sarah only calls me Izzy when she thinks I'm fucking up."

"Look at me." Lillian gently tipped Izzy's chin up. "I don't think you're fucking up." It was possible they were both fucking up in some massive emotional-disaster sort of way Lillian could barely anticipate since she'd barely had any emotions with women. "And if your inner truth was signing women's names with an organic Sharpie, I wouldn't be here. Can I call you Izzy?"

"Yeah."

"Izzy Wells." It fit her.

"Are we going to do this again?" Izzy finally looked at Lillian, her eyes guileless.

"Did you get me out of your system?"

"Never." Izzy's eyes drifted closed as though remembering pleasure or anticipating it.

The thin curtains let in the dark luminescence of the night sky, casting the room in blue shadows. It made Izzy's pale skin look paler, like a magical creature descended from a castle on the moon. Lillian had seen the best dancers in the world perform the most challenging moves, but no body and no one had looked so beautiful. Izzy blinked her eyes open, then closed again.

Lillian brushed a lock of damp hair off Izzy's forehead.

"Go to sleep, Izzy." She kissed Izzy's forehead.

Izzy sprawled on her side, instantly asleep, smiling, like she was still bathed in the pleasure of her release. But Lillian stayed up for a long time. *I wanted to date every girl who'd leave because they were passionate about something that wasn't me.* That was Lillian, and the thought of hurting Izzy made her want to curl up in a ball and never leave the cottage. *I won't. I won't. I won't.* But there was no way to end this without breaking both their hearts, not after calling Blue's name in bed, not after learning Blue's name was Izzy.

chapter 27

Izzy woke up slowly. She felt wet, aroused, and satisfied at the same time, her body limp and humming. The room smelled pleasantly of sandalwood and sex. Rain beat a gentle white noise on the roof. Izzy drifted off again, then woke to a shock of embarrassment. She'd masturbated in front of Lillian: alone-in-her-own-bed masturbation, horny-teenager masturbation. She'd grabbed Lillian's hands and…she could still feel the desperate way she'd clasped Lillian's hand to her. It had felt so good. She loved going at her clit just the way she needed while Lillian's fingers crooked inside her, pulling her toward orgasm. She wanted that again. Right now. But she couldn't. She must have looked like she'd lost all control.

And shit! Her head was on Lillian's pillow. Her breasts pressed against Lillian's lean side. She was lucky she hadn't thrown her arms and legs around Lillian, because that was what Izzy's body wanted. This was why she had to leave before she fell asleep. At some point endorphins would send her to sleep and then her body would give in to what she wanted: to cuddle against a woman in the tremulous hope of being held in return. But drooling peacefully on a stranger's pillow ruined the illusion, like going backstage after a show and seeing the drag queens untaping their business.

Hopefully Lillian was a sound sleeper. Izzy edged away. The bed shifted under her weight.

Lillian opened one eye.

"Sorry. I know you don't cuddle," Izzy said.

Lillian draped a sleep-heavy arm over Izzy's hips.

"I don't," Lillian said, pulling her closer. "You can get up to pee or get coffee but then come back to bed." Lillian opened both her eyes. "I mean if you want to."

Of course Izzy wanted to. She got up, peed, and then splashed water on her face. When she came back, Lillian was sitting up against the headboard. She pulled Izzy to her so Izzy was sitting between her legs, her back against Lillian's chest.

"I already broke my no second-night-stands rule." Lillian wrapped her arms around Izzy. "Why not break *no cuddling in the morning*?"

"Did *you* always want shooting stars?"

Lillian hadn't offered that information when they were walking on the beach, but maybe that was just because Izzy hadn't asked. Izzy held her breath waiting for the answer.

"No."

That was the answer Izzy wanted to hear. If Lillian had wanted a relationship once, maybe she'd want one again.

"Professional dancers do date, have relationships, even marry," Lillian said as though Izzy had said the opposite. "I just haven't had time. But there was a girl in high school. I thought she was my true love. I'm sure she wasn't. We were just kids. It didn't end well. Maybe that made an impression on me. My mother disapproved. She said the girl was a distraction."

Izzy wrapped her hands around the arm Lillian had wrapped around her.

"We started going to movies together and sneaking carbs we weren't supposed to have. We got older. It got more serious. We started talking about what we'd do when we started our careers."

"Did you want a relationship then?"

"Yeah." Lillian sighed. "Did you google me?"

"A bit."

Lillian squeezed Izzy. "Did you see the stuff about the lawsuit?"

"I saw something about a lawsuit. I didn't go in deep. It seemed...personal." And not nearly as exciting as watching a leotard stretch over Lillian's body as she danced. "I was more interested in your videos."

"Please tell me you got off to me dancing in *The Nutcracker*."

"Lillian, that would be wrong!" Izzy tilted her head back to look at Lillian. "I only got off on Sleeping Beauty. I imagined I was the prince. But what about the lawsuit?"

"I went to a famous dance school, but they didn't cast Black dancers in any of their important recitals, so my mother sued, won, and now everything is great." Lillian spoke quickly as though this was an unfortunate fact that needed to be gotten out of the way.

"Is it?"

"The school changed their policies. They let some people go. It was a landmark case."

"I bet it was hard."

"I was sixteen." This time Lillian's words came out at a crawl. "I was talented. And I didn't get cast as a principal or soloist. I wasn't building up a vita because I was always in the ensemble roles. The school said, pretty clearly, that they weren't casting me because I was tall and Black. Choreography specifies size and uniformity. So my mom sued. The lawsuit went on and on. And from the day we filed the suit, Eleanor said we had to prove she wasn't some jealous dance mom who thought she could cry racism to get her daughter better parts."

"But you *were* good."

"I was a prodigy."

Izzy felt Lillian's chest rise and fall.

"But that wasn't enough. I had to be beyond perfection. I rehearsed for twelve hours a day." She rested her cheek on the top of Izzy's head. "My mother made me break up with my girlfriend. She was a distraction. I broke her heart. I'm sure she recovered, but at the time…she asked how I could have chosen dance over her. I said we all put dance first. We wouldn't be at the school if we didn't. But she said we could have both. Dance and a relationship." Lillian set the next words out carefully, like it hurt to speak them. "I told her *she* could. I told her she didn't understand the privilege she had as a white dancer. If she didn't understand that, she didn't understand me."

Izzy thought she heard a tremor in Lillian's voice. Why was the world like this? Why did this kind, beautiful woman have to give up love to succeed? It wasn't right. Lillian knew that. She didn't need Izzy to tell her, but Izzy said it anyway.

"It's not fair."

"Yeah."

"It wasn't your fault."

"No."

Izzy wrapped her arms around Lillian's, wishing she were sitting behind Lillian so she could cradle Lillian's whole body in hers.

"What happened?" Izzy said quietly.

"My girlfriend said it sucked that the dance world was racist. It wasn't fair that some people had to work harder. Sometimes one person in a relationship had to give up more than the other. That was shitty, but it was true, and that didn't mean love wasn't worth it. I didn't tell her she wasn't worth it, but we both knew that was what I thought."

Lillian's body had gone stiff.

"And I was right. A high school crush wasn't worth giving up ballet. It would have been ridiculous for my mom to say, *Oh sure, give up on everything you've worked for so you can date the girl you fell in love with in ninth grade.* I guess that was what the lawsuit was about." Lillian paused as though the thought had just occurred to her. "Eleanor, my mom, always talked about making opportunities for Black dancers. Maybe one of those opportunities would be having what my girlfriend had. To be great but not *the best* and still get the role and have a personal life. I spent a lot of time frustrated before I realized I could just have sex without all the rest of it." Lillian laughed low in her throat. "Once I figured that out, I thought I had everything I wanted."

I thought I had.

Izzy felt Lillian relax, but somehow it felt deliberate, like Lillian was controlling her muscles and making them relax. Izzy stroked Lillian's arm. That kind of rhythmic touch always calmed her, although it had been a long time since a woman had stroked her like that.

"I'm supposed to do an interview for this documentary about Black dancers. I probably shouldn't tell them that part, should I? It was hard being a ballerina until I realized I could have casual sex. I almost got out of doing the documentary too. It's almost finished, but my mother told the director she really needed to get my perspective." Lillian gave an annoyed huff. "What perspective is that? I can't imagine fitting someone else into my life because no one would put up with my schedule and I don't like to be distracted at work? Ballet killed any chance I had of being romantic or spontaneous?"

"You're spontaneous. You're in Captain Cozy's Cottage on a cliff that will probably slide into the ocean next year, naked, with a burlesque dancer. That seems go with the flow to me."

"You make me sound good."

Izzy drew Lillian's hand to her lips and kissed her fingertips. Lillian's forced relaxation softened.

"I know that you aren't looking for anything romantic, but getting stuck in a cottage by the sea is ten on the romance scale. I mean for other people." No need to mention how mind-blowing last night had been. No need to remind Lillian what Izzy's face must have looked like when she came.

Izzy admired their arms wrapped together. Lillian's skin was as dark as pure cacao, as French roast coffee beans, but none of those things compared. They weren't even an approximation because Lillian glowed the way the night sky glowed when there was no moon. Radiant and dark. A beauty that owed nothing to stage lights. Against Lillian's skin, Izzy looked like something that had lived under a mossy rock without sunlight for a long time.

Lillian was quiet for a moment. When she spoke, she was matter-of-fact.

"As much as I like the breathtaking sexual tension of pretending we're not going to have sex again," Lillian said, "we could just devour each other every chance we get until we go our own ways."

Izzy felt a shy smile spread across her face.

"You mean amend our previous agreement and give in to our base nature?"

"If you have to put it that way." Lillian pinched Izzy's thigh. "Yes. Until one of us gets voted off in the finale, we'll have...fun. Like comets instead of shooting stars. What do you think?"

I'd give you the moon. Marry me. Give it all up because we are so wonderful together.

"That could be fun," Izzy said.

chapter 28

Eventually, Izzy went out in search of coffee. Lillian felt light. She rose from the bed and floated around the cottage naked. The lacy curtains barely hid her from view, but so what? She could hear Eleanor's shock. *Decorum! A Black dancer has to…standards…judged differently…* But for once her mother's voice wasn't front and center. Front and center were thoughts of kissing Izzy at the Lynnwood Terrace, out of sight of the cameras, sneaking around the greenrooms after everyone had left, of pulling Izzy back to bed.

Izzy returned a few minutes later with coffee in hand and a brown paper bag tucked under one arm. She looked endearing, smiling in her puffer coat, wearing Lillian's tank top, which was gloriously tight on her. She held the two ceramic coffee mugs proudly, like she'd hunted and gathered them for her mate.

"Good news and bad news," Izzy said.

"Okay?"

"They didn't clear the roads." Izzy looked like a kid who'd just learned summer vacation went for another week.

"We have to get out of here," Lillian said before she could suck it back.

Izzy's face fell.

"What's the good news?"

"Tock checked the contract. In the event of natural disaster—this counts—if the contestant is unable to be at the competition, the show will film an episode without them. There's a whole bunch of stuff about how if our people lose, we can't go back and complain, but we get to stay here for...a while."

"I have the company's dance almost done, but it's in Benesh Movement Notation. That's a kind of shorthand for dance moves. It's like musical notation."

"I know. And it's incomprehensible." Izzy handed Lillian a mug and sat down on the sofa on the far side of the room, which didn't say much—the room was probably ten by ten—but Lillian felt the distance. Izzy set the bag on a nearby table and pushed it away from herself. Izzy had been looking forward to spending time with her. She'd practically bounded in. And damn it, it would be fun to spend the day having sex. Talking. They could walk along the beach. Izzy could charm the retirees and the Dutch again. They could make a fire in the sooty firepit in the center of the cottages. It wasn't raining.

But her dancers. This was why she couldn't get distracted. She had to think about the company.

"Benesh Movement Notation just takes careful study," Lillian said for no reason except Eleanor would say that.

"Okay." Izzy wrapped her hands around her mug, pulling into herself a little.

Truth: Benesh really was incomprehensible. Many of the best choreographers didn't use it. They'd use movement patterns, counts, music, placement, and film instead of a notated score.

"Okay, it's really hard," Lillian conceded. "Imani is the only one who can read it, and it takes her hours. I can't send her the choreography." Lillian rubbed her hand over her face. "She doesn't have time to interpret it, and then it'll be on her if they mess up. But it's on me."

If she had her undeveloped app, she could just upload her notation or sketch out the moves without notation, sharing it with the company in real time. But her app was an idea and a book full of sketches.

"And I need to rehearse them. I need to be there for them. I need to *show* them what I've written." And she needed to kiss Izzy and hold her face between her hands. *I want to spend the day with you, but I have to get back.* Lillian struggled into her pants, not bothering with underwear. Not that there was anywhere to go, with or without underwear. She paced across the room. "I didn't tell them about Reed and Whitmer shutting us down, and now I'm here. I didn't prepare, and I didn't support them." *I put what I wanted first.* "If they lose, they're going to find out the next day that they don't have jobs, and the whole time I was...I was..."

"With me."

"What are *you* going to do with Velveteen Crush?"

"They'll figure it out. Members of Velveteen Crush usually do our own acts, so we're all ready to choreograph a dance or design an act. Can your people rehearse without you?"

"Rehearse what?"

"Their own thing?"

How did she politely tell Izzy that in ballet, unlike burlesque, the company did not make up their own dances?

"This is my fault." Lillian sat down, still topless.

Izzy looked patient, like someone who knew the answer and was waiting for a friend to come to it themselves.

"How is a landslide your fault?" Izzy asked.

"You said we should turn around."

"You work twenty-four seven and you wanted to walk another mile on the beach."

"I don't work twenty-four seven."

Izzy raised an eyebrow. "When was the last time you took a walk in the rain before that?"

"It doesn't rain in LA."

"In all the places you tour? New York? London? Any rain there?"

Lillian listened for a note of irritation in Izzy's voice, but she didn't hear it.

"Okay. I never walk on the beach. That's the point." *I don't fuck up.* She was on the stage at the Lynn Bernau School of Dance recital. *Perfection is not enough.* She was in the bathroom throwing up as the dance masters scored her. She was in the courtroom waiting for the judge's gavel. She felt her mother watching her. *You must be beyond reproach.*

"Come sit." Izzy motioned for Lillian to sit next to her.

Lillian sat. It felt good to be close.

"I can't let them down."

"Let's brainstorm," Izzy said. "What can you do?"

A brainstorming session wasn't going to move a landslide. Maybe if Lillian had another twenty-four hours in every day, she'd have learned to program and written her app. She'd send the choreography to Imani in an easy-to-view file.

"I had this idea for an app." Why had Lillian mentioned it?

Izzy didn't look confused by the non sequitur. She nodded. "What would your app do?"

"It's nothing. An idea for an app is not going to save me."

"But what is it?"

Lillian hadn't even mentioned it to Kia.

"I have sketches of the moves, and you'd be able to put them together to show the choreography, but you'd be able to adjust the drawings with a stylus, pull an arm up here, stretch an arabesque penchée." Lillian folded her legs into the lotus position, which, despite the flexibility required to sit comfortably in it, showed, according to Eleanor, *nervous self-containment.* "You could make your own collection of personalized clips. I could just compile and hit send. If I had that, I could fix this. Or I could build a helicopter and fly over the landslide."

"Maybe everyone could contribute their modifications." Izzy nodded like this was a real idea. "Like the way people add templates to Videoleap. Have you done any work on it?"

Lillian turned her phone over in her hands. This was Izzy's job. Even with the binary code tattoo, it was easy to forget she was a programmer when she was strutting around in glittery corsets. But she was. And from what little she'd said about it, she was good at it. Lillian couldn't show her an app idea. Amateurs were embarrassing.

"Can you see something and then unsee it?" Lillian asked.

Izzy put a hand on her naked shoulder, the portrait of empathetic listening, and then asked, "Is there some weird, kinky sex thing?"

Lillian burst out laughing despite the fact that her dancers had no choreography, Imani couldn't read what Lillian had written, and she was stranded in a cottage that was one tsunami away from washing out to sea.

"If it's your naked body, no." Izzy's lips quirked in a coaxing half smile. "I could never forget that."

"I'd be offended if you forgot." Lillian opened the animation app on which she'd saved a 1.8 second clip, the product of an entire

LAX to O'Hare flight. A drawing of a woman moving one arm up and down. She held it out to Izzy.

Lillian folded and refolded her legs.

Izzy watched the clip over and over, her lips pursed. She tapped the air above the screen as though making a quick calculation.

"The collaborative part would be hard. You'd need a lot of server space. But the basics...Did you do the drawing?" Izzy asked.

Lillian nodded.

"Is this the only one?"

If she'd shown Izzy the animation, she might as well show her the files. She accessed the cloud and handed the phone back to Izzy, open to photos of her sketchbook drawings. Dancer after dancer. Move after move. Hand position after hand position.

"These are lovely. If I had more time, I could probably design this. I don't think I could build it in time to send Imani your choreography." Izzy sounded apologetic, as though building the app were only *slightly* out of her reach, not a totally fanciful impossibility, just more work than she could whip out in a morning. Lillian would enjoy watching her work, that easy confidence put in motion. She could imagine Izzy's hands flying over her keyboard the way they'd flown over Lillian's body. A woman who knew what she was doing.

"You're sexy," Lillian said.

"Because I can make an app?"

"Exactly."

"Yeah right." Izzy put a hand over her binary code tattoo.

"I am right."

Izzy looked back at the phone and kept scrolling.

And then it occurred to Lillian...she photographed all her drawings or scanned them into her computer. Even the picture that Kia had seen of Izzy, fully drawn and shaded, not a sketch but a piece of art. Izzy lying on her side, naked except for her underwear, the shading accentuating the weight of her breasts. Now was the right time to snatch the phone back.

"You have hundreds," Izzy said.

Izzy scrolled for a moment, then stopped.

"Oh." She stared at the screen. Bit her lip. Looked from the screen to Lillian. Then her smile widened like she'd been handed the perfect Christmas present. "I'm flattered. Is this from…?"

"Our first night."

"You said no scones, but you drew my picture."

"I like to sketch, and you're an attractive model." Lillian affected an arch tone, then swept in and kissed Izzy on the cheek. "Don't get cocky."

"You can't resist me." Izzy grinned. "So, anyway, I don't have time to make your app in the next twenty minutes. If only I had forty." Izzy's grin filled with pride. "What if you take some of these drawings—probably not this one." She flashed the picture of herself to Lillian. "Send your company a rough sequence. Then tell them to improvise."

She couldn't abandon her dancers. Improvise? That was like putting someone on a raft and pushing them out to sea.

"You say they're incredibly talented," Izzy added.

"That's why I have to do everything I can to help them."

"Tell them you're giving them a chance to expand their skill set. That's helpful."

"It's my job to do this *for* them, not to push it off on them."

"You said you have to do everything you can to help them." There was that patient, coaxing look again. "What else can you do right now?"

The room felt brighter. Lillian's body felt lighter.

"Are you going to tell me that all we can do is do our best?" Lillian pretended to scowl.

"People have said that occasionally."

Lillian pictured Imani's face when she called and told Imani she had to finish the choreography and lead rehearsal. If she put it on Pascale, Pascale would panic. But Lillian could see the gleam in Imani's eyes that said, *Now we're really going to have fun.*

"I think Imani would like to lead the rehearsal," Lillian mused.

Hadn't Imani said she wanted to be a dance master when she retired from dancing?

"See? Perfect," Izzy said. "She can handle it, and you can handle it."

"You mean handle not being in control of everything all the time." Lillian tried to put her scowl back on, but she'd lost it.

"Exactly." Izzy stood up suddenly. "There's more bad news." She didn't look upset. She picked up the bag she'd brought in under her arm and held it out triumphantly. "All they have for breakfast at the lodge are scones."

Izzy stepped out so Lillian could work alone. Around noon, Lillian texted Imani and shared the file containing a string of images, mostly drawings Lillian had done before but a few new ones to accommodate the Lie in Wait theme.

Lillian: *Change whatever you like. Just make it work.*

Imani: *Want us to film it and send it to you?*

Lillian typed *absolutely*, then reconsidered. Did she? Izzy was waiting for her. By the time Imani and the dancers filmed the dance, Lillian would, hopefully, have Izzy's clitoris gently situated between her lips and her tongue. Then her phone would ping. She'd have to watch the video, give feedback. Eleanor had always told her to stay focused. You couldn't focus on going down on a woman when you were waiting for a text from work.

Lillian: *I trust you.*

Lillian got up, put on her coat, and went outside. The sky was a bright gray. The smell of pines freshened the wind blowing off the ocean. Everything felt clean. It felt like the day after a show ended. Yes, as soon as one show ended, it was time to start preparing for the next one, but you got one day. One day when you could walk down the street and not feel like you should be rehearsing. For twenty-four hours that weight lifted. The world came back into focus: This is what trees look like. This is what car horns sound like. This is what coffee smells like.

It felt like that.

Lillian found Izzy in the not-so-grand lodge with the Dutch tourists and a few retirees. Izzy lounged in an armchair that looked like years of use had melted it down to twice its original width and half its height. She waved. When Lillian drew closer, Izzy looked up at her.

"Everything okay?" she asked quietly.

"Perfect."

Izzy beamed and patted the cushion next to her. Lillian hesitated. There was room for them both but not we're-just-friends room. But they weren't just friends, so she fit herself in next to Izzy, hip to hip. Izzy put her arm on the back of the chair with a questioning look. *Is this okay?* Lillian smiled. Izzy settled her arm around Lillian's shoulders.

"You two are so sweet," one of the retirees said. "You'll remember this forever." He looked lovingly at the man sitting next to him.

Under the guise of kissing Lillian's cheek, Izzy whispered, "I told them we were on a second date when we got stranded."

"I guess we were," Lillian said.

We just didn't know it.

Had she just said they were dating? Not as in "relationship" dating but as in "not just a second hookup"?

"The manager says there's a town a mile south," one of the tourists said. "We're going to walk in. He says it's usually too dangerous to walk on the road, but there's no traffic because of the slides. Will you two join us?" He looked at the retirees. "And you?"

It took an hour to gather everyone, but an hour later five young Dutch tourists, eight retirees, the cottage manager, his two shepherd mix dogs, and two stranded reality TV stars were walking down Highway 101. The lack of traffic should have felt apocalyptic, but it just felt like someone had set real life on pause. The tourists and the retirees tried to name songs that all of them knew, then tried to sing them, to much laughter and bungled lyrics. The cottage manager told a story about a pirate named Vladivostok von Wellington, which got wilder and wilder until everyone was calling, "No way" and "You cannot possibly think we'd believe that." The manager kept dropping his voice lower as he imitated the fictional Vladivostok.

And Izzy held Lillian's hand.

Or Lillian held hers.

"Do you know what I'm going to do to you when we get back to the cottage?" Izzy whispered, her words hidden by the sound of Vladivostok threatening to drain the sea and ground every ship before he'd give up his gold.

"Read that seafaring book to me?"

"Or make you read it to me while I..." Izzy whistled a few notes and swung their joined hands, which was the kind of silly, playful thing that would have made Lillian pull away if it had been any-one else. Since it was Izzy, it was wonderful.

The "town" was a rock shop, a café, a garage, and two churches. The café was closed, but the manager went around back to a little house on the property. A few minutes later, a woman opened the café, and half an hour later she was delivering pancakes and fruit salad.

When they were back on 101, heading back to the cottages, to-go coffees in hand, Lillian whispered, "Tell me more about how I'm going to read this seafaring book to you. Is that your kink? What was his name? Roger?"

"*Rogan: A Seafaring Journey to Manhood.* How could you forget, Lillian? It's our story."

"I'm pretty sure it's not *our* story."

"It's how I'll always remember you. The woman who led me to Rogan." Izzy opened her eyes wide. With her cheeks rosy and her puffer coat puffing and her hair blowing in the wind, the blue of her hair looked more like a teenager's home hair dye than a rebel burlesque performer's signature look.

"I'm going to make you listen to the whole thing," Lillian said. "As punishment."

"Ooh. Have I been a bad girl?"

God, there were so many things Lillian would like to try with Izzy. Would Izzy like to be spanked? Tied up? Lillian never both-ered with things like that. It was too much communication and boundary setting for a hookup. Maybe Izzy would enjoy it if Lillian strapped on. That was one of Lillian's favorite pleasures: to thrust into a woman. It was a pleasure Lillian didn't get to enjoy nearly as often as she'd like. Bringing a harness and dildo to a hookup was very, very extra, as Kia would say. But with Izzy...they could pick out the size and shape for her. Lillian would be careful to get it right. The strength in her hips exceeded anything a normal person could imagine, and she would use only a fraction of her strength on Izzy. She'd take care of Izzy. It was all so delicious.

Lillian's thoughts turned her on. She was horny. She needed Izzy and she needed her soon. And even though Lillian could control every muscle in her body, there was nothing she could do to control the desire mounting inside of her, and it was wonderful to be just a little bit out of control and wonderful to know that at the end of this beautiful, breezy walk, Izzy would put her lips around her clitoris and—

Their phones rang simultaneously. Lillian and Izzy looked at each other, then answered. Somehow Bryant had managed to conference call them without a link or a meeting ID number.

"They've cleared enough of 101 to get an SUV through," he said. "DOT gave us special permission to come get you. Be ready in an hour."

chapter 29

One of the crew arrived in a monster SUV that looked like it was designed for military operations rather than rescuing people from inadvertent coastal vacations. Lillian wished it had gotten stuck in the mud. She and Izzy were quiet as they rode back to Portland. It had been too much to hope for one day off. Totally off. Nowhere they had to be, nowhere they *could* be.

They arrived in Portland a half hour before the Reed-Whitmer Ballet Company went on. One of the runners met them at the door and led them to the sound booth.

"You can watch from here. They don't want you in the greenrooms. They're pretending you're still stuck in the landslide."

The booth was more like a mezzanine, a long room that spanned the back of the soundstage, panels of lights glowing in the darkness. The three sound techs seemed relaxed. One of them removed her headset and pointed to a table of snacks.

"Help yourself. You can talk up here too. Nothing here is miked."

On the floor of the soundstage, Bryant ran through the usual checks. They took their seats near the plexiglass window that looked down on the studio audience and the stage, still not talking. It wasn't an unfriendly silence, but it wasn't comfortable either. One of their groups had to lose. Maybe today. Lillian should be kissing Izzy in the cottage.

Soon her company would perform. She had to focus, but visions of lying on top of Izzy teased her. Swimming on the beautiful fullness of her body, one hand tucked around Izzy's thigh, massaging Izzy's clit, asking her how many fingers. Why couldn't she be doing that now?

She jumped when Kia vaulted over the seat beside her and plopped down.

"Y'all survived!" Kia said.

Izzy looked confused. Kia flashed her influencer badge.

"Works every time. So how was *the coast*?" Kia said with a ridiculous amount of innuendo.

Lillian blurted, "Comfortable." Her company was going on in minutes. This was not the time! Plus, Izzy was right there!

"Blue's going to be offended that that's all you've got to say." Kia leaned over Lillian. "Hi, Blue. Offended?"

"Crushed," Izzy said cheerfully.

"Don't worry. Most women only get *acceptable*."

"Kia!" Lillian protested. They were talking about her sex life. "The *cottage* was comfortable."

"Nice towels? Good baseboard heaters?" Kia directed the question at Izzy.

"That's definitely what I'll remember from the night. Baseboard heaters."

Izzy smiled. Kia looked back and forth between them. It was fun. Easy. Some of Lillian's anxiety and guilt over not being with her dancers ebbed.

"Can we please talk about the show?" Lillian protested with mock indignation.

What would it be like if she and Izzy were a real couple and Kia was always teasing them about sneaking off together?

"Don't worry," Kia said. "Imani's got the company covered, and Sarah's getting everything ready for your show, Blue."

Bryant called action. Hallie and Harrison bantered, looking even whiter and more cheerful than usual. Then it was time.

Izzy squeezed her hand.

Kia said, "I saw them practice. It was great."

The soundstage went dark. A techno version of Debussy's *La mer* blared from the speakers. Imani entered stage left, performing the first moves of the choreography Lillian had sent her. She'd let her braids down. She looked magical. The lights flickered like lightning. The sound of rain drowned out Debussy. Elijah, Malik, and Jonathan emerged from the wings, half tumbling and half dancing into the shape of a monster. Jonathan's legs were the monster's hind legs. Elijah and Malik somehow managed to shape themselves into huge teeth, chomping toward Imani. It was like a ballet company had morphed into a giant lantern fish in a thunderstorm.

The audience laughed.

And there came Pascale, whirling in wearing the bear deflector jacket, racing toward Imani with another hideous Lie in Wait costume and draping it around her shoulders. Black light illuminated the clothing's neon appendages. Straps. D rings. Something that might have been a float. The monster shuddered. Pascale and Imani strutted on pointe with a touch of cockiness they might have gotten from Blue Lenox.

The audience roared with laughter.

The monster disintegrated into something like a caterpillar.

Jonathan was its head, and Elijah pulled up the rear. After one last flash of Lie in Wait neon, the caterpillar raced offstage, leaving Imani and Pascale to bow.

It was terrible. It was hysterical. It was oddly gorgeous. The Star Maker looked like it wanted to explode past one hundred.

"Well, that was a new style," Harrison said. "Alejandro, what did you think about it?"

"This is a reach for a professional ballet troupe."

Izzy squeezed her hand again.

"But I think it was a good reach," Alejandro said.

Christina clasped her hands together. "Their message really resonated with me."

The Prime Minister said, "So much going on. I think I got vertigo looking at that one. But…imma have to give it to 'em. Creative! Reed-Whitmer creative!"

Reed-Whitmer had made it to the next round. Without her. She wasn't invited to the dancers' friendship circle, but she was always part of this. Except this time she wasn't. For a second, she felt like a little girl left out of a party. And behind that feeling was relief. They didn't need her. She didn't have time to dwell on her thoughts. Velveteen Crush was next. She held her breath. Next to her, Izzy looked like she wanted to jump out of her seat and rush down to the soundstage floor.

Even without Blue Lenox, Velveteen Crush was fabulous. Bizarre but fabulous. (Not that Lillian could say much about *bizarre* after the Reed-Whitmer performance.) America would see Lie in Wait in a new light after Velveteen Crush's quasi striptease, which was staged to look like a silent film and accompanied by eerie carnival music. It shouldn't have worked. It did.

*   *   *

The runner asked them to stay in the sound booth until well after the last performance, not that Lillian would have missed watching the competition; that was her job. But finally Hallie and Harrison summed up the challenge. Mood of Motion went home. Counting the judges' votes and the Star Maker votes, the hip-hop group, Effectz, was in the lead for the highest overall score. Next was the Dream Team Marchers. Then the Liam Ronan Irish Dance Company. Followed by Reed-Whitmer. Dance Magic. Velveteen Crush was one from the bottom, but there was a big gap between them and the lowest scoring Spice Angels.

The runner returned their phones to them and released them. Kia checked her messages.

"Our people are having a little celebration," she said.

"*Our people?*" Lillian asked as they exited the soundstage and stepped into the mild but relentless Portland rain.

The street was dark. Fatigue was catching up with her. Had she slept last night or just dozed in postcoital bliss? It seemed wrong to fall asleep with Izzy cuddled against her. How many more times would she feel Izzy breathing next to her? How many times would Izzy's full breasts rest against Lillian's arm? So alluring. Why did she sleep with rock-hard dancers when that had never been her type? When she was back in LA, she'd look for curvy hookups. But no. She wasn't longing for a woman's curves. She longed for Izzy.

"Your people," Kia urged. "Your dance company that you've dedicated your life to? You know? Imani who's like a mini you and who you love even though you only show it by criticizing her?"

"I do not."

Did she?

Kia rolled her eyes at Izzy.

"She totally does. Blue, Sarah told you to come too. Everyone's hanging." With that, Kia doubled back. "I gotta talk to one of the guys from Effectz. He's got a great recipe for reimagining the Tater Tot. I'll see you over there."

"Let's get to this party," Izzy said.

"I'm exhausted." Lillian could see the disappointment on her dancers' faces if she walked through the door.

"Me too. Someone kept me up all night. But this is their big win."

A feeling Lillian always kept at bay flooded her before she could stop it. It would be wonderful to be included, to be wanted.

"They don't want me there."

"Of course they'd want to celebrate with you."

"I'd kill the vibe. I'm supposed to tell them not to party. I'm supposed to scare them with how one drink is going to ruin their career."

"If they're afraid of you, do some flaming shots with them. Let loose."

"I'm a dance master. I'm not supposed to let loose."

Izzy stopped, cupped Lillian's face, kissed her, and then said, "You get to let loose. You don't have to unravel."

Lillian could hear music and laughter from down the hall as she approached the apartment assigned to Imani and Pascale. Lillian stopped.

"They're having fun," she said to Izzy.

"Come on." Izzy pushed her toward the door. At Izzy's knock, Jonathan flung the door open. Behind him, the company had piled into the living room. Someone had bought champagne and pizza. Nineties hip-hop played from a Bluetooth speaker.

Jonathan let go of the door handle like it was hot. The party froze. Pascale shut the lid of the pizza box.

"The party don't start 'til I walk in!" Izzy said, bounding through the door.

"I read the choreography," Imani said, her chin tilted up. "I did my best."

"She was up all night," Jonathan added.

"Grace under pressure." Lillian didn't mean it to sound like a backhanded compliment. She tried again. "Well done."

Izzy tapped Lillian on the arm. "They were the best thing ever."

Lillian felt as naked as if she'd missed a grand jeté. *This is me.* She'd worked her whole life to be the woman who killed a party.

"I'm sorry I wasn't there for you," she said.

"Did you hate it?" Behind Imani's controlled expression, Lillian saw how much this meant to her.

"It was..."

The room was absolutely still.

"Fucking fantastic," Lillian said.

Izzy beamed. The members of Reed-Whitmer remained frozen for a split second, the way a dancer in midleap appeared to stop at the top of the arc.

Then Elijah said, "Fuck yeah it was!"

The room burst into the kind of laughter that comes after calamity.

"Ooh, look. Champagne!" Izzy said.

"Straight from the 7-Eleven," Elijah said.

Someone passed Lillian a Solo cup. Suddenly all the dancers were talking at once.

Pascale squealed, "Did you really like it?"

"I loved it."

Someone turned up the music. Tupac and Biggie rolled over in their graves at being stuck on a playlist with each other and

"Thong Song." Imani refilled Lillian's cup. An hour in, someone put on the Zipper song. The party arranged itself in lines, raising and lowering their imaginary zippers. Izzy raised an eyebrow and smiled at Lillian.

"No," Lillian said calmly. "Never. No. Absolutely not."

Her dancers cheered.

"I will not."

Izzy didn't say anything, but her smile was as warm as the sun rising.

Lillian set her empty Solo cup on the floor.

"Lillian can tear up a stage," Elijah said.

"Show us your moves, Ms. Jackson," Malik said.

"It's Lillian," Lillian protested as she rose. "You can't call me Ms. when I'm drinking champagne out of a Solo cup."

If Lillian had been tired before, she was delirious after two hours of nineties hip-hop and cheap champagne. She left with Izzy.

"I want to ravage you," Izzy said, when they'd turned a corner in the hall, "but I think call is at five a.m."

"Maybe since we missed the last performance, we should be alert for tomorrow."

Lillian's body warred between the need for sleep and the need to kiss every inch of Izzy. There was a middle ground: falling asleep next to Izzy's naked body without having sex. That was scones-land, but she was about to suggest it anyway when Izzy said, "How about tomorrow? You and me and Seafaring Rogan?"

"Tomorrow." Lillian pulled Izzy closer and kissed her gently. "I'd like that."

chapter 30

The next day was a blur. The only thing Izzy wanted was to get the bridal brief, plan whatever they were going to do with the challenge, race through practice, and fall into Lillian's bed. But everything took forever. Bryant needed Izzy to film a conflict scene with the leader of Effectz while Arabella, Tock, Sarah, and Axel filmed a happily-hanging-out scene with the Spice Angels. The rep from the bridal company didn't like the way the costumers had fitted their outfits and wanted them retailored. It was eight o'clock before all five members of Velveteen Crush were in the same room together. Then they were all off their game. Arabella looked as angry as a wet cat in her white dress. Axel didn't know how to be onstage in men's clothing. A competing politician had accused the senator Tock worked for of financial malfeasance, and Tock was beside himself without his phone and a chance to do damage control. Only Sarah liked her flirty white outfit, but she agreed that the troupe's energy was frazzled. During a break, Izzy followed Tock out of the building so they could check their phones. She wrote a text to Lillian.

Izzy: *I'm going to be here all night. I wish I was with you.*

That sounded too intimate.

Izzy: I'm going to be here all night, wish we could hit it

Ugh. No.

A text came in from Lillian while Izzy pondered.

Lillian: I'm so sorry. I'm going to be tied up all night.

Izzy: Not an unattractive picture

Lillian: With rehearsal!

The next day, with their act generally in order, Izzy and the troupe sat on the sofas in their greenroom watching Dance Magic on the large TV screen.

"It's all a heteronormative, capitalist conspiracy," Arabella said.

"Love spends," Axel said.

Arabella leaned her shoulder against his.

"Truth."

Arabella was right, but weddings were magical too. What would it be like to have one person commit themselves to you, mind, body, and soul? Yes, there was the whole patriarchal, ownership-of-the-woman thing, but if you could rewrite that…

For a moment, in the cottage, it had felt like Izzy and Lillian were the only people in the world. It was a taste of the forever a wedding promised. For a moment, Izzy wasn't her past or her future. And at the same time, it felt like Lillian saw and accepted all of her. Velveteen Crush's performance was going to capture that kind of magic with a big dose of LGBTQ+ pride. She performed opposite Sarah. Axel paired with Tock. Really, it should have been Axel and Arabella. They were a queerer couple than wholesome Axel and suit-wearing, tap-dancing Tock, but everyone had agreed this was time for the gay marriage angle.

Izzy's heart raced as though she were standing in front of an audience for the first time. They had to make it. Lillian had to make it. Tonight she'd see Lillian. She remembered Lillian sitting half naked in the cottage, so elegant and strong. Izzy had to feel that strength again. This couldn't be their farewell. It just couldn't.

Bryant interrupted her thoughts, opening the greenroom door without knocking.

"Blue," he said matter-of-factly, "your mother's here."

Izzy stood up, peering around Bryant.

"Not *here*," Bryant amended. "In the audience. We're going to have a special moment with you two after you perform. Got it? Joy. Love. Mom. Daughter. Wedding magic. Okay?"

"She really came?"

Izzy could feel Sarah's empathetic eye contact through the back of her skull.

"Yeah. She's excited, pumped," Bryant said. "She's playing really good on camera. You ready to give me some joy?"

She really came.

"Yes. Yes. Yes!" This was the perfect performance for Megan to see, all about love and trust and the future. Izzy cleared her throat. "I mean, yeah. I didn't know she was coming, but that's cool."

"She told you she was coming," Sarah said when Bryant closed the door behind him.

Izzy sat down quickly.

"I didn't..." All those times Megan had promised to be there. *I'd never miss your starring role. Opening night. Closing night. Your last show in high school.* "I didn't know...think...she'd actually come. To see me." Just this once she met Sarah's deep eye contact with her honest feelings. "With everything going on with Bella's wedding, she still made time to see me. Like I...matter."

Sarah drew her into a hug. "Of course you matter."

If all the world was a stage, Izzy had walked into a magical play. Megan had come all the way to Portland to put her first, even though Bella was getting married and Megan surely had Harmonious Terra-cotta napkin holders to hand monogram. And Lillian had listened to her sad-child story and seen her hideous orgasm face and accepted her. Despite a rough rehearsal, Velveteen Crush's performance was going to slap. Maybe love was real, and Lillian would stay, and the Prime Minister would declare them both the final winners, and she'd save the theater, and everything would be okay.

Izzy closed her eyes. Was she imagining everything? Was this feeling just the high of performing? The moment when she transformed into the untouchable Blue Lenox? No. This was real.

"How do you feel?" Sarah asked.

"I'm happy." Totally and completely happy.

Their performance was flawless. The judges loved them. Izzy blinked into the lights. She felt her friends beside her, all of them glowing, even Arabella (although her glow was more an ominous, red glow).

The Prime Minister declared their performance the only one that didn't make him feel like he'd been trapped in a copy of *Modern Bride* magazine, to which Bryant yelled, "Redo!" On second take, the Prime Minister said their performance was beautifully unified around the themes of love, marriage, and movement.

Bryant called cut again, but before Velveteen Crush could exit the stage, he called out, "Blue Lenox, stand there." He hurried onto the stage. "Be sure you're looking at Camera A when Hallie announces your mother's here."

Izzy scanned the audience, but the lights were too bright to make out faces. Bryant silenced the set and called action.

"We have a special surprise for Blue Lenox," Hallie declared with enthusiasm that suggested she was about to offer them a combination of Megabucks jackpot and the Second Coming.

"Blue told us she's so excited to be on the show, but she's missing her sister's bridal shower and dress fitting," Harrison said.

"Her sister's getting married!" Hallie effused.

The studio audience let out a collective "awwww" that was too simultaneous to be spontaneous.

"We brought your family all the way up from California so you *can* do the dress fitting!" Harrison said.

Wait. Not the whole family, just Megan.

"And the Allure Bridal Collection is going to provide the custom-made dress and bridesmaids' dresses. And today, we're sending you to the River Vista Resort and Lodge to pick the perfect Allure Bridal Collection dress for the big day."

This wasn't supposed to be about Bella.

Someone was running down the aisle, cameras following them: Megan, rushing toward her, arms flung wide.

"Izzy, Isadora, Izabelly, peaches."

Megan flung her arms around Izzy, bathing her in Megan's familiar drugstore perfume. And over Megan's shoulder, Izzy saw a mirage of women wearing the same white T-shirt printed with pink sparkly letters, the same pink jeans, the same small puff of lace above their heads. In the middle of them stood Bella in a white dress with a sash across her chest reading BRIDE.

Megan pulled back holding Izzy by her bare shoulders. Megan wore the same shirt, printed with pink sparkly letters reading MOTHER OF THE BRIDE.

"You look amazing," Megan said. "That was the best performance I've ever seen."

A few paces behind her stood Rick, in pink jeans, looking

embarrassed. His T-shirt read FATHER OF THE BRIDE. Beside Bella, a small person with short hair was wearing jeans and a white T-shirt reading SPOUSE OF THE BRIDE. And behind that, an army of pretty white girls, their T-shirts declaring BRIDESMAID in pink script.

"What? No," Izzy said.

Bella looked exactly like a grown-up version of the kid Izzy had known. Big blue eyes. Open smile. A little shy. Her hair looked windblown, as though she'd been too busy chasing butterflies to comb it. Like someone who had spent most of their life happy. That kind of happiness left a glow on people, like a light tan. Like the sun-kissed streaks in Bella's hair. A cold lump formed in Izzy's throat. Megan hadn't come for her. Megan had come to get free dresses for beautiful, happy, sun-kissed Bella or maybe just to get the bridal party on TV.

Bryant called cut. A runner appeared at Izzy's side, shoved a change of clothes at her, pushed her into an empty bathroom to change, and then guided her to the exit. Before she knew it, someone was bundling her onto a tour bus.

"Where are we going?"

Megan was right behind her, talking without taking a breath. "The Allure Bridal Collection is taking us on a girls' getaway bridal dress fitting. I can't wait to see you in a bridesmaid's dress. Can you believe the show's going to pay for everything? Bella is so excited. Her partner is nonbinary. Did you know that? So it's not really a girls' trip. Ace is part of the LGBTQ-plus community, just like you. You'll love them. Rick's coming too. Poor guy. He can't tell a tulle from a rayon, but he wants to be part of everything. You and Bella! My darling girls. My kiddos. My littles."

You left me with a shit trailer in the middle of nowhere and a wad of cash.

Izzy didn't have a bag she could put on the seat beside her to say, *Don't sit here.* Megan plopped down and kept talking.

"Bella and Ace's colors are just lovely. Did you get the bridal planning packet I sent you? I went to your cousin Marley's wedding, and she picked taupe and mint green…"

Two camera operators positioned themselves in the bus. The sweat from Izzy's performance was cooling. The bus's air-conditioning chilled her. The rest of Bella's party piled in.

"I have cousins?"

Why did she ask? She could just get Ancestry.com.

Megan started counting. "Marley. Tiffany. Alex. Jenny." She listed more names. "That's on my side. Then on Rick's…" She went on, oblivious to the fact that Rick was not Izzy's father. Rick was the man Megan married who'd always seemed embarrassed by having a teenage girl in the house and solved that problem by treating her like an Airbnb guest, putting out clean towels for her but never talking to her.

It was too much: The high of the performance fading. Her clit aching for Lillian's lips. Everything Sarah had said about her inner child coming true. Reed-Whitmer hadn't performed; what if they lost? And here was Megan crooning about Bella's partner. And Izzy was going to burst into tears. She dug deep inside to pull Blue up like a shield, but she couldn't muster her. She needed Sarah to tell her to breathe. She needed Arabella to tell her this was all capitalist bullshit and Tock to say they could file an injunction. She needed Axel to misquote an inspirational saying. And she needed Lillian to hold her. And she was stuck on a party bus with her mother, stepfather, half sister, Ace, and a dozen girls with clouds of white netting attached to their tiaras.

chapter 31

Two hours later, the bus pulled up in front of the River Vista Resort and Lodge. A runner hurried them into a conference space redecorated to look like a bridal trade show. Banners reading ALLURE BRIDAL COLLECTION covered every wall. The company's signature bubblegum pink branded everything. Bella and her friends rushed at the racks of dresses staged around the space, oohing and aahing as though they'd never seen fabric before. Rick stood by the exit, staring at his phone and looking like he wanted to be anywhere else. He wasn't her father, but Izzy sympathized. She'd grab him if she made a run for it. It was good to break heteronormative traditions by bringing the father to the dress fitting, but not if it made that father look like he was trying to will an aneurysm on himself.

"Your father is so silly," Megan said, following Izzy's gaze. "He won't even come in the bathroom if there's a box of tampons on the counter, says he doesn't want to intrude."

Had Megan rewritten history entirely?

"He's not my father." It came out sounding angrier than Izzy felt. *I want to clarify that you do know where babies come from, and that Rick and I share no DNA.*

"He thinks of you as his daughter. We both do."

Yes. You ought to because you *are actually my mother. Not that you act like it.*

Izzy wanted to cry. She wanted to scream. And part of her just needed to sit down and say, *How the fuck are we having this conversation?*

Megan continued with a detailed description of the wedding, oblivious to Izzy's barely contained meltdown.

Bella stayed focused on her friends, not glancing at Izzy once.

A woman wearing a suit in Allure Bridal Collection pink beckoned them closer.

"Let's get going," an assistant producer said.

The cameras waited.

The assistant producer showed Megan, Bella, Izzy, and Bella's friends how to enter the set as though walking into a real store. Ace, in their SPOUSE OF THE BRIDE shirt, followed.

"Not you," the assistant producer said. "Not dad over there either."

Rick looked relieved.

"We're doing girls only."

"Ace is nonbinary," Bella said with surprising vehemence. "We're not doing all that heteronormative stuff."

"How about it's bad luck if the spouse sees the dress before the wedding," the assistant producer said with a sigh. "That's not heteronormative. It's just weirdly superstitious."

What followed—in the starts and stops of somewhat unscripted television—was a wedding dress shopping party.

Bella's friends burst into the fake store like confetti.

"This is my sister." Bella introduced her friends Michaela, McKenzie, McKenna, someone else, someone else, and Brooke.

Michaela, or maybe it was McKenna, went in for a hug. Izzy's flinch must have told the others not to try.

"Brooke and McKenzie drove here all the way from San Diego," Bella said, putting her arms around her friends' waists.

"It's nice to meet you," Izzy said.

It wasn't Brooke and McKenzie's fault Izzy's mother hadn't loved her.

The clerk disappeared through a door leading to what would have been a back room if any of this was real. She returned with an armload of pink dresses.

"Sorry about all this," Bella said, handing Izzy a dress. She seemed more annoyed than apologetic.

Bella's friends took their dresses and rushed into a row of dressing rooms giggling.

"Try on your dress. Don't be shy, Izzyboo," Megan said. "You're going to look lovely." She looked a little worried. "I hope I told them the right size."

The dress wasn't designed for a woman Izzy's shape. And she didn't need to look like a twig. She could wear anything she liked. She could wear a glittering G-string that disappeared between her ass cheeks, and she could strut across the stage like a white Gladys Bentley or twirl pasties like Flame La Mache. She took the word *woman* and expanded it like her waistline. Beautiful. Big. Real. Except no matter how well you subverted gender norms and conventional beauty standards, society crept in.

"Come on out, Izzy," Megan said. "We're all girls here."

Stripping in front of an audience of thousands would feel safer than this.

"This is so much fun," one of Bella's friends exclaimed. "I can't believe we're going to be on TV."

If Izzy wanted to have fun, she could go find some yellow jackets or give plasma.

"Izzy does burlesque," Megan said. "Don't tell us you're too shy to wear off the shoulder. We can get another style, can't we?" Megan was probably asking the Allure Bridal Collection representative. "We just want everyone to have fun and feel comfortable." Megan's voice lilted with joy.

Megan must have pitched this wedding idea to the show, but Megan wasn't trying to rekindle her lost stardom. She wanted Bella to have the perfect wedding. The thought struck Izzy hard, as though the metal scaffolding holding up the dressing room had collapsed on her. This was worse than Megan wanting to be a star. Star Megan got stuck with a child she didn't want, but she'd left microwave mac and cheese in the cupboard for Izzy. She'd kept the power on and the water running. The first time she'd left Izzy alone for a weekend, Megan had offered to buy her a .22. That was awful parenting but pointed, vaguely, to the idea that she wanted Izzy to feel safe. But Megan was capable of being a great mom, she just hadn't bothered to do it for Izzy because she hadn't wanted her in the first place.

Tears filled Izzy's eyes. She wiped them with the back of her hand, staring at her face going blotchy in the dressing room mirror.

"Come on, Izzyboo," Megan said. "We want to see you."

All of this was happening so Bella could have a dream wedding. All this was happening while the Reed-Whitmer Ballet Company was performing. Lillian was dancing. If they lost, the show would whisk them away without a chance to say goodbye. That just wasn't fair.

Slowly she disrobed and stepped into the dress. It was too small. If Arabella was here, she'd show Izzy how to make a bomb out of tulle and a lighter, but Izzy was alone like she'd been when Megan drove out of Broken Bush.

"Do you have a corset in my size?" Izzy called to the Allure Bridal Collection rep.

The woman popped her head in. "You mean shapewear?"

"No. A real corset. Like lingerie." It was a long shot. Allure probably wanted women Izzy's size squeezed into tight spandex shapers. *You'll never be a size 6, but we'll do what we can.* "Never mind. I'm guessing you don't. How about this dress in a bigger size?"

The woman looked miffed.

"Of course the Allure Bridal Collection spring line has a corset. It's part of the honeymoon set."

"In my size?"

"The Allure Bridal Collection is size inclusive," the woman said, still offended. "One moment. I'll get them for you."

Izzy felt a little better in a bejeweled corset and flowing silk pants (in a shade of red somewhere between Congenial Fuchsia and Moderately Hospitable Scarlet). She straightened, adjusted her breasts to their full advantage, wiped away her smeared mascara, and stepped out.

"Oh," Megan gasped when Izzy appeared. "You have never looked so beautiful."

They spent the next three hours watching Bella emerge wearing dress after dress. Finally, a runner returned their phones and led them to their hotel rooms with the promise that they were welcome to complimentary mani-pedis at the on-site salon and a shuttle would take them back to Portland tomorrow morning.

Bryant texted them the call sheet. It'd be another *away game*, as the runners called the out-of-town challenges. Someplace in LA called the Mimosa Resort. Someone would pack her bags for her.

Finally alone, Izzy fell onto her bed and opened her phone. Sarah had texted a dozen times. Izzy scanned until she saw the one that mattered.

Sarah: *Reed-W made it. Spice Angels went home*

Izzy closed her eyes and held the phone to her chest.

"Thank you," she said to the ceiling.

Lillian had texted the same news with a smiling emoji. Then another text.

Lillian: *Are you ok?*

Izzy: *Just watched my sister try on 100 dresses*

Lillian: *Was it alright?*

Izzy walked over to the window and looked out at the Columbia glistening in the darkness beyond the dog-walking area and a bike path.

Izzy: *Fine*

One word. One lie. It shouldn't matter. The lump Izzy had been swallowing all day rose in her throat. Her phone rang. Her heart made her touch accept before her brain told her not to.

"Hey," Lillian said.

"She's doing it for Bella," Izzy said before Lillian asked. "She wants the dress or to get her on TV, or maybe she just wants me there so she feels like we're a family, like I'm a matching napkin ring. Complete the set. Just to make it perfect." Izzy's voice broke. "I'm sorry. I don't care. I don't know why, I'm—" She gulped a breath to steady her voice. "I'm fine. It's just been a long day."

"It's okay to be upset."

"I wish I didn't have to go to the wedding."

"You can say no."

"Just say, *Sorry, Bella, I can't come to your wedding because our mother once forgot me outside my elementary school because she'd gone to Burns to get a tattoo of a chili pepper?*"

"Sweetie, that's the best reason anyone has had for skipping a wedding."

Sweetie. Izzy's heart skipped a beat. In a good way.

"Bella didn't leave me to get a tattoo."

"You can say no just because you don't want to. Your feelings matter. You get to do whatever you need to do to protect yourself."

"You sound like Sarah."

"Sorry, but it's true."

"Why do I believe you more than I believe Sarah?"

Lillian's low chuckle dispelled a bit of the childhood/family dysfunction gloom that had settled over Izzy.

"Because I don't take my own advice," Lillian said. "Because it's been so long since I protected my feelings, I don't even know where I left them. Probably backstage somewhere in a locker. Someone's going to open it up and be like, *Shit. What's all this baggage?* So it's okay to tell me about it."

And suddenly Izzy was spilling the whole story, going over everything she'd told Lillian on the beach but in detail, scattered memories and conversations. The girls she'd liked. The smell of the range. The sound of the trailer creaking in the wind. How Megan looked at Bella like she was a sunflower and pretended Rick was Izzy's father as though she forgot all the nights she went out on dates with Rick and missed Izzy's performances. And how it shouldn't hurt but it did. And every few sentences she'd remember that Lillian didn't need to hear all this. No one wanted to hear about how hard it was to be a healthy, young white woman with a good job, a thousand fans, a spot on TV, a free Allure Bridal Collection outfit, and her own house (for now). "I'm sorry," she said every few sentences, like a swimmer coming up for air every few strokes. Each time, Lillian said, "Izzy, you don't have to apologize." Her words felt like a balm. And finally, *I'm sorry* turned into *I'm fine*, and then *really, I'm okay*. Finally, they got off the phone. Izzy lay in the cocoon of Lillian's kindness...for about five minutes, until embarrassment hit her full in the face.

She'd just poured her heart out to Lillian for an hour. She'd lost track of time. What if it was *hours*? It was one thing to tell Lillian a little bit about her childhood, but she'd gone on and on. She'd cried at one point. Her stomach knotted. Lillian had probably been watching the minutes pass, thinking, *How do I get out of this?* Tomorrow Lillian would look at her, and Izzy would see that look. *You're not who I thought you were. Not tough. Not glamorous.* Lillian saw through the Blue Lenox act, but that didn't mean she wanted *this* part of Izzy.

Izzy tried to push the thought away. What was the mantra Sarah was always pushing?

I am worthy of love?

I am worthy of love.

I am worthy of love.

Being worthy of love didn't mean that people loved you. How self-pitying had she sounded? Sarah would tell her it would all feel better in the morning. Izzy looked at her phone. It was well after midnight, so it was morning. She'd be a mess today, all pale and drawn.

Go to sleep. I am worthy of love. She rolled over. *Bitch, go to sleep.* She shouldn't use the female as a pejorative. Had anyone ever fallen asleep by snapping at themselves? She turned on the TV and flipped through channels, one inane show after another. She turned it off. A ship passed on the river, blowing a low horn. The lonely sound brought fresh tears to her eyes, making her a healthy white woman with a good job and a free Allure Bridal Collection outfit crying over a foghorn. She wiped her eyes with the edge of the pillowcase. She'd look worse if she cried again. Then she'd be puffy *and* pale and drawn. *Go to sleep.* Maybe the Allure Bridal Collection rep could hook her up with makeup before they left. She'd snag the corset, put on some lipstick, pull herself together.

She had almost fallen asleep, had at least exhausted herself enough to lose track of her thoughts, when a knock at the door brought her back. It was too soft and polite to be one of the runners dragging her to another bridal hazing.

"I think you've got the wrong room," she called without getting up.

"Izzy?"

Izzy rubbed her eyes. She *was* awake. Maybe Sarah had come to rescue her. The voice just sounded like … Lillian. She got up. Her reflection in the mirror told her she'd already achieved pale, puffy, and drawn. No way to fix that now. She peered out the peephole in the door. Lillian's white suit shone against the dark wallpaper in the hall. She was so beautiful. Izzy's breath caught. She opened the door.

"What are you doing here?"

"We have to be back in a few hours, but I thought you might like company." Lillian reached for Izzy's hand. "We don't have to do anything. You look tired." She touched Izzy's cheek. "I know you're fine, but." That was the end of the sentence.

"You just … ?"

"Borrowed the car that the show loaned Kia because she's an *influencer.* And drove up." For all her poise and the fact that she was wearing a perfectly ironed suit at three in the morning, Lillian looked nervous as she stood in the doorway, holding

Izzy's hand but not looking at her. "Was that too much?" Lillian shrugged, but her shoulders didn't lower.

"You drove up here for..." *Me?*

Lillian stepped inside and closed the door. "Okay, actually, you didn't sound fine."

"Sorry."

"Izzy." That was the same tone Sarah used when Izzy was making bad emotional choices. "Stop apologizing."

Izzy was so tired. She stepped forward and rested her head on Lillian's shoulder, then remembered her smeared stage makeup and pulled back.

"Sor—"

Lillian placed a soft kiss on her forehead.

"Come on." Lillian led them toward the bed. "I didn't mean to wake you up. I mean...I did, but only for a minute. Is it okay that I'm here?"

How could Lillian even ask?

"Of course it is."

"Good." Lillian's confidence returned. "And tomorrow I can drive you back...unless you want to take the shuttle back with your family."

"And listen to my mother talk about wedding napkin holders. Please save me."

"I got you. Now get in bed and back to sleep."

Izzy lay down and watched Lillian undress until she was wearing white panties and a white silk camisole. How could Izzy possibly sleep with Lillian *here*. Lillian nudged Izzy to scoot over, then nudged her to roll over, and then put her arm around Izzy's waist. By the time Lillian had nestled herself against her, Izzy was asleep.

chapter 32

Lillian sat on a chartered jet headed for one of *The Great American Talent Show*'s premier sponsors, the Mimosa Resort. Ordinarily, a luxury flight to a high-end resort would be all right, but she was restless. She and Izzy had only had a few hours before they needed to get back to the soundstage. Then they were whisked to the airport in different shuttles, bundled onto different planes. Lying next to Izzy without touching her or being touched had been a sweet torture. She wanted the relief of their bodies melting together. But more than that, she'd wanted to keep Izzy safe. Izzy had felt small and fragile in her arms. And her apologies broke Lillian's heart. *You don't have to apologize for being human.* And seeing Izzy smile in the morning made all the frustration and anxiety of the show worth it. If it wasn't for *The Great American Talent Show*, she wouldn't know how Izzy's cheeks rounded when she smiled or how her eyes filled with flirtatious mischief. Lillian wanted to make sure Izzy was still smiling.

But a voice in the back of her head nagged at her. Izzy fell for successful women who put their art and their careers first. Did Izzy stick to hookups because she'd given up on love? Because she thought she wasn't worth more? If Lillian could just look into Izzy's eyes and speak to her without words. *You're worth everything.* But, realistically, when this was all over, wouldn't Lillian leave like the rest? Either to keep dancing with the Reed-Whitmer Ballet Company or to take the fellowship or a place in another company? She tried to shake the thought.

The first two days at the Mimosa Resort were technically days off, but that just meant no competition. Bryant said they would be filming the teams frolicking. His exact words were *frolic the fuck out of that resort.* Looking at the schedule, Reed-Whitmer was frolicking on one side of the complex, Velveteen Crush on the other. Lillian longed to trace the edge of Izzy's bathing suit where it dipped between her thighs, and—

Kia, in the seat beside her, gave her a little shove. "You're cheesin' so hard for her. You gonna jump her in the lobby or what?"

"Kia!" Lillian snapped, but she didn't have anything to say after that.

She let out a long sigh.

"Talk to me, coz," Kia said. "You're smiling. You're angsting. I haven't heard you tell your dancers that relaxation is the gateway to failure since we got back from the coast."

When they got to LA, she'd have to do the interview with Ashlyn Stewart for her epic documentary. Soon Izzy would go to the wedding. So many obligations. And they both would do the things they didn't want to do because . . . why?

Lillian turned around.

"Relaxation is the gateway to failure," she called over her seat.

Imani tossed a balled-up napkin at her. An airplane bottle of Fireball traveled from hand to hand. Imani tossed the bottle in Lillian's lap.

"Imani Ojiki," Lillian scolded in Eleanor's haughtiest tone.

"When in Rome," Imani called over.

"We're not in Rome. There is no Fireball in Rome."

"I don't think that's true." Kia took the Fireball from Lillian, cracked the cap, and handed it back. Her dancers laughed, but it wasn't mean.

"Oh hell," Lillian groaned, and downed half the Fireball.

Her dancers cheered.

chapter 33

The Mimosa Resort was a jungle of palms, pools, and jasmine vines. Arabella said it was a monolith of capitalist excess. At that, Axel had thrown her over his shoulder and dunked her in the pool, both of them giggling.

Now the camera operators were packing up. Resort staff were passing around pool towels. It had been a lovely day except that Bryant had decided Velveteen Crush should frolic with the Liam Ronan Irish Dance Company. They were perfectly nice, but Izzy had spent the whole afternoon scanning the tropical paradise for Lillian. Presumably she was frolicking somewhere else. More likely she was standing on the sidelines watching her dancers with pride and love. Would she jump in the pool without prompting from the camera operators? Was drinking champagne from a Solo cup enough to show her that she could banter with Imani? That she could splash Malik? Or cannonball into the deep end? Izzy smiled at the thought of Lillian cannonballing. Lillian didn't have to be the untouchable dance master, but those habits were hard to break. Izzy knew.

Last night had been...everything. It didn't matter that Izzy had slept for only a few hours. The hours she'd spent in Lillian's arms had healed something inside that she didn't think could be fixed. She'd poured her heart out to Lillian, and Lillian hadn't turned away. She'd come closer. She wasn't annoyed by Izzy's outpouring. She had driven two hours to hold Izzy. No performance, no applause, no crowd of fans, and certainly no hookup had ever felt as good as Lillian's arms around her. She just had to break away from the show, find Lillian, and enjoy the two days they ostensibly had off before the next challenge.

Izzy dangled her feet in the water, so perfectly pool blue. The bird-of-paradise flowers on stalks nearby, so perfectly red and purple. Sarah snapped a towel at her, breaking her out of her reverie.

"We're going back to the rooms," Sarah said. "Coming?"

Lillian might be back too. Izzy scrambled up, tossing a towel over her shoulder. She'd be dry by the time she reached the resort buildings. Plus, she looked divine in an iridescent-green two-piece she'd sewn herself.

Back in her room, Izzy showered and changed. Sarah knocked on her door a few minutes later. Everyone was hanging out by the pool…well, another pool. Without cameras. Where they could frolic in whatever ways they did or did not want to frolic. There was only one person Izzy wanted to frolic with right now, but she didn't know Lillian's room number, and Lillian hadn't returned her texts. That was just because the show had locked up Lillian's phone. That was all. It wasn't a rejection. And oddly, when Izzy told herself that…she believed it. Last night had been real.

Izzy followed Sarah down the hall and out to another tropical paradise lined with white sun umbrellas and stations serving pitchers of freshly squeezed juice and every kind of alcohol known to humankind. Her friends were already there. Tock on his laptop.

Axel doing push-ups on the edge of the pool. Arabella back in a black gown, sunken deep into the pillows of a chaise longue, reading a book with a puddle of blood on the cover.

However, when Izzy and Sarah arrived, Tock shut his laptop. Axel stopped doing push-ups. Arabella closed her book and held up her phone.

"They started running the candids today."

"TikTok. Insta. They still have Facebook," Axel said.

They were all looking at Izzy. Sarah looked a little guilty.

"What?"

Sarah patted a lounge chair next to the one she'd plopped onto. Someone had designed the chair to ergonomically induce idleness. Izzy sank to the bottom of it like she'd fallen in a sinkhole.

"You two are adorable." Tock said it like this was a legal fact.

"Aww, that's cute," Arabella said.

Axel looked at her with comically wide eyes.

"What? I can say it's cute and still hate cuteness," Arabella said.

"They've got a supercute picture of you and..." Sarah's grin finished the sentence.

Izzy almost dropped her phone in her rush to check *The Great American Talent Show* feed. Apparently, the show had profiles on about a thousand social media sites she'd never heard of. She went for Instagram and scrolled down.

"Keep going," Sarah said.

Then there it was. Izzy touching Lillian's shoulder as she drew her toward herself, their cheeks almost touching as she whispered in Lillian's ear. The photo made it look like they were holding hands, although Izzy remembered the moment and they hadn't been. Below it a fan had posted ⊞♡♡♡♡ *SO CUTE!!!*

"She's going to kill me." Izzy didn't really feel it, but she still heard Lillian's words: *One viral video of Elijah twerking could ruin his career*. "No one's supposed to know." This was the kind of thing Lillian had worked so hard to avoid. The spotlight focused on her but for the wrong reasons. "She's a dancer. She's not a...holy shit, someone made a GIF out of it."

It was just a heart exploding around their faces, but it was a *heart*. A heart when they were keeping it professional. On the surface. Despite the fact that Velveteen Crush had clocked them immediately. And the Reed-Whitmer Ballet Company didn't seem to be in the dark either.

"It's one picture," Sarah said. "Relax."

"The show has a solid nondiscrimination policy," Tock said. "There's not going to be any problem with you two being gay. Or if she's bi or pan. Bi and pan are specifically mentioned in the policy."

"It's the photo. I have to tell her." Would Lillian's mother see the photo and be mad? Give Lillian some lecture that made her feel even more driven toward perfection?

Arabella waved to someone coming down one of the orchid-lined paths.

"Hey, Kia. Over here."

Kia strolled over. "My favorite burlesque troupe!"

When Kia got closer, Arabella held up her phone.

"Tell Blue not to freak out about this. She thinks Lillian will be pissed."

"I saw that. Hella cute," Kia said.

"Do you know where Lillian is?" Izzy asked.

"About that, want to have dinner with my family?" Kia said, the invitation clearly for Izzy only.

"Your family?"

Lillian's family?

"Actually, it's at my aunt and uncle's house. Lillian's folks."

Lillian's parents' house?!

"Lil told you about the documentary, right? She's doing the interview today. She'll pretend she doesn't care, but it'll trigger her a bit."

"Did Lillian invite me?"

Kia plucked a flower out of one of the nearby planters and tucked it behind her ear.

"She'll be really glad you're there."

chapter 34

There was nothing Lillian wanted more than to be with Izzy, but she'd committed to the documentary. Her parents sent a car to the Mimosa Resort. Being chauffeured to her parents' house felt like traveling back in time. Except for Ashlyn Stewart asking a few probing questions that Lillian would answer with sound bites, dinner with the Jacksons would be exactly how it had always been. They'd eat a catered dinner. Eleanor would praise Lillian for being iconic or something like that, but Eleanor would joke with Kia and Uncle Carl. Wouldn't it be nice if, just once, Eleanor took a motherly interest in something other than Lillian's career?

When Lillian arrived, Eleanor ushered Lillian into the living room. Presumably, the woman setting up a camera was the documentary's director, Ashlyn Stewart. From the corner, the bust of Socrates watched her critically.

"Would you like anything, Lillian? Water? Sherry?" Eleanor asked.

I grew up here. I know where the water is. Lillian didn't say it.

"Your mother is lovely," Ashlyn said when Eleanor had left.

Ashlyn was wearing ripped jeans and a Cat Power T-shirt, her hair pulled back in a messy bun. She wore a collection of rubber bracelets that looked like shredded tires from some bygone eighties punk era. Izzy would appreciate the outfit.

Ashlyn brushed her hair out of her eyes. "Thank you for doing this. I just have to set up a light box here and pull the curtains, and we can get going."

Ashlyn had a pleasant, laid-back confidence. She gestured to the sofa.

"I understand you didn't want to do this." She held her fingers up in a square, capturing Lillian's face, then moved her camera a fraction of an inch. "You don't have to."

"I owe it to my mother."

Ashlyn looked at her with a gently questioning expression.

Lillian sat very straight, a perfect ballerina's posture.

"We can talk about that in the interview," Ashlyn said. "And anything you say that you don't want to be in the film, just let me know. I'll show you the transcript. I won't include anything you don't want."

"Don't documentarians want to expose the truth?"

"I do." Ashlyn pulled a rubber band off her wrist and knotted her hair up some more. "But not at the expense of the people who've agreed to share their lives with me. This is art." She hovered her hand over her camera. "This is history. It's important. But your real life is worth more than art."

"Eleanor would never say that."

"Let's talk about it. Ready?" Ashlyn asked.

Lillian nodded. Ashlyn touched something, and a red light appeared on the front of the camera.

"Can you tell me about this bust of Socrates?"

The non sequitur must have been a way to set people at ease... or catch them off guard.

"I feel like it should be Janet Collins or Alvin Ailey. If you can't get a famous Black dancer bust, maybe MLK. I don't know why Socrates."

"Have you asked your parents?"

Had her parents discussed it? *Which Greek figure would you like to go in the room we never use?*

"Seems rude. They can decorate their house however they like."

"What made you fall in love with dance?"

Was *love* the right word now? Was it *drive*? *Obsession*?

"I think it's in my DNA. Like how birds fly south in the winter. Their whole body, being, soul is meant to do this thing. That's how I felt as a kid. Then I realized I was really good. And then I wanted to win."

"How old were you when you decided you wanted to win?"

"About seven."

"How do you feel about that?"

"Maybe it was a little extra."

Ashlyn chuckled.

"Did you have a happy childhood?"

"My mother didn't force me to dance, if that's what you mean. But once I said I wanted to be a professional, she took me seriously, and you have to work hard if you want to be a professional dancer. The younger you start, the better. I missed out on some kid stuff."

"Like what?"

"I've never built anything with Legos. Never had a big birthday party. Never played video games. Never been to a water park. It's a long list."

When was the last time you walked in the rain?

"Your mother says you made a lot of sacrifices for ballet. Do you regret any of them?"

"I'm glad I didn't give up my career for Legos."

Ashlyn nodded at the joke.

"I do and I don't regret it," Lillian said. "That's how life is, right? Every time we choose something, we give up something else." Like a beautiful, blue-haired woman flying kites at the beach. "But... first you give up Legos. That doesn't matter. Then you give up riding a bike, having a pet, going out with friends. Then dating."

She saw Izzy unzipping her sweatshirt, felt Izzy's arms around her as they waltzed. When she finally saw Izzy again, she'd tell her about the interview, spelling out all her conflicting feelings. Izzy would listen. Then Lillian would tell her about Socrates and Eleanor's forest of orchids. They'd laugh. Izzy would understand how Lillian could love her family but also want something to disrupt the family status quo, some disruption to shake up the way things had always been. Maybe they'd lose the show and that would be the disruption. But no... that'd just send her down a different fork on the same path. If you wanted to change your life, you had to be your own disruption.

"If you want to keep being the best, you have to keep giving stuff up."

"Are you dating anyone?" Ashlyn asked.

Ashlyn was known for her use of silence to, as the critics said, *reveal truths behind the words people speak.* This would be one of those silences.

"Um." Lillian swallowed. "It's complicated." Was it? "There's someone I care about a lot. She'd take me to the water park if I asked." Or walk in the rain or fly kites or make love or waltz.

"Would she build Legos with you?"

Lillian hadn't expected Ashlyn to tease. She'd expected her to be a cinematic version of a stern dance master.

"I think she'd build the hell out of some Legos with me if I wanted that."

Ashlyn would capture the smile that spread across Lillian's face at the thought of Izzy sitting on the floor surrounded by Legos.

"Are you still as passionate about ballet as you've always been?" Ashlyn asked.

"Yes, of course." Lillian reined in her smile and tried to remember the party line. What was it? *I love being an icon*? *I wouldn't change a thing*? She folded herself into the lotus position on her chair and wrapped her arms around herself. On-screen, she'd look anxious. Maybe that was okay. What she was about to say did make her anxious. "I'm still passionate about ballet, and I don't know who I'd be if I wasn't a professional dancer. But I think I might be ready for something new."

chapter 35

The Jacksons' house looked like the quintessential rich people's house from the movies. Circular driveway. White columns. Front doors opening onto a high-ceilinged foyer. Kia led Izzy to the dining room. At one end of a long table sat an elegant woman with gray dreadlocks coiled into an artful arrangement. Eleanor Jackson. It couldn't be anyone else. Beside her a man in a tweed blazer and white goatee leaned back in his chair. Across from him sat a man of about the same age, wearing a Hawaiian-print shirt.

"This is my aunt." Kia indicated Eleanor Jackson. "Uncle Erik. My dad, Carl. Is Lil still in the interview?"

"She is. Have a seat," Eleanor said.

Izzy sat.

"The woman who has intrigued our unflappable Lillian," Carl said, leaning his elbows on the table. "Tell us everything about you."

Eleanor shot her brother a look. "Ms. Wells didn't come here to be interrogated."

Lillian's uncle thought Izzy intrigued Lillian? Izzy kept her posture relaxed so Carl wouldn't think she was nervous. She had to hear what came next. Intrigued was good when you were talking about a person, right? She couldn't stop the flush of excitement warming her face.

"My niece is being interrogated in the other room," Carl said.

"Ashlyn Stewart is not interrogating her," Eleanor said.

Carl continued as though she hadn't spoken. "Our Lillian has not taken an interest in a particular woman for a long time."

Lillian had talked about her. She was interested. Izzy was *particular*. It shouldn't make Izzy's heart glow. She shouldn't want to do pirouettes around the table at the thought of Lillian talking about her. Their relationship...fling...interlude...what was it? It had an end date. One last night. The final dégagé. But if Izzy was *intriguing* and *particular*...Sarah would urge her to set reasonable emotional boundaries. Forget reasonable emotional boundaries.

"Do you insist on putting her on the spot?" Eleanor asked. "What else are you going to do on your two days off, Ms. Wells?"

Ideally, bury my face in your daughter's...

"Sightseeing."

"*La bayadère* is at the McHaelen Performing Arts Center," Eleanor said.

It sounded like a test.

"I studied *La bayadère*. I double majored in computer science and dance." She sounded like a kid. Eleanor didn't care what she studied in college. But if this was a chance to show she understood just a little bit of Lillian's world, that she cared about dance too, she wasn't going to miss it. "Nikiya, the temple dancer. Two powerful men, only one is honorable. The part in act one when Nikiya is commanded to dance...if it's choreographed with the jeté battement and pas de bourrée..." *Please let that be the right term.*

"Breathtaking," Eleanor finished.

Izzy thanked her younger self for studying so hard that the French had stuck in her mind.

"Lillian danced Nikiya. She was divine." Eleanor poured herself a fingerful of liquor from a crystal decanter and offered another snifter to Izzy. Then Eleanor's expression grew thoughtful. "She sacrificed so much for her career. She still does. It's admirable."

"Our little puffin is smitten," Carl said.

Izzy pursed her lips to stop from grinning.

"You know nothing about it," Eleanor said.

"I intuit."

"You live on a yacht in a fantasy of your own making," Eleanor said, the sternness in her tone defeated by the affection in her smile.

Eleanor's formality seemed like an in-joke. *Look at me. I'm playing the role of strict matriarch. Do you buy it?* She was a lot like Lillian.

"Kia and I will force Lillian to take a week off and we will take the lovebirds sailing after the show," Carl said.

"With your overabundance of spaniels?" Eleanor asked.

"So few," Carl said. "Will you come, Ms. Wells?"

A thousand times yes.

"I'd love to."

There was more talk about spaniels and yachts. Eleanor and Carl clearly loved the back-and-forth. Kia teased her father about his favorite spaniel having the personality of an angry diva. Carl offered to help Izzy get a Cavalier King Charles spaniel, not that she had asked.

"They're always like this." Erik folded his hands over his belly and smiled at Izzy. "Next my beloved wife will show you her orchids."

A smile lit Eleanor's face.

"The *Diuris laevis* is in bloom," Eleanor said.

Her family groaned.

"Don't do it to her," Kia wailed.

How was it possible? As if the universe had conjured the moment out of Izzy and Lillian's flirtatious banter. Eleanor was actually going to show Izzy her orchids. As if the things they'd joked about weren't jokes at all but the start of a relationship.

"Come, my dear." Eleanor rose, smiling at her family like she'd just gotten away with something. She led Izzy down a long hallway to a large sitting room that had been retrofitted as a greenhouse with rows of orchids sitting under sunlight lamps.

"You can tell me which one you like, and I'll ship you your favorite," Eleanor said. "I promise I'll only show you the bloomers." She started with the first table. "This is a pink moth orchid, the phalaenopsis."

From down the hall, Izzy heard Kia's voice. "Don't tell her about all of them, Aunt E. We want to eat sometime this year."

Eleanor cupped an orchid blossom between both hands.

"Lillian gave me this one when she was ten. It blooms every year. I've propagated twenty new starts from it, so if it dies, I'll always have a copy." She pointed to a high shelf by the window. A row of orchids sat in matching pots.

Did Lillian know Eleanor kept twenty orchids because Lillian had given her one? Eleanor loved her daughter. In a way that mattered.

"This is the bane of my existence." Eleanor pointed to a manifold attached to a large control box. "It's supposed to time the water, mist, temperature. There's an app. It never works."

"Would you like me to take a look at it?" Izzy really was the suitor trying to impress the parents, but how could she not? She remembered a little about dance; she knew everything about bad apps and their better replacements.

Eleanor handed over her phone and pointed to the app. It was a miserable piece of software. But Izzy had built an app called TimerMax that worked around the proprietary code for smart devices so you could run them all on one app. It wasn't exciting, but it worked. She downloaded it for Eleanor and showed her how to use it.

"It is brilliant," Eleanor proclaimed when they were back at the table. "A marvel of simplicity."

Izzy let her whole smile show.

"The caterer will be setting up in just a minute," Eleanor said. "I'm going to check to see if Ashlyn and Lillian are done with the interview."

chapter 36

Eleanor appeared in the doorway just as Ashlyn Stewart was packing up her equipment.

"The caterer is almost ready to serve," Eleanor said, "if you're done, of course."

Ashlyn nodded. "We are. I'll just close down a few things here."

"Take your time." Eleanor indicated which overly grand hallway led to the dining room.

But she didn't go that way herself. Instead, she motioned for Lillian to follow her to one of the terraces. Because Eleanor had terraces, not porches. Lillian followed Eleanor out the French doors and to the stone railing. Eleanor looked like a Greek statue herself in her flowing caftan. The lights of LA below them caught in Eleanor's eyes, giving them a mischievous sparkle they didn't have in real life.

"I like your friend," Eleanor said.

"She seems nice." It wasn't Ashlyn's fault Lillian hadn't wanted to do the interview.

"I will concede, just this once, that my brother is not entirely misguided. At least, if you feel the way he suggests." Eleanor spoke with uncharacteristic hesitation.

Kia told Uncle Carl how Lillian felt about the interview, and Uncle Carl told Eleanor. Lillian sighed.

"I approve," Eleanor said.

Really?

"Not that you need my approval for anything. Mind you, you will not hear me extolling the magic of serendipity like Carl does. But the four of you and all those hideous dogs floating to Catalina Island…" Eleanor shook her head, with a rueful smile. "I can see it."

"Us and Ashlyn Stewart?"

"You and your friend, Ms. Wells."

"Izzy?"

How could Eleanor know?

"Kia said you were seeing her."

Ah. Uncle Carl told Eleanor about Izzy. Damn their deep sister-brother bond. Uncle Carl got to be a gossip and Lillian had to be an icon.

"I won't let her be a distraction." Why did that come out so naturally, like she didn't even have to think about it? Izzy was the only thing she'd been thinking about. She drove Lillian to distraction with a smile.

"I like her for you. I showed her my orchids. *All* of them." Was Eleanor hiding a grin?

"Mom, no!"

Eleanor had so many. Izzy didn't sign up to meet Mom's orchids. Lillian took a step back.

"Wait? When?"

Eleanor shouldn't even know about Izzy except that Kia and Uncle Carl didn't respect boundaries.

Behind them, someone cleared their throat.

"Erik wanted me to tell you that dinner is ready." A familiar voice.

Lillian turned.

Apparently, you didn't always have to be your own disruption.

Izzy looked dashing. Their eyes met. Lillian's mouth dropped open. Izzy looked from Lillian to Eleanor and back to Lillian. Then Izzy pressed her fingers to her lips in an adorable look of shock.

"You didn't know Kia brought me."

No. She did not know that her cousin had invited her lover to have dinner with her parents along with a famous movie director. And the look on her mother's face said Eleanor didn't know that Lillian didn't know. She didn't know that Izzy didn't know that Lillian didn't know.

"Kia Jackson," Eleanor said in a scolding tone, although Kia wasn't there. But Eleanor never lost her poise. "We're having sea bass for dinner with a tarragon-infused asparagus mousse," Eleanor said casually, as though Lillian's worlds hadn't just collided. Eleanor brushed past Izzy. "Come on, you two."

Had Eleanor said she liked Izzy *for* Lillian?

"If you don't want me here, I'll go." Izzy's eyes widened with distress.

Finding Izzy in her parents' house was like stepping onstage to find the director had changed all the choreography. But it had been too long since she'd seen Izzy. And they only had a few weeks left, maybe only a few days. She reached Izzy in three steps, spoke the only clear thought she could muster—"Oh my God, you look gorgeous"—and kissed her. "I don't even have words," Lillian said when she released Izzy.

I'm going to kill Kia was one possibility. *You're so gorgeous. Let me take you to my childhood bedroom and make love to you while my family eats tarragon-infused asparagus mousse* was another option. Instead she fell back on her training.

"What a delightful surprise." She meant it even though her brain was going to explode.

"Why, thank you, Ms. Jackson." Izzy held out her arm. "Shall we have dinner?"

chapter 37

≈

Izzy's mind reeled as Lillian led her back to the dining room and paused before they entered.

"I can't tell you how weird it is to see you in my parents' house, but I'm glad you're here."

Izzy's heart sang. Eleanor liked her *for* Lillian. And Lillian had kissed her on a porch at her parents' home. It was amazing Izzy could still form words, but she managed to whisper, "Me too."

Izzy tried to collect herself as she sat down at the table. Ashlyn Stewart's wife had arrived while Izzy was gone. They introduced her—Rose Josten—like the couple were family friends. Izzy scanned Lillian's eyes for a clue to how the interview went. Lillian didn't reveal much emotion in front of her family, nor did she say much, although conversation was light and cheerful, and it was easy to jump in with a joke or story. But Lillian didn't seem crushed. Occasionally she giggled at something Izzy, Kia, or her uncle said, and, although her laugh was quiet, it was giddy. No one mentioned the documentary. Finally, dinner came to an end. Kia rose.

"Lil, take my car. I'm going to ride home with my dad." She glanced at Izzy. "I'm sure you don't mind riding back with Lil?"

They were quiet as they walked to the circular drive where Kia had parked. Kia drove a vintage sports car, a make and model car enthusiasts probably coveted. Izzy had barely noticed that it was stick shift when Kia was driving, but Lillian putting the car in gear and heading down the hill into LA traffic with one hand resting on the gearshift was so breathtakingly sexy that Izzy thought she might pass out. But that wasn't the important thing right now.

"Do you want to talk about the interview?" Izzy asked.

"Not yet. I'm still trying to sort it out." Lillian moved her hand on Izzy's knee. "Eleanor didn't give you a hard time, did she?"

"She was sweet. She said she'd give me an orchid. They were beautiful!"

"Oh God. She showed you all of them, didn't she," Lillian said.

Hopefully that meant the interview hadn't been too hard.

"Not nearly. I showed her an app she could use for her watering system."

"An app you made?"

"Yeah."

"That's so damn hot. How do you do it?"

"Make a universal remote control app?"

"All of it. Charm my mother."

It had felt good having the matriarch of the family bustling around her and offering her a gift and praising her app.

"She was…the way a mom should be. Maternal, I guess."

"Maternal?" A puzzled look replaced Lillian's smile.

Hopefully she was too focused on the road to notice Izzy watching her.

"Sweet? Nothing about Eleanor is sweet or maternal." Lillian paused. "I'm sorry."

"For what?"

"I didn't think about what Eleanor would look like if you'd had...your mom." Lillian's voice was gentle now.

"My mom never gave me an orchid." It came out too wistful.

"She really will send you one. I'll give her your address. I shouldn't complain about my mom. She was there for me. I can say that."

"You can complain about anything you want."

Lillian merged onto a crowded freeway. Izzy recognized the signs to the freeway that would lead them back to the Mimosa Resort. Lillian was going to miss it.

"That way." Izzy pointed.

"Oh." Lillian glanced over nervously. "I didn't even ask. Do you want to come home with me? We don't have to be back at the resort yet."

Izzy's world burst into bloom like every magnolia and bougainvillea in California had opened simultaneously, like the wind had picked up the scent of lemon blossom and curled it around her in a swirl of pixie magic.

"I wouldn't mind."

Lillian's house was a low, midcentury-modern stucco, near the top of a hill of equally understated homes. A small garden of rocks and cacti graced the front yard. Lights set in the landscaping shone on the walls, making them glow a peach color. A fountain burbled in front of the entrance.

Inside, Lillian switched on a table lamp by the door, but she barely needed a lamp with the stunning wall of windows on the other side of the room. Izzy hadn't realized how high they'd climbed. Below them, the city lights glowed, the thoroughfares like veins of light. Inside, a stone foyer welcomed them into an open-concept living room furnished in hues of white and beige. It was gorgeous, but the space felt very still, as though no one had been here for a long time.

Lillian poured them both a glass of water and a glass of dark red wine. They sat on opposite ends of a large couch, their legs resting against each other in the middle, Lillian still wearing her white pumps. Izzy was surprised that Lillian put her shoes on the sofa. It seemed like a leave-your-shoes-at-the-door kind of house. Still, Izzy felt at ease.

"I can see where you could put some houseplants," Izzy said. "Maybe a tillandsia."

"If I knew what that was, I'd order one." Lillian smiled.

"It's an air plant. You just mist it or hang it in your shower. It's the one you can travel with. I'll get you one."

To remember me by.

"Do you want to talk about the interview now?" Izzy asked quietly. "You really do have a right to complain or not talk about it. Whatever you want."

"I said most of the right things." Lillian gazed out the window. Her stillness mirrored the stillness of the house.

"Did you say wrong things too? I mean, if you felt them, they aren't wrong. Did you go off script?"

"Ballet cost me *so* much life. So many things I haven't done. When you do what I did, you only get to be one thing." Lillian turned back to Izzy. "Ashlyn asked if it was worth it."

"What did you say?"

If Lillian said no, that meant she wanted something more than a life of travel and ballet. The hope Izzy should be trying to quash rose like the sun.

"Yes."

Somehow Izzy's hopes refused to be quashed.

"I think so," Lillian amended. "There've been times when I executed an impossible move and got it perfect. Not just that the audience and the critics thought it was perfect, but I knew in every cell of my body that I got it right. Every fiber of every single muscle and all my heart." A fierce joy filled Lillian's eyes.

You're worth it. All the heartbreak that might follow after the show…it was worth it to see that look in Lillian's eyes. To see her be so real. When Izzy was unguarded, her inner child emerged. When Lillian let all her guard down, she was a goddess.

"You don't know what it's like if you haven't been there. For that one split second, you're immortal. There's nothing else. And in that moment, it's all worth it." Lillian's energy faded to something warmer and more human. She took a sip of wine and put her glass on the floor. She rested her cheek against the top of the sofa. "But I think…and I told Ashlyn…just because those sacrifices were worth it then doesn't mean they'll be worth it forever. And I know that I shouldn't worry about what Eleanor thinks. I'm too old to be doing things for her approval."

"Don't worry," Izzy said. "It's really hard to get rid of your inner child. Trust me. I'm trying."

Lillian nudged Izzy's knee with hers.

"I like your inner child."

"But go on," Izzy said. "You don't want to do things for your mom's approval but…?"

"If Ashlyn puts that in the documentary, I'm worried Eleanor will feel like she wasted her time. She gave up a lot too. She sacrificed so much to make me a…unicorn. If I gave up ballet, I'd just be a woman with really great abs trying to figure out what to do with her life. And I do like being a unicorn. I can't lie. It's fun to always be the best. To always win. Except for this damn

TV show, I don't know what it's like to lose. I know I won't like it even though I will be losing to you." Lillian traced her fingers along the sofa in an unconscious caress that made Izzy's body tingle.

"You'll win," Izzy said.

Nothing was guaranteed, but how could Velveteen Crush possibly beat Lillian and her dancers?

"Nah, it'll be you," Lillian said. "And I'll be terribly jealous, but you'll make it up to me in bed on our last night together."

Lillian hesitated on the word *last*. Could she be feeling what Izzy felt?

"I don't want you to lose." Izzy meant it.

"I don't want *you* to lose."

Lillian tipped her head back with a sigh that sounded both regretful and amused.

"Who are we kidding," Lillian said. "Effectz is going to kick all of our asses."

Izzy rolled her eyes. "Are they even human? Their moves!"

"The important thing I told Ashlyn is that I've missed out on a lot of things, and it was worth it, and I think I'm ready to make up for some of those things."

Izzy would help her make up for anything. Did Lillian want to go to medical school? Izzy was ready to help her study. Did Lillian want to climb the Himalayas? Amazon Prime could get Izzy ice cleats by tomorrow.

"I don't know…just sit somewhere and watch the sunset every night for a month. Explore one of the cities I've danced in but never seen. And go to a water park, a real one with slides."

Izzy laughed at the image of dignified Lillian Jackson whooping as she shot out of a waterslide.

"Hey." Lillian play slapped Izzy's leg. "I get to have my dream."

"Oh my God. Of course you do! I love it. I'll take you to every waterslide in America."

Oops. What she was supposed to do was break up with Lillian in a couple of days or a couple of weeks. That was the plan; plans could change.

"I'd like that." Lillian tucked her hand under the cuff of Izzy's pants and stroked her skin. After a moment, she said, "Enough about my poor rich-girl life."

Izzy touched Lillian's white pump. When she was sure Lillian didn't have more to say, Izzy asked, "Do you always wear your shoes in the house?" Izzy's hand was still resting on Lillian's pump.

"As long as you're here, I will."

"Why?"

"My feet are ugly. All dancers' are. It's a price we pay."

"I don't care. Show me." Izzy stroked the smooth leather of Lillian's shoe.

Lillian pulled her feet back a few inches. "No," she said with indignation that sounded half-pretend, half-real.

"I've seen you naked." Izzy offered Lillian a touch of Blue's smile. Was it too soon? Had they moved from real talk to flirtation?

"I have a beautiful body, but did you look at my feet?" Lillian's pretend scowl broke. "No. You were too busy looking other places."

"How could I not?"

"I always look at feet, and I like yours," Lillian said. "They're like little white sea creatures."

Izzy burst out laughing. "Lillian! That's the worst compliment I've ever gotten."

"They're lovely," Lillian protested. "They're all pale and soft and perfect because they live under the sand."

"I can't believe *I* was thinking about your pussy and *you* were thinking about my pale fish feet. Are you going to wear socks to bed now, so I won't look?" Izzy squeezed Lillian's foot, the leather barely yielding. "I've spent every second of free time building up a burlesque troupe that's dedicated to the idea that people don't have to be perfect to perform, to be seen, to be loved."

"And you do all of that under the guise of Blue Lenox."

The comment might have sounded harsh except for the tenderness in Lillian's eyes and the coaxing way Lillian tilted her head. Izzy had never felt so seen, not even by Sarah, who had known her for years.

"I don't take my own advice." Izzy looked everywhere but at Lillian. "Some of the best people I know don't take their own good advice."

"Fine," Lillian said, closing her eyes.

Slowly, she kicked off one pump and then another. Her skin was rough, her big toe turned in. The joints looked perpetually swollen. Izzy felt a wave of tenderness for Lillian's feet.

"May I?" She readjusted her position so she could draw both Lillian's feet into her lap.

Lillian nodded.

"These are wonderful feet."

"Liar," Lillian said.

"Even though they don't look like pale fish. You've got to work on your compliment game." It was so easy to be together, so fun to tease Lillian, and Izzy felt happy. It felt like stepping out of an airport into a new city. This wasn't the exhilaration of performing. It wasn't the giddiness of having a drink too many with her friends, her Blue Lenox persona fully in place. This was the comfortable, uncomplicated happiness that couples had.

Izzy gently pressed her thumb into the sole of Lillian's foot and rubbed. Lillian let out a moan of pleasure more intimate than the way she'd cried out during sex.

"You'll ruin me for all the others." Lillian closed her eyes and sighed. "God, that feels good."

"Did you see the picture on the show's Instagram?"

"What picture?"

Izzy reached for her phone.

"Don't stop," Lillian groaned when Izzy took her hands off her feet.

Lillian picked her own phone off the floor. Izzy returned to massaging Lillian's beautiful, imperfect feet. Lillian scanned through the pictures.

"It's of us," Izzy said, happiness giving way to uncertainty. Lillian couldn't be *that* upset, but if she looked at Izzy with reproach, said, *This can't happen again*, that would hurt.

"Check the top of their feed," Izzy said.

Lillian studied the picture.

"It looks like we're holding hands," Lillian noted.

"Is it bad for you to have this out there? They'll probably try to get more photos of us if people like that one."

"Seven hundred and thirty-two likes and a lot of rainbows."

"Will it hurt you in auditions?"

"Something like this? Nah. No one cares that I'm a lesbian," Lillian said but her lips pursed in a slight frown. "As long as it doesn't hurt the company. That's all I care about."

Lillian closed her eyes. Izzy kept touching her feet. Slowly, the tight lines around Lillian's lips softened.

"Tell me all about these air plants I'm going to start collecting so I can be just like my mother with a house full of exotic plants no one can tell apart."

To make Lillian laugh, Izzy began to explain in the most minute detail she could.

"Some of them have a lot of thin fronds, but they're probably not called fronds. And they're silvery, but not so much that you think they're dead."

She went on until Lillian laughed, "It's too much. I can't take any more fronds."

Then the conversation drifted to everything and nothing. Show gossip. Favorite restaurants. For the first time since Izzy had met her, Lillian seemed to totally relax.

They talked dreamily until eventually Lillian said, "I have a beautiful Jacuzzi tub I never use. Would you like to do that with me?" In the bathroom, Lillian picked up a candle from an attractive arrangement on the counter. She showed Izzy the wick. "See? Never used."

Luckily she did have matches. Soon they were deep in vanilla-scented bubbles from a bottle Lillian had also never used. Lillian rested Izzy between her legs, pressing her back to Lillian like she had at the coast, but this time she slid her hand between Izzy's legs and gently bit her shoulder as Izzy arched into her hand. Izzy needed every circle of Lillian's fingers, every delicate press and release, Lillian's fingers just barely inside her. Everything felt good, and everything drove her crazy, but in between nibbling on her shoulder and kissing her neck, Lillian still checked in. "More? There? Here?" Until Lillian must have sensed Izzy was too close to know exactly how hard or which side of her clitoris was more pleasurable.

Izzy mounted higher, reaching for something to clutch, her hands slipping off the slick tub, then clutching Lillian's legs. Lillian's touch was so light. So light. Then harder. Izzy knew exactly when Lillian found the perfect firm, fast circles. Exactly what Izzy wanted.

"There!" Izzy gasped. "Don't stop."

She didn't need to say it. Lillian knew not to change anything so close to the edge. Izzy came with a howl of pleasure.

When Izzy had caught her breath, Lillian drew her out of the tub. They toweled each other off. Izzy admired every sinew of Lillian's body. In bed, they took their time. Izzy worshiped Lillian's small breasts, feeling her hard pectoral muscles, admiring Lillian's nipples, which were the same gorgeous ebony as the rest of her skin. Their bodies were so beautifully different. Even Lillian's vulva was different. Izzy's was discreet, almost Barbie-like, until she was really turned on. Lillian's vulva was lush and big and full, like a secret extravagance when the rest of her was so sculpted and contained. Izzy worshiped that too. They took turns until Lillian came and Izzy came again. They kissed some more, slowing down as fatigue claimed them. Izzy melted into the blankets. Lillian covered her eyes with her arm.

"Damn, girl." Lillian drew out the words, praise and satisfaction in two syllables. She took Izzy's hand without looking at her. "Just in case you were wondering, I want you to stay the night."

chapter 38

Really, Lillian wanted Izzy to stay forever. If only they could cocoon themselves in her house and never leave. They spent the rest of their time off moving between the bed and the couch, savoring each other's bodies, then devouring Grubhub delivery and talking and watching the city. Food had never tasted so good. The view from her living room had never been so magnificent. When Kia texted to check on her, Lillian texted back *I'm with her* and added three hearts. She turned her phone off before Kia could tease her about the hearts or say anything about little puffin flying free. Did puffins fly? It didn't matter. Nothing existed outside of her home and Izzy's embrace.

Except the world did exist, and way too soon they were back at the Mimosa. The next days of filming passed in the now familiar commotion. Plan. Rehearsal. Talk to the costumers. Wait for Bryant to implode in a flurry of carabiners and hiking socks. Then Lillian stood in front of the judges, her heart racing but only with nervousness. You couldn't raise your heart rate skipping around a faux straw cabana. They'd been good though. Somehow. She barely remembered rehearsals. Mostly Imani had directed them. The judges liked her work.

The highest scoring teams were Effectz—as always—then Dance Magic, then the Reed-Whitmer Ballet Company. The lowest scoring teams in the Mimosa challenge were the Dream Team Marchers, the Liam Ronan Irish Dance Company, and Velveteen Crush. Bryant lined them up in front of a wall of pink flowers and a sign with the show logo. He directed the performers to hold hands in a variety of poses.

Lillian stood on the sidelines. There were greenrooms inside the resort, but Bryant allowed the teams to stay outside and watch. Kia stood beside Lillian.

"She's got this," Kia whispered. "Liam Ronan bombed."

They had. Irish dance just didn't say, *Let paradise into your life at the Mimosa Resort.* Lillian still felt like she was going to pass out or throw up. How was this as bad as stepping out on the Palais Garnier stage for the first time? She was supposed to want all these people to lose. Her dancers counted on her to somehow annihilate all of them, even Effectz, who were probably superhumans designed by NASA. But what about Izzy? How much work did her theater need? Izzy had said, *If the bank doesn't take it,* and laughed it off, but what if it wasn't a joke? What if Izzy was in trouble? What if she needed the prize money to salvage her dream? How could Lillian want to beat her then?

Lillian wanted to leap over the snaking video cables and fling her arms around Izzy. She wanted to take Izzy to Kia's food truck. Maybe Lillian and Izzy could doze on the couch pretending to listen to podcasts. They could bake scones together. Had Lillian ever baked anything? No, but there were instructions. Izzy should be in her bed while Lillian made love to her slowly as the sun set over the city. *Made love. Love.* It couldn't be.

Bryant arranged and rearranged the contestants until the Prime Minister called out, "If you think there's a perfect arrangement of emotionally manipulated reality TV stars holding hands, I am here to tell you there is not. Live with the imperfection."

Bryant hurried off camera and called action.

As expected, the Liam Ronan Irish Dance Company went home. And Lillian did something she hadn't done since she was at the Lynn Bernau School of Dance—ran to the bathroom and threw up from nerves.

By the time she'd collected herself, a runner had hustled the remaining teams into one of the resort conference halls, where each of the groups had been assigned a set of tables, water station, plates of tropical fruits, and enough champagne and orange juice to bathe in. Lillian tried to catch Izzy's eyes, but Izzy was giving one of her signature pep talks. Lillian caught Izzy's words through the buzz of conversation and mic checks.

"...your true self...authentic, invincible...nothing to fear!"

But there was so much to fear. Finally, Izzy met Lillian's gaze. She saw her own longing and her own apprehensions reflected in Izzy's eyes.

"We got a lot to do." Bryant's voice projected through a lavalier mic. "You'll be flying back to Portland in a few minutes."

A sigh rippled through the group. They wouldn't be back at the Lynnwood until after midnight.

"Tomorrow, we'll be filming reaction takes about the Mimosa Resort and about the team challenge. That's next. You know what that means. We bring back one of the groups that got voted off. That'll be Retroactive Silence. Teams will be—remember how you feel when you hear your partner team. You'll need to re-create that feeling for the reactions tomorrow." He checked his tablet. "Retroactive Silence and Effectz."

Effectz: the best team according to pretty much everyone. Retroactive Silence: the weakest link.

Lillian's heart pounded. *Please let it be Reed-Whitmer and Velveteen Crush.* Or was it *please don't let it be*?

The judges would vote off either one team or two. It was one of the show's highlights. How many teams would go home?

Bryant continued the pairs. "Dance Magic and Dream Team Marchers."

That meant…

"Velveteen Crush and Reed-Whitmer."

Beside Lillian, Kia whispered, "Fate."

"Our corporate sponsor for the show is Shape of You Dancewear," Bryant said.

A collective groan issued from the crowd.

"You'll have to be more enthusiastic tomorrow," Bryant said dryly.

Beside Lillian, Kia, the omnipresent influencer, whispered, "That company's shit."

"I know," Bryant went on. "Shape of You Dancewear has had some image problems, which is why they've asked to be one of our corporate sponsors. You've all seen their recent TV commercials, but the company's apologized, and this is their chance to show America they're not all about vaguely racist fat-shaming." He looked pained.

"Not *all* about?" Izzy called out. "Just *somewhat* about?" The crowd laughed and bristled at the same time. Izzy was joking and she was dead serious. And she was Blue Lenox and she was magnificent. Izzy straightened, pushing her breasts forward, tucking her hands in the pockets of her black jeans, and adopting her sexy, curvy lesbian–James Dean slouch. "Do you think—"

"I do." Bryant cut her off. "Whatever you're going to say, I do. And I didn't want the sponsorship either, but the execs did, and Shape of You is paying bank."

How was Izzy going to fit into anything by Shape of You Dancewear? Their slogan was *Only the Finest for the Fittest.* Their sizes went from 0 to 4. Before the socials started hating on them, they were going to launch a minus size line. Izzy was confident. Blue Lenox was practically untouchable, but that didn't change the fact that she wouldn't fit the plus-size line the company had thrown together: sizes 6 through 8. And that was the company saying, *Your body is wrong.* Even if everyone knew it was bullshit, that had to hurt. And was Lillian going to put on pale pink athletic wear that Shape of You sold under the slogan *Only One Skin*? Elijah was the lightest-skinned performer in Reed-Whitmer, and he'd still look like someone painted a white girl's leotard on him.

"If Shape of You wants to rehabilitate their image," Izzy went on, "they need to do that on their own, not on a show that kids across America see and—"

"Blue." Bryant sighed and shook his head. "Don't fight fights you can't win."

Even Blue Lenox couldn't stop the wheels of reality TV from grinding on.

"And no contact between pairs until we've got the cameras on you," Bryant said. "All planning for the team challenge happens together."

Izzy caught Lillian's eye from across the room and dropped her chin in the perfect impression of the disappointed-face emoji. So cute. Lillian didn't let the words *I love you* settle in her mind.

chapter 39

The next day, Izzy stood in front of the members of Velveteen Crush and the Reed-Whitmer Ballet Company in the large rehearsal space allotted to them for the group challenge. Two camera operators circled them. Izzy had to glance at Lillian every few seconds to take in just how beautiful she was and that she was still real because their nights together had been the most magical of Izzy's life. If only she could talk to her, touch her. Anything. But the cameras were on them.

"Blue. Blue." Arabella's voice drifted into her consciousness. "Are you listening? Shape of You Dancewear uses child labor. I'm not going out there unless I'm covered in the CEO's blood."

"She doesn't mean it," Axel said.

Tock said, "We have plausible deniability."

"Blue," Sarah said and elbowed Izzy. "Blue, weigh in here."

"I think it's a great idea," Izzy said.

"You aren't listening." Sarah tapped her again. "Arabella wants to cover her shapewear in blood."

"Real blood?" Izzy asked.

"The CEO's," Arabella said.

"Of course not," Sarah said.

Lillian stood several paces away, watching Izzy with an amused half smile.

Malik pulled a pair of peach-colored tights from Jonathan's hand.

"We can't wear this. Look at these colors. *Only one skin*? These are like Aryan Nations tights."

"I dyed my pointe shoes when I started dancing," Pascale ventured in a peep. "My teacher said I had damaged them. They weren't damaged. They were mine."

"Give me neon," Elijah said. "Magenta. My clothes don't have to match my skin, but they better match my soul." He gestured dismissively. "And my soul is not white-person Band-Aid color."

Then everyone was talking at once except Izzy and Lillian.

"*Make it bleed*," Arabella said.

Elijah said, "Those leotards wouldn't cover my—"

"We don't want to know." That was Imani.

"Ms. Jackson?" Pascale said in much the same tone Sarah had said, *Blue, weigh in here.*

The voices intensified. No one was listening, but the number of *hell yeah*s suggested they all agreed on something.

As long as Lillian was watching Izzy, they were the only people in the room. And the weak winter sun coming through the high windows held all the magic of summer. If they could just stand here forever...if they weren't about to enter a competition that could send one or both their troupes home. Home? Where would that be if Lillian was in LA and their connection dwindled to a few texts? How could Izzy be so elated and terrified and exhausted and energized? She should have taken Sarah's advice and processed some feelings, because now she had too many.

Suddenly, Izzy felt laughter welling up from deep inside. Like one of those soda machines that shot CO_2 into whatever beverage you wanted. A bubble of laughter broke through all her other feelings. Lillian was trying to keep her serious face on too. Izzy snorted. Lillian lost her last bit of composure. No one paid attention. Izzy hurried over and put a hand on Lillian's shoulder. For a moment, they bent over, Izzy's forehead to Lillian's shoulder, Lillian's cheek resting on Izzy's hair, and they just laughed the kind of laugh that made you feel like the world would never end.

The debate over Shape of You Dancewear got louder. Axel's voice rose over the rest.

"The coat is a prison, if the cat is still cold."

Everyone stopped.

"What?" Imani said.

"The coat is a prison, if the cat is still cold," Axel said like it was obvious.

"What coat?" Elijah asked.

"What cat?" Arabella raised her eyebrows in an *explain yourself* look.

And then everyone was laughing.

"I don't want to do blood," Pascale said when the group had caught their breath, "but I don't want to wear this stuff the way it is."

"We can't fit it." Sarah's gesture took in herself, Arabella, Izzy, and Axel.

"They're not even good capitalists," Tock added. "They could make ten times the money if they made inclusive sizes."

"There's no such thing as good capitalists," Arabella said.

"We could show them what these things should be," Pascale piped up.

Sarah looked at the camera operators and then at Izzy. "You make half our costumes." Sarah motioned for everyone to come closer. They huddled like a football team. "Let's go back to your house. Dye the leotards. Tailor the clothing. Make this stuff fit us, not the other way around."

"I'm up for that," Malik said, "but would the show let us do it?"

"I don't think we can let them know," Sarah said.

The huddle moved in closer.

"The Prime Minister is always saying he wants realness. What's more real than making something that fits us?" Sarah said.

It really should be Blue giving this speech, but Izzy couldn't do it.

"It's a risk," Pascale said.

"I'm in," Elijah said.

Imani said, "We can pretend to be working on whatever today, with the cameras. Tonight...where do we go to do this?"

"Blue's got all the stuff we need, right, Blue?" Axel said.

"Perfect," Imani said. "We fake doing it their way today. When we get out, we go to your house, Blue. We rip this shit apart and dye the hell out of it. Tomorrow's a day off, so we can practice the real act in secret. Then another day in front of the cameras and then show time."

There was a chorus of whispered *yeah*s and *it's worth it*s.

"Wait. Lillian." Izzy grabbed Lillian's hand and pulled her into the hall. "You haven't told them about Reed and Whitmer pulling their sponsorship." Izzy clasped Lillian's other hand. "They don't know what's at stake."

"Have you told them that you need the money for your theater?"

"No, but that's just me. That's not them. If we ripped up the Shape of You Dancewear...it'll be our star performance or our last. They could vote us both off." Izzy squeezed her eyes closed. "Everything I did"—starting Velveteen Crush, welcoming the worst performers, buying the theater, getting on the show—"I did it so some girl in Broken Bush would see us and think, *I can be myself*."

"Not *I have to squeeze myself into some size two body shaper*."

"Yeah."

Lillian didn't go pale, but something vibrant drained from her face.

"Everything I did," Lillian echoed, "was so my dancers would belong in ballet, not just shove themselves in around the edges."

"Basically we'd be endorsing a brand that refuses to recognize us."

"Yeah."

Izzy let go of Lillian's hands and drew her into an embrace.

"We have to tell them." Lillian rested in Izzy's arms for a moment longer, then pulled away. "I'll tell them about Reed and Whitmer. You tell your friends about the theater."

"And it should be unanimous. If anyone doesn't want to do this, we won't."

"Agreed."

Back in the rehearsal space, Lillian drew her company to one side. Izzy drew Velveteen Crush to the other.

"We'll only do this if everyone wants to," Izzy said. "We're family. You can say no." She looked at each of her people in turn. Everyone nodded.

"What about you, Blue?" Sarah asked. "Do you want to?"

Izzy had to want this. Every time Velveteen Crush performed, she'd told her troupe that they were reaching people they'd never meet, representing diversity in gender, race, size, sexuality, and aesthetic. She couldn't turn around now and go along with Shape of You Dancewear's brand image.

"We're not going to treat this fabric like some sacred thing that can't be changed," Izzy declared, loud enough that Lillian's dancers looked over, "just like we don't take society's expectations and treat them like some sacred thing." She was Blue Lenox doing what Blue did best. Rallying. Inspiring. Standing on top of the mountain at dawn saying, *Follow me!* "We define beauty."

Lillian walked back, flanked by her company. They looked somber, but Lillian nodded.

"Let's do this."

An Uber van let the Reed-Whitmer Ballet Company out in front of Izzy's house. Lillian wasn't sure what she expected. A trailer covered in glitter? A high-rise with framed posters of famous strippers? In real life it was a small bungalow on a narrow street lined with terraced gardens and enormous oaks. Patches of daffodils sparked out of mossy rocks. Judging by the music pouring out from the front door, Izzy's people were already there.

Izzy stepped out, framed by the light of the open door, just as she had been silhouetted in the door of the cottage on the coast.

"Welcome to my house!" she said with a theatrical bow. She beckoned the Reed-Whitmer dancers inside. "Make yourselves at home."

From inside, Lillian heard cheers and greetings.

Izzy stepped outside and closed the door behind her. They stood on the dark porch.

"Welcome to my home," Izzy said quietly, without the bow.

Shadows hid them from the street.

"I don't usually invite women home," Izzy said.

Lillian wore a sleeveless hoodie she usually used as a warm-up jacket. Izzy had told her this one time she'd have to sacrifice her principles and not wear a white suit. Now Izzy traced her fingers up Lillian's arm. How could such a delicate touch light her up like this?

"You're so strong." Izzy's fingertips lingered on Lillian's bicep.

Lillian was stronger than all the women she slept with, even the other dancers. She didn't think much about it. Now she felt a surge of something sweet and primal, her body flexing to say, *I can protect you.* Although the things Izzy needed protecting from weren't physical, so instead she asked, "How are you holding up?" and they talked until they heard a roar of laughter from inside.

Inside, the house felt more like a craft party than the night that might make or break their careers. Someone had brought a tray of vegetables, and someone had set out bowls of dark chocolate. Three sewing machines were set up in front of the windows.

"Look at this, Ms. Jackson." Pascale held up a leotard twice the size of Shape of You's largest XL. "Malik fixed it. Did you know he could sew too?"

"My gram taught me," Malik said.

Lillian glimpsed a home office. Three large desks held six large screens. A giant office chair sat in front of one of the computer stations, an enormous set of headphones hung over the top of the seat.

"My work," Izzy said.

What did Izzy look like when she worked? Hyper-focused? Restless? Did she listen to music on her headphones or use them for gaming? This was Izzy's everyday life. She sat at that desk. She drank from the Darth Vader head mug on that table. What would it be like to wander into the office and rub her shoulders when she'd been working for too long? Lillian snapped herself out of the domestic scene in her mind. She wasn't moving into Izzy's house.

"Elijah and Jonathan are out back, dyeing Shape of You Dancewear actual human colors," Malik said.

"I suppose we've got to pitch in," Izzy said, glancing longingly at the staircase that probably led to the bedroom.

Lillian wanted to go straight upstairs, but even if that had been an option, she didn't want to miss this part. Malik showing Pascale how to use Izzy's machines. Jonathan singing Boyz II Men. Pascale catching a drink before it tipped over with the grace of a well-trained mother. Arabella and Imani seemed united in quality control, checking fit on the altered garments and comparing skin tone until Jonathan and Elijah had perfectly dyed outfits. They even ran Izzy's leotard through a light bleach bath to capture her moonlit complexion.

Izzy and Lillian helped out where they were needed, both of them hanging back a little, touching as they moved around each other. Lillian brushed a smear of glitter off Izzy's face.

"How did you get glitter on you? We're not even making anything with glitter," Lillian whispered, loving the feel of Izzy's warm skin beneath her fingertips.

"Hazards of being in a burlesque house."

Lillian tucked a strand of hair behind Izzy's ear. Behind them, she heard Elijah's knowing "I called it" and Imani say, "Did you see the picture on Instagram?" They all knew. It felt good. Lillian turned around.

"Gossiping about your dance master is the first step to…to…"

"Having fun," Imani called out.

chapter 40

After everyone had left, Izzy said, "When this is over, I'm going to sleep for a month."

"We can sleep if you want to," Lillian said.

"Later." Izzy gave her Blue's signature wink. She held out her hand and led Lillian toward the stairs and to her bedroom.

"I don't want to presume." Lillian took a step toward Izzy.

"Do you think I took you up here to see my plant?" Izzy gestured to a mile of viny houseplant curled around the room.

Lillian ran her hand up the back of Izzy's neck, took a fistful of hair, and kissed her hard. They were standing in the middle of the room with nowhere to lean. Lillian held Izzy firmly around the waist as she bit Izzy's lip, then gently kissed the same place. Izzy trembled in her arms and moaned. Izzy clung to her neck, and Lillian held her up. Maybe all her training was for this moment.

"Do you like toys?" Lillian should have asked earlier, but she'd hesitated. Now though, the thought of running a vibrator over Izzy's vulva or moving a dildo inside her felt irresistible.

"Did you bring something in your purse?" Izzy gasped theatrically.

"I thought you might have something," Lillian said.

"A few."

"Do you have a harness?" Lillian asked.

"Well, yeah." Izzy caught her breath long enough to say it like Lillian had questioned her credentials. "Would you like me to strap on? I'd love to."

"That would be lovely...but...also...do you like to be the... recipient?" Lillian asked. "It's okay if it's a no."

"I...um..." Was the surprise in Izzy's face a yes or a no? "Just when I've been with women and we used a strap-on...Blue Lenox is a top. That's what they wanted."

"What did *you* want?" Lillian softened her grip around Izzy's waist and trailed a light kiss up her neck.

"I like to wear a strap-on, but...I did always think...it'd be fun if a woman would do that for me....strap on...if she wanted to...give me that gift."

Lillian ran her teeth along Izzy's ear, burying her face in the sweet smell of Izzy's hair.

"Nothing would get me off like strapping on for you."

"Please," Izzy said quietly. She led her to the closet, where an array of sex toys were organized in clear plastic shoeboxes. It was so Izzy: practical and sexy.

The tension that filled the air burst, and Lillian giggled. She touched one of the boxes.

"You're so organized." She wrapped her arms around Izzy and squeezed her.

"Hey!" Izzy protested, pretending to push Lillian away but only pulling her closer. "I've been waiting my whole life for a woman like you. I don't want to be digging around in some unlabeled box."

Their laughter, mingling in the air, turned Lillian on like a touch.

"I like this one." Izzy tapped one of the boxes.

Lillian looked at Izzy's collection and selected what she needed.

"I'll just wash this real quick." Izzy held up the dildo. "I haven't used this on anyone but myself."

"Not an unattractive picture."

Back in the bedroom, they undressed and lay down on Izzy's velvet comforter. The room was the perfect temperature. They kissed for a long time. Lillian straddled Izzy and rubbed her thigh between Izzy's legs. Then with the speed and grace of an entrechat, she glided down the bed and ran her tongue down Izzy's inner thigh in one slow stroke. Izzy lifted her hips. Lillian breathed in her scent. Like roses after they had bloomed out, musky and clean.

Lillian guided Izzy's thighs open so she could see her labia shining in the soft light. Her small clit. Her downy hair. Lillian explored Izzy's opening for a long time, licking the uneven ridges of her aroused flesh, lazily dipping her tongue into Izzy's body.

"Tell me when you want me to strap on," Lillian said between kisses.

Izzy sighed magnificently. "Now would be a good time."

Lillian exhaled a soft breath against Izzy's delicate wetness.

"Okay, sweetheart," Lillian whispered softly.

Izzy groaned when Lillian got out of bed, and Lillian felt the same loss. She moved quickly, stepping into the harness. She mounted Izzy, bracing herself over her. With one hand she stroked Izzy's cheek.

"Like this?" Lillian pressed the tip lightly against Izzy's opening.

"It's very nice of you to be . . . gentle. Very. Thoughtful. Lillian." Izzy grabbed Lillian's hips, pulling her down hard.

It was awkward. The dildo missed her opening. Lillian reached between their bodies and guided the dildo, then lowered her weight onto Izzy. Izzy clung to her. Lillian controlled her thrusts, to match the rhythm of Izzy's need, not her own. She used only a fraction of her strength. It took willpower, but she was strong enough to hurt Izzy if she wasn't careful. Lillian focused on every muscle in her own body so she could make it just right for Izzy, enough and never too much. This dance was more important than any stage. She searched Izzy's face. Izzy met her gaze, her eyes stormy with urgency and a breathtaking vulnerability. And affection. It almost looked like love.

Eventually, Izzy clasped Lillian's back and pleaded, "Now I want to feel your skin."

Lillian knew what Izzy meant. Penetration was fun, but the dildo wasn't touching Izzy's clit.

"Can I pull out?" Lillian whispered.

Izzy nodded.

Lillian wriggled out of the harness as fast as she could, then settled her leg between Izzy's, rubbing up and down until Izzy moaned, "Like that." This time when Izzy came, it wasn't a wild spasm. She came with a long, slow, happy sigh, her body going limp beneath Lillian.

"That was amazing," Izzy said. "How are you so good at that?"

"Of course I'm good. I'm a dancer."

When Izzy had rested, she rolled Lillian over.

"Now tell me how I can ruin you for all others."

chapter 41

≈

Izzy woke in Lillian's arms. She'd slept with Lillian in her own bed, like a couple, like they'd do this again and again. But she had to respect Lillian's boundaries. After they'd snuggled for a few minutes, Izzy reluctantly pulled away.

"Our people will be here by nine," she said. "Do you want to… get a coffee or something so you can come back in like you didn't spend the night?"

"Do you want me to?"

"Of course not."

"Why of course not?" Lillian asked, putting her arm across Izzy's belly and pulling her back in.

"The most gorgeous woman in the world in my bed? I don't mind if my friends know you spent the night."

But Lillian might mind. There was discreetly flirting in front of the Reed-Whitmer Ballet Company, and there was sitting at the kitchen table first thing in the morning glowing from great sex.

"It wouldn't help." Lillian gave Izzy a playful kiss. "I'd be wearing what I wore yesterday."

"I could loan you something."

"Maybe a corset? That would be much more subtle. Why don't you make me a coffee here."

Izzy would have liked to spend all day lazing around with Lillian, but Velveteen Crush and the Reed-Whitmer Ballet Company arrived before nine. An air of revolution vibrated in the house as they designed their routine and rehearsed. Izzy was ready to give a Blue Lenox speech to inspire the group, but Sarah had beat her to it and plus they didn't need inspiring.

Around nine p.m., the teams left.

"I thought we'd never get done." Lillian dropped onto the sofa. "Who am I? I'm always the one saying, *Work more. Stay longer.*"

Izzy sat next to her. "You trained them well." She rested her head on Lillian's shoulder. "There's only four teams after us. Dance Magic, Effectz, Dream Team Marchers, and Retroactive Silence."

"I can't believe they brought them back."

Should Izzy ask? *What happens with us?* Broken Bush echoed in the moment, all those times Izzy had sat with a girl and wondered if she should say how she felt. Would that open the door to something wonderful or just ruin a beautiful moment?

Lillian took a breath to speak. Would it be an apology or a proposition? If Lillian said, *I like you, but you know this won't last,* Izzy would have to muster all of Blue's strength not to cry. If Lillian suggested they stay together, rainbows would dance across the night sky. But then if she changed her mind, like every woman eventually changed her mind, the stars would go out.

"I want to show you something," Izzy blurted.

If there was a chance Lillian might choose her, Lillian had to see all of her, including the part that looked like a vintage (i.e., decaying) theater.

"I want to see anything you want to show me," Lillian said earnestly.

*   *   *

An hour later, Izzy unlocked the back door to the theater. At least back doors were supposed to look shabby. Right? Walking through the lobby with its shredded carpet and exposed wires where sconces once hung screamed, *Crumbling mess*. A fluorescent tube flickered above their heads.

"Even better than the basement of the soundstage," Lillian said, looking around.

"It's a wreck."

"I like a beautiful woman in a dark hallway." Lillian kissed her.

The hallway disappeared, and Izzy's heart rested peacefully between beats.

"This lighting says, *Serial killers live here*," Izzy groaned when they broke away from their kiss.

"I'll protect you."

Izzy led Lillian onto the theater stage. Izzy flicked on the light switches mounted in a questionably wired panel at stage left. In the dim glow, the theater looked...okay.

"It's beautiful," Lillian said.

"I thought it could be."

Izzy sat down at the end of the stage, her legs dangling. She pulled off her sweatshirt and spread it out to make a seat for Lillian.

"Everything in this theater is grungy."

Lillian sat down beside her.

"So why did you buy it?" Lillian asked without a shadow of criticism in her voice.

"We had some bad experiences performing. Axel got kicked out of a men's bathroom when he was in drag. But they wouldn't let him use the women's bathroom either. Tock was ready to sue, but you know how that goes..." Izzy put a hand on Lillian's knee.

"You didn't want to spend two years filing motions?"

"Seemed like that could be really hard."

Lillian leaned her shoulder against Izzy's.

"Then what happened?" she asked.

"We did a show in Seattle. After the intermission, the bar decided we were too *unconventional* for their customers. Velveteen Crush is a no-audition troupe. Anyone can join. That means a lot of people come who are working through stuff. I'm a professional. That bullshit doesn't touch me."

Lillian's arm around Izzy's shoulders said, *I know that's a lie, but I'll let it slide.*

"But I was setting them up for something they weren't ready for. I owed it to everyone to create a safe space."

"You owed it, or Blue owed it?"

Izzy searched for the answer. Around them the theater rested in its former glory and its current disrepair, beautiful and broken.

"When I bought the theater…I don't think I knew the difference."

Lillian kept her arm around Izzy.

"It's not just a money pit." Izzy might as well put it all out there. "It's in foreclosure."

"Oh, Izzy."

"I double mortgaged my house to buy it."

"You're not going to…?"

"Lose my house? Maybe. I don't know. I've been trying not to think about it."

Lillian wrapped her arms around Izzy. For a moment, it didn't matter what happened to the theater or the house. Then Lillian released Izzy from her embrace, keeping her hands on Izzy's shoulders as she'd done when she'd first hugged her on the beach.

"What kind of lawyer do you have? My father knows a lot of

people in real estate. Didn't you say Tock was an attorney? Who are you talking to about this?"

"I haven't told anyone."

"Wait? What about your troupe when we agreed to cut up the Shape of You? You were supposed to tell them. They needed to know what was at stake for you."

"We need to show the world body positivity. That's what's at stake."

"You know that's not the whole truth."

"If you knew your dancers would be fine and it was only you with something to lose, would you have told them?"

Lillian hesitated.

"No," she said quietly.

"We don't take our good advice, do we?" Izzy said. "Can I show you why I fell in love with the theater when I first saw it?"

She rose. Lillian followed her. For an hour, she showed Lillian the cornices and frescoes she loved because they were so traditional, and she wanted her people in that classic space. Eventually, they returned to sitting on the stage.

"Thank you for showing it to me." Lillian kissed the top of Izzy's head. "I want to show you something too."

Whatever Lillian wanted to share, Izzy wanted to see.

"Nothing we've done on the show has challenged our skills as ballet dancers," Lillian said. "I mean, it's hard to come up with performances the judges will like, but that's not the same thing. I gave up *everything* to be a dancer, and eventually I'll age out." She shrugged as though it was funny—so young to be too old—but she stiffened as though she were falling off a stage. "I know we said we weren't going to stay together after the show."

Are we? Lillian's eyes seemed to say.

"But before that, I want you to see me dance. I want to show you why I gave up so much. I want to show you why it's all worth it." Lillian took her arm off Izzy's shoulder and folded herself into the lotus position. She rested her chin on her steepled fingers. "At least I think it's worth it."

Izzy didn't speak as she watched Lillian get ready. Lillian spent a long time walking up and down the stage, testing the spring of the boards, occasionally picking up a bit of detritus. Then she took off her jacket. Then she called up something on her phone and handed it to Izzy.

"I'll give you a count of three and then press play. I don't have pointe shoes, so I can't go on pointe."

Lillian walked to the side of the stage, her steps measured like a diver walking to the end of the springboard. She turned.

"One, two, three, play."

The first strains of music played. Izzy knew Lillian was good. She'd seen videos. She'd seen Lillian perform on the show. But Izzy hadn't understood. Now Lillian leapt. She wasn't just good, she bent the laws of gravity. She floated in the air and chose when to step down, and when she did, she did so as lightly as if she were stepping out of a silver carriage. But up close, Izzy could see every muscle in Lillian's legs. Every striation belied her weightlessness. When Lillian bent the laws of gravity, she bent steel. Impossible that a human being could be this strong. Her grace so controlled and so fierce. And it made sense: Lillian's relentless drive, the striving for perfection. Lillian was trapped in a diamond box of her own making, all so she could land the final move with a grace that rippled the silvery edges of the universe.

All Izzy had ever wanted was for her lovers to put her first, but would it be fair to ask Lillian to put Izzy before ballet? To reorganize the universe Lillian created and shattered in a single leap? Wouldn't that be like fencing a unicorn in your backyard?

Lillian turned to Izzy with a little bow.

"Not bad, eh?" Lillian said, but her eyes said she knew how much better she was than *not bad*.

chapter 42

Once again, Lillian stood in the space behind the stage, waiting to go on, except this time Velveteen Crush waited with the Reed-Whitmer Ballet Company. They were last. The other groups had done well. Velveteen Crush and Reed-Whitmer needed to top the Star Maker and get two out of three judges to vote for them. The suspense held her by the throat. What would she do if Reed-Whitmer disbanded? Go to Paris? Get the next part she auditioned for because she was that good? Quit dance? Move to Portland? Reupholster theater chairs with Izzy? And how could she be this nervous and not know what she wanted?

"And now for one of the most dynamic pairings we've seen on *The Great American Talent Show*," Harrison sang out. "Velveteen Crush and the Reed-Whitmer Ballet Company."

The lights dimmed. Izzy stepped out onstage. Everyone else fell in line behind her. Eleven people from two groups running on no sleep and minimal rehearsal couldn't be perfect. But she and Imani had come up with a good routine. The stage was set to look like an opulent bathroom. Each of the dancers would come up to a mirror in which they would see something they weren't. Izzy would compare herself to tiny Pascale. Pascale, holding a rigid cou-de-pied, would compare herself to Sarah tossing her red hair around like a party girl. Jonathan would touch his dark face as he stared at Elijah's light skin.

Lillian remembered every second of her first performance of *Carmen*. Now she moved on pure muscle memory.

"Cut," Bryant yelled.

Had they finished without her noticing?

The Prime Minister called from his dais, "They fucked with your precious shapewear." He drew out every word with satisfaction.

"You can't say *fucked*." Bryant also seemed to be having an out-of-body experience, perhaps dreaming of hiking the Pacific Crest Trail with only a nail file and a Nalgene bottle. He pulled off his headset. "What the literal fuck?!"

"Don't say *fuck*." The Prime Minister chuckled.

"We have to redo this." Bryant pointed at the performers. His attention seemed to focus on Izzy. "*All of you*. Go backstage and change into authentic Shape of You Dancewear. Now!"

The Prime Minister let out a slow, fake laugh. "How have you gotten to the point in life where you can say *authentic Shape of You Dancewear* with a straight face. Let's just film a quick critique."

Bryant hurried over to the judges. He gestured toward the sound booth to cut all the mics.

Lillian released her breath and tried to gasp in another one. But she couldn't find the proprioception that allowed her to open and close the sacks in her lungs. Nothing was in her control.

Bryant stepped back.

"Okay. Roll." He looked like he had swallowed a fishing lure.

Lillian had a bit of sympathy for him. Sometimes you couldn't will away the fishing lure.

"What exactly are you wearing?" the Prime Minister began.

Izzy stepped forward. "Shape of You Dancewear doesn't fit us. It wasn't our color." She cocked her head a little, as though the thought had just occurred to her. It was Blue's swagger...or it was Blue but tempered with something calmer and more reserved. "So we changed it."

"Anyone can wear light nude," Hallie said, but she sounded uncertain.

"The great cry for racial equality," the Prime Minister said. *"Band-Aid pink belongs to everyone."*

"Cut that in postproduction," Bryant yelled, not bothering to call cut.

"I just think you're brave," Christina said. "But part of the performance is following the brief. You can't decide you don't like the costumes."

"Performance is a collaboration," Alejandro added. "You may have collaborated with each other, but you haven't collaborated with Shape of You Dancewear."

"Do you think we'll be sending two teams home today?" Harrison asked with a mix of delight and horror.

"I think we have to," Alejandro said. "They destroyed their costumes."

"Companies like Shape of You Dancewear destroy people's self-esteem," Izzy said. "They define their brand by judging who belongs. There is no line that divides us into the worthy and the unworthy. There is no body type, weight, shape, gender, sex, or color of human being that's wrong. People make mistakes. Sometimes we're train wrecks. But who we *are* is never wrong."

God, she was amazing! Izzy was amazing and Blue was amazing. Izzy and Blue weren't continents apart like it sometimes seemed. In this moment, Izzy and Blue held hands: sweet, modest, vulnerable Izzy Wells and fierce, flirtatious, uncompromising Blue Lenox.

"Shape of You Dancewear promotes healthy weight loss through the inspiration of fine fashion," Christina said.

The Prime Minister skewered his colleagues with a look that the wall-mounted screens captured in high-def. "The unhealthy lifestyle of wanting to live without shame?"

"Cut!" Feedback screeched over Bryant's voice.

Lillian tried to catch Izzy's eyes, but the way they'd been lined up, she couldn't see her behind Axel. They'd both go home. They'd walk into the Portland rain and Izzy would be crushed by debt. The Reed-Whitmer dancers would be unemployed, reality TV losers looking for places in a dance culture that wanted them for their novelty. It would be Lillian's fault for not being perfect when their careers were at stake. She had no right to pray, *Please, let Izzy win.*

"Just call it." Bryant projected his voice over the sudden chatter in the studio audience.

Hallie and Harrison brightened their smiles another watt.

"This is so close," Hallie said. "Reed-Whitmer and Velveteen Crush both need two yeses from the judges to stay on. I can't wait to see what they say."

The Prime Minister bowed, showing the camera the intricate map of braids on top of his head, then he looked up dramatically.

"This is the realness I've been waiting for. I want to see what both of these teams have to show us in the final rounds. I'm yes for both."

The crowd cheered.

"Reed-Whitmer," Alejandro said, "you've showed amazing skill this season, but you could have done this the right way, and you didn't. I'm so sorry, but I think Reed-Whitmer has to go home. Velveteen Crush, altering the Shape of You Dancewear, this kind of subversion is on brand for you."

Since when was wearing clothes that fit a subversion?

"But it's too much. I'm voting no for Velveteen Crush also," Alejandro finished.

Lillian's fate and Izzy's had come down to Christina-Margarita Ebb Bessinger-Silas, whose opinion about every performance, regardless of how she voted, was that she felt something. That was it. You felt something about traffic. You felt something about a nice restaurant.

Christina dabbed her eyes.

"This performance moved me. I was in one emotional space and then this performance, the teamwork, and your message, and that brought me to another emotional space. Then it was like I went forward into another space."

Did she have a blueprint of all these spaces? If Izzy was standing near her, Lillian would whisper, *It sounds like a storage unit place.* Izzy would chuckle. Lillian would clutch Izzy's hand, and it would be all right because it had to be.

"But I just don't think I ended in the right emotional space," Christina said. "I vote no on both."

It was over.

She'd given the Reed-Whitmer Ballet Company her best. It hadn't been enough. Despite what Izzy said, her best was wrong. She was vaguely aware of voices around her, Jonathan telling Elijah, "I'm not going anywhere without you." Malik said, "We'll get the company back together." Imani had her arm around Pascale. "You *will* find another company. They can't turn you down because you have kids." They were all wrong. Jonathan and Elijah wouldn't end up in the same company. The company wouldn't be back together. Pascale would have a hard time convincing a serious company that she could be a professional ballerina with kids. And Lillian would have to tell Eleanor—as soon as the contract allowed her to talk about it—that she'd failed her dancers at a competition that was beneath them.

She wanted to cry, and she wanted to beg for forgiveness, but beneath the roiling sea of grief and shame and disappointment, she felt something else. This was the last straw. She was free. She hadn't said yes to the fellowship in Paris yet. She could do anything, go anywhere, be anything. The ballet community would think she was slinking off in despair. Let them think that. She could stay in Portland. All Izzy's life, women had left her. Lillian would stay. Not just date but ask Izzy to let her move in. Lillian had given up her life for ballet. Now she could have it back.

She had to find Izzy. A runner blocked her path. Vans were ready to take Reed-Whitmer to the airport. Per contract, competitors had to leave after the judges voted them off. Someone would pack their belongings for them.

"Wait," she called after Izzy, who was also getting hustled away, although leaving for her house across town was less dramatic.

Izzy turned. Lillian held out her hand. This was their moment. She pulled Izzy past the crew, down the stairs, and into the basement where they'd kissed. They turned a corner. Lillian glanced behind them. They'd lost their pursuers like action movie heroes. She pulled Izzy into an empty greenroom.

As soon as the door closed, Lillian wrapped her arms around Izzy. She waited for a moment to feel whether Izzy yielded or stiffened. Izzy melted against her, and Lillian kissed her. Hard and slow and deep. Drinking her in. Why had Lillian let ballet eclipse everything? The pain of Reed-Whitmer's loss was a purifying fire. She could see clearly now. She could see the possibilities. She'd help Izzy. They'd save the theater.

Lillian only pulled away when she tasted tears on Izzy's lips. Izzy was crying.

"I'm sorry." Izzy turned away. "I should never have agreed to cut up the Shape of You Dancewear. I said yes and I sacrificed your company."

"Everyone agreed to it." Lillian turned Izzy's face toward hers, stroking away her tears. "This was our idea. My company. Your troupe."

Izzy buried her face against Lillian's shoulder.

"I will miss this so much." Izzy's voice was rough.

Lillian wrapped her arms around Izzy.

"This is everything you've been fighting against." Izzy spoke into Lillian's shoulder. "Your company is better than all the other groups."

"We're not—"

"You know you are. And you earned it. But you didn't win. The fight's still rigged. This is like what happened to you at your dance school." Izzy drew back, wiping her eyes.

Lillian led Izzy to a sofa, and they sat. The room must have belonged to one of the teams that got voted off. No sweatshirts draped over the chairs. No abandoned coffee mugs on the tables. The lights were dim.

"Shhh. It's a stupid TV show. It's all rigged. We knew that. But, Izzy—" Lillian tipped Izzy's chin up so she could look at her. "I want to talk about us." *I'm falling in love with you.* "Let's not end this. I can help you with the theater." She clasped Izzy's hands. "I'll give up ballet. Fuck the fellowship in Paris. I want to stay in Portland. With you."

This was a beginning, not the end. That pain in her heart—like a cracked rib that she felt every time she thought about leaving Izzy—she'd healed. She wouldn't lose Izzy. She wouldn't be one more woman to break Izzy's heart.

She could sell her house in LA. That would probably cover the theater and buy Izzy's house outright. That was probably not the best way to start a relationship but whatever. She'd been disciplined her whole life. If she wanted to give up everything for a woman she'd known for a few weeks, she could. And if it crashed and burned, Uncle Carl would let her live on his yacht with his spaniels.

"All of it. Today! I don't need to dance. I want to give it up for you."

Sunshine was supposed to break through Izzy's tears, and it did. For a second. Then Izzy looked confused.

"You can't," Izzy said.

"There's no more Reed-Whitmer Ballet Company. I can do anything I want. I'm free. I'm finally free. Ask me to move in."

Izzy looked pained. Lillian had come on too strong.

"I'm sorry. That's too much. We'll be long distance or casual or whatever for as long as you want. But, Izzy, I don't want anyone else."

Izzy wanted a relationship. Lillian felt it in the way Izzy kissed her. Izzy wanted to let Lillian in.

Izzy didn't speak. She looked like someone standing on the edge of a cliff working up her courage to jump.

I won't hurt you like those other women.

Finally, Lillian said, "Breathe," because she wasn't sure Izzy had taken a breath.

"I can't believe I'm saying this." Izzy pressed her hands into her eyes so hard, Lillian grabbed her wrists to stop her. "The answer is no," Izzy choked out.

For a second the word didn't register. Of course Izzy would say yes. Izzy would wrap her arms around Lillian. They'd laugh. They'd make love. She could almost taste Izzy, like rainwater mixed with a drop of ocean. A siren.

Izzy shook her head. Tears streaked her stage makeup.

"I love you, Lillian." Lillian wanted to cut in with *I love you too!* But Izzy spoke too fast. "I know it's too soon, but I do. And I see you. You love to dance. I know you hate it sometimes too, but when I saw you dance at the theater, I get why you gave up so much. And I know you think you mean what you're saying, but you just got voted off. You're spiraling."

"Jacksons don't spiral."

Please let Izzy laugh.

Izzy pulled away. "Lillian, you wouldn't be here if you hadn't gotten voted off." There was no anger in Izzy's voice, just sadness. "Look at me and tell me: if Reed-Whitmer won the show, would you have given it all up?"

Lillian opened her mouth to speak, but the answer escaped her, like blanking on familiar choreography the moment you stepped onstage. You knew it but the lights were so bright and the stakes so high.

Izzy closed her eyes.

"I've seen you dance." All the praise Lillian had received in her life didn't hold the reverence in Izzy's voice. "You're a unicorn. You're following in your mother's footsteps. She loves you so much. Did you know she's cloned an orchid you gave her?" Izzy stood up, spreading her hands. "And tomorrow morning or next month, you'd see it yourself. Your star is still shining. So many people will want you. You'll dance everywhere that matters. No one will care that you lost some stupid TV show. And I love you too much to get in your way."

Lillian stood up too. Izzy was backing toward the door. She had to stop her. She had to turn back time, just a few seconds, and erase that moment of hesitation. *I want you. I do. I'm scared. Who am I if I'm not a dancer?* But Lillian couldn't get the words out.

"The women I dated," Izzy said, taking another step back, "who left me because they were passionate about their careers…they weren't assholes. They just loved something more than they loved me, and that's okay. But I guess I've absorbed enough of Sarah's self-help books without reading them. I love myself too much to keep walking into relationships I know will hurt me. I know dancers can't dance forever. Come find me then? I'll probably be free." Izzy's whole face trembled with her efforts not to cry more than she already was. "You've ruined me for all others."

"Will we at least be friends?" Lillian choked out. She didn't want to be friends. Well, friends, yes, but not *at least* friends. They should be friends and lovers, conspirators, partners.

"Friends." Izzy spoke the word like she was handling a sharp rock. "What would we do as friends?"

"Text each other memes?"

"When have you ever texted memes?"

"I could start."

"What kind of memes? Dogs with sunglasses?" Tears streamed silently down Izzy's face. "I don't even get why people think dogs are funny in sunglasses." No one should look so sad speaking those words.

"Text me about your life. Tell me about your troupe and the theater. Show me the costume for your next act. Tell me how you're taking all the good advice I gave you. Tell me…" *That you're happy.*

Izzy stopped backing away, stepped toward Lillian, and wrapped her arms around her.

"I'm so sorry that this hurts you now." She rocked Lillian gently. "But in a week or a month, you'll see I'm right. Baby, I know. I've lost so many times. When you're coming off a loss that tears you up like this...whatever you think you want, you don't. Don't make a big decision right after the world knocks you down. It'll be the wrong thing. That's my good advice. You're going to be great at that fellowship. Or you'll get another job. All your dancers will. And you're going to be amazing. Imagine me out there, cheering you on, always."

With that, Izzy left, closing the door gently behind her, and Lillian burst into tears.

chapter 43

Izzy shoved her feet into a pair of flip-flops someone discarded, hurried down the windowless halls, and ran to the trailer where various assistants kept the dancers' phones, and pounded on the door.

A man she vaguely recognized opened it, looking worried, maybe because Izzy was wearing only dancewear and flip-flops.

"Whatcha need?"

If Lillian had followed her and tried to convince her to stay together, she'd crack. She couldn't say no again. Her mind wouldn't let her cause herself so much pain, but it would hurt more when Lillian realized Izzy was right. And if Lillian wasn't running after her, if Lillian accepted what she'd said and went back to Reed-Whitmer's greenroom to freshen up before catching a van to the airport…If Izzy had to face that, she would lie down on the sidewalk and never get up again. There was no good option.

"I just need my phone for an Uber."

By the time Izzy got home, Sarah had called her a dozen times. With speed that beat Amazon Prime, the show returned her luggage to her a few minutes after she arrived home. Izzy left her suitcases by the door. The living room was still a wreckage of Shape of You Dancewear. She didn't turn on the lights. She just stood in the center of the room. What had she done? The hurt in Lillian's face killed her. How could she hurt the woman she loved? How could she ruin everything?

Izzy was still wearing a leotard. It was ridiculously cold. She pulled out her phone to text Lillian. *I didn't mean it. I did it for you. I want you to be happy. I love you.* She opened her texts. She had to be strong. She texted Sarah instead.

Izzy: I'm home. I'm okay.

Sarah's call beeped through.

Izzy: I'm so sorry we lost. I know it means a lot to you and everyone.

Sarah: Fuck the show. What happened? You ran off with Lillian. Imani texted that Lillian's crying and she never cries.

Izzy: I don't want to talk about it

Sarah's call beeped insistently.

Sarah: Pick up

Sarah: You don't have to hold this in

Sarah: Whatever you're feeling is valid.

Her call went to voicemail, and she called again.

Izzy scanned the row of unread self-help books on the shelf by the window.

Izzy: I'm really upset, and I'm not ready to talk about it.

Sarah: Don't go into yourself like that. You need people to get through this

Izzy: I need to be alone. I don't know how to talk. It's too hard. I've made so many mistakes, I can't look at them with someone else.

She should stop. That much feeling would have Sarah on her doorstep in seconds.

Izzy: I need you to respect my boundaries.

She waited for Sarah to text that wanting to be alone wasn't a valid feeling. When Sarah's text came back, it was a paragraph.

Sarah: I'm so sorry Izzy. You've tried to tell me before, and I never listen. I'm just sad that I can't be there for you, that none of us ever really can. You don't have to open up if you don't want to. But I'm here for you! Okay?! We all are. Always.

Izzy: Thanks.

Izzy silenced her phone and walked into her office. She pushed aside the stack of bills, woke her computer, and cruised the internet for reviews of animation software. She chose one with a hundred-dollar-a-month subscription fee. Price didn't matter. She'd only use it once.

She didn't have Lillian's drawings, but she sketched out some rough estimates of the human form. The software was intuitive. She got one of the figures to raise an arm. She created another clip of a figure doing one pirouette. Slowly the force of her concentration muted the pain in her heart, not by taking it away but by taking her away, leaving nothing but lines and code and commands and the lightning-fast work of her computers. She started with classic moves and poses, building up a library of little clips. None of them were good, and she'd have to build an app to hold them, menus to allow the user to arrange the clips and alter the movements, ways for the choreographer to share the sequences, for other people to edit and comment, because art was always a collaboration. She'd build enough of it so that Lillian could hire another programmer to refine it and make it exactly what she wanted. The prototype would show Lillian it was possible, that Izzy had paid attention to everything Lillian had shared with her, that Izzy wanted Lillian to fulfill every one of her dreams.

chapter 44

It felt like Izzy worked on the app for an eternity, but it could only have been a couple of days. But she had to face the theater, and she owed Bella a call because she was finally going to take good advice. She couldn't go to the wedding. Not after everything that had happened. It'd be too hard.

Rain hit Izzy as soon as she stepped outside. She hurried to her van and across the river to the Roosevelt Theater. She might as well face everything all at once. The air inside the theater felt colder than outside. She sat down on the stage and took out her phone. The show had given her Bella's phone number. It was strange to get your sister's number from an assistant producer's contact list.

She half expected the call to go to voicemail as Bella rejected the unknown number, but maybe Bella had programmed her number in too. Bella answered on the second ring. Izzy had practiced what she was going to say, but saying it out loud made it final, like sending Lillian away was final. She'd been carrying hope around like a candle, the hope that someone could love her for her, the hope that someone would put her first. Now she was blowing that candle out.

"I really want you and Ace to be happy," Izzy said. "But I can't come to the wedding. It's too hard. I'm not a part of your family. I didn't even know we had cousins."

Izzy liked Bella for not saying, *Nooooo, you're my sister.*

"I wasn't going to invite you." Bella sounded sympathetic. "I mean, I don't mind if you come. I just thought it'd be weird to invite you after not seeing you for years, like I just wanted a wedding gift. But Mom wants you there." Izzy could hear Bella shush someone on the other end. "Ace and I didn't want to be on TV with a fluffy wedding dress. We want our wedding on a beach with just a few friends."

Izzy could picture Bella on the beach, hazy orange sunlight catching her hair like it did when she was a child running across the range. "But as soon as we told Mom we were getting married, she said we had to have the whole family together. Then we had to do the show. We don't *want* all that." Bella didn't say anything for a moment. "I just couldn't say no because she's doing this for you."

"That doesn't make sense."

"There are pictures of you *all* over our house." Bella snorted. "She prints every Insta picture where you're not naked. Our house is like a shrine to you."

"I didn't die or anything." Izzy shivered in the cold theater. Why were the boards she sat on damp? Was that a leak from above or water seeping in from some yet-undiscovered disaster under the stage?

"She feels like you did," Bella went on. "I used to be jealous of all those photos. There're some of me, but not nearly as many. But Ace helped me see that she feels like she failed you. She heard you were on the show, and she saw the sponsors, and I don't know how she pulled it off, but she got the producer to do the surprise bridal shower. She planned this whole thing because she thought it'd get you back in our lives. She's using *my* wedding to try to get *you* back. Rude." Izzy could hear the scowl in Bella's voice. "Actually, it really hurt at first when we realized what she was thinking. Ace and I shouldn't have to learn an official wedding dance because Mom didn't take good care of you when you were a kid."

Bella angry was like a kitten walking sideways with its hackles up. Harmless but foretelling the fierceness that would come as it grew up. Izzy could come to like this woman. Her sister.

"You can tell her from me: I'm not coming. Do your beach wedding if you want to." Izzy felt a lump forming in her throat. It was time to say goodbye. "If I did reconnect with her, I'd want her to reconnect with *me*, not put on some big show. My Insta pictures aren't who I am. If she wants pictures of me that mean something, we'll have to build a relationship slowly, and then maybe we can take a real selfie." She held the phone in her cupped hands. "I want you to be happy. I really do. Don't let her make this about me. I'm not worth it."

Bella's voice drifted up to her.

"Yeah you are. That's why Ace and I went along with it in the end. If you did come back ... I'd love to have you as a sister. Would you like to reconnect? Without matching Sympathetic Gilded Rosy Terra-cotta napkins?"

"Who even knows what color that is?"

"I know!" Bella said. "She kept sending us paint chips because we didn't know what Lucid Ecru was."

Their laughter was tentative, but it felt like a first step to something real.

"I'll stay in touch."

It'd been good to talk to Bella again, but taking the first step toward that family made all the holes in her heart feel bigger. A hole for Megan. For Bella. For the theater. For the community that loved her as Blue but not Izzy. And a bigger, wider emptiness like a beloved house stripped of everything that made it home: the place where Lillian should be.

"But, Bella," Izzy said before she hung up, "be sure to keep the dresses. They've got great resale value."

chapter 45

Kia let herself into her cousin's house and sat down on the sofa next to Lillian, surveying the room. On the coffee table, Lillian's sketchbook lay open to the picture of Izzy because Lillian wanted to torture herself. A bottle of crème de violette and a pizza box sat on the coffee table as well.

"Lil' puffin." Kia put her arm around Lillian's shoulder.

Lillian shrugged away.

"That nickname doesn't even make sense."

Nothing made sense. Izzy wanted her, cared about her. It was so clear. And Izzy wanted commitment, but she had pushed Lillian away. Izzy had left crying about a breakup *she* caused. Anger surged in Lillian for a second before hurt and confusion doused that flame. Why?

Kia picked up the bottle. "How much have you had to drink?"

"Just that."

"It's a third gone. When did you open it?"

"When I got home."

Lillian had slept on the sofa. The bedsheets were still rumpled from Izzy's visit, and sleeping on them would break her. Changing the sheets and washing Izzy away would break her too.

"That's three days," Kia said.

"Don't give me shit about it." Lillian's head ached. Her eyes ached. Her heart ached. Not the good pain of exertion, the pain of an injury.

"Girl." Kia let the word out on a sigh. "You drank a third of a bottle of crème de violette in three days?" She looked at the bottle. "If you're trying to get drunk, it's not gonna happen like this."

"I tried, but the stuff is awful."

Even liking horrible liquor made Izzy special. Everything about her was unique.

"You don't know how to do this heartbreak stuff, do you? You gotta drink tequila shots." Kia lifted the pizza box lid. "And you've eaten nothing. You're supposed to binge on junk food. I'm going to open a bottle of wine and we're going to talk. Then we're ordering Thai food, and I'm taking you out to go therapy shopping. There's this great lingerie store in West Hollywood."

"No one will see it. I'm never going to have sex again."

"Right." Kia wandered over to the wine fridge in Lillian's kitchen and peered inside. "Would you feel better if I opened this fancy Chardonnay?"

"No."

"Say yes. I want to try it."

"Yes."

Kia handed her a glass and sat cross-legged on the other side of the sofa, probably transferring flecks of neon paint from her hand-painted overalls to the leather. It didn't matter.

"Now tell me what happened with Blue?"

"How did you know?" Lillian asked.

Lillian had crashed and burned. For the first time since she was a teenager, she'd tiptoed into the realm of real feelings and offered her heart to Izzy, and Izzy had said no.

"A, because I've loved you since we were, like, two," Kia said. "And B, you were crying after the show."

"Everyone was crying."

"Actually, they weren't," Kia said. "We were all trading numbers with Velveteen Crush. We want to do a reunion trip. Maybe meet down in Mexico. But no one could find Blue. Sarah says Blue hasn't talked to anyone since then. Sarah made her do a proof-of-life live chat, but Blue just said she wasn't ready to talk about it." Kia set her glass down and shifted to face Lillian, her sneakers leaving dust on the sofa. The sofa where Izzy had rubbed Lillian's feet and told her she didn't have to be perfect. Kia's expression was dead serious. "Lillian, did you break up with her?"

Kia was supposed to know her.

"How could you think that?"

"Well," Kia said slowly, "a lot of reasons. You don't do relationships. You're moving to Paris."

Lillian sat perfectly upright. If she let an iota of control slide, she'd cry.

"You're going to do everything you can to make sure everyone lands in a good place now the company's broken up," Kia went on. "You're going to start auditioning, which means you'll be training more than ever. *I* don't think you lost the competition because of Blue, but I know you, and *you're* telling yourself you got distracted and that's why everything is your fault."

Harsh but true.

"I think the person you were before you started the show would definitely break up with Blue." Kia shook Lillian's knee. "Look at me. I think the person you are now wishes she hadn't. The show isn't your fault. The only part of this that is your fault is breaking up with someone you care about because you're...I don't know. Driven? Scared? Why won't you let yourself have this?"

Lillian whirled toward Kia.

"She broke up with me!" She wasn't mad at Kia. She wanted to muster up anger at Izzy, but she couldn't when she could still hear Izzy crying in the hallway. She was mad at the world for just...being the way it was. "She said she loved me, but she wouldn't be with me because I'd always put dance first, and she couldn't distract me from my career because I'm an...an icon! I told her I'd give up dance."

"She said *icon*?" Kia frowned.

"No, Eleanor said *icon*." The fire went out of Lillian.

Kia passed her her wineglass.

"That's bullshit. She doesn't get to know you better than you know yourself."

"And what's worse, I don't even know if she believes that. She says she always falls for women who leave her for their careers. One of those law-of-attraction things. Her mom left her when she was still in high school. Just picked up with her new husband and her sister and drove away, like, *There's food in the fridge. Have a good life*."

How could Izzy's mother have done that to her daughter? Eleanor might be overbearing, but she'd give Lillian a kidney. Or her heart.

"She said if we'd stayed on the show, I wouldn't have wanted to be with her."

"Would you?"

"Yeah."

"And given up dance?"

Could she really give up ballet? She hesitated.

"See, you don't know," Kia said. "You're not sure she's wrong."

"I want her to be wrong." Lillian gulped her wine. Why did people drink when they were sad? Sadness made the wine sour. "She doesn't have anyone to talk to." Izzy needed someone, even if it was another lover. The thought tore her heart. Most people didn't know you could tear your heart, but you could. A dancer with a torn heart never recovered. "She doesn't even open up to her friends."

"And they obviously love her," Kia added.

"She thinks they only love Blue Lenox."

"Blue Lenox is an act."

"I know. I think they do too."

"Let me roll this out for you," Kia said. "She's got abandonment issues. She doesn't run her ideas by anyone. She's afraid you'll ditch her for your career, and even *you* aren't a hundred percent sure you won't."

"I don't want to." *I don't. I don't. I don't.* Her life was a river dragging her away from Izzy even though she wanted to cling to her.

"Did you accept Paris?" Kia asked.

"Yeah, I sent them an email."

Kia raised her eyebrows as if to say, *I prove my point.*

"If Izzy came back, I'd bail on them. I'd walk out in the middle of class. I don't care what the school would think."

"So here it is. Yeah, she should have believed you when you said you wanted to be together. Generally, the whole I-know-what's-best-for-you thing is some condescending bullshit. But she had enough reason to be scared. And people carry stuff around with them. *You* walk around like all you want is Eleanor's love when everyone knows she'd do anything for you."

Izzy had been touched by Eleanor's offer of an orchid. What was it like to grow up without love or safety? Eleanor had always been there for Lillian. Always.

"What do I do?"

"What do you want to do?"

She could see Izzy at Bella's wedding. She'd dress up. Not burlesque up. But something nice that said she tried. She'd stand on the sidelines. There'd be a slow dance. Izzy could have any bridesmaid she wanted, but she wouldn't ask. Izzy would be too raw, the night too fraught.

"I wish I could go to her sister's wedding with her."

"Text her."

"Just text her and say, *If you need a plus-one, I'll still go?*"

"Yes."

Kia picked up Lillian's almost-dead phone.

Lillian stared at it until Kia's body language said she was going to text Izzy for her. So Lillian texted.

Lillian: *No pressure but if you don't want to go to the wedding alone, I'll still go with you.*

It didn't seem like enough.

Kia looked over. "Just send it."

chapter 46

With the phone call to Bella out of the way, Izzy lay down on the stage and stared at the ceiling. Why had she bought the theater? Why did she have to be a so-called community leader? Why couldn't she have stuck with amateur burlesque? Then she'd never have gone on *The Great American Talent Show*. She wouldn't have met Lillian. And she wouldn't be so miserable.

To make the whole thing so much worse, Lillian had looked devastated. In a few weeks, Lillian would realize Izzy was right. Izzy wasn't worth Lillian giving up her career. Lillian was a shooting star, and no matter how much Lillian *thought*, in the moment, she wanted to be with Izzy, she wouldn't stay. And Izzy couldn't ask that of her. But Lillian didn't know that yet, and the thought that she'd hurt Lillian. So. Much . . . She couldn't bear it.

Izzy had held her tears in. Now she wept.

Izzy didn't know how long she'd lain on the stage when she heard the theater door rattle. Then voices. Laughter. Someone was singing.

"Let's get a ton of work done." That was Axel's voice.

Izzy staggered to her feet.

A crowd of Velveteen Crush members poured into the theater, led by Sarah, Tock, Axel, and Arabella.

Someone said, "Dang it, she's here. We can't surprise her."

One of the new performers, a title insurance agent who'd said burlesque was the first time she'd had excitement in her life, waved up at her.

"Work party." The woman spread her arms to encompass the crowd. "We were going to surprise you with how much we got done." Her voice trailed off as she took in Izzy's face.

They were all wearing tool belts. Axel and a trio of men Izzy didn't recognize, each holding a clipboard, looked ready to organize everyone.

"Wait," Izzy said.

She couldn't let them spend all day working on the theater only for her to tell them it was going into foreclosure. She'd wanted to tell them in an email, not like this, with Lillian's departure burning a hole in her heart. But there was nothing for it.

"I'm so glad you're here." She wiped her eyes. "Your dedication…" Everyone was staring at her, waiting for the speech. She searched for the words. "Go home." It came out flat and harsh.

No one moved. They were waiting for the punch line. For Blue to turn that rejection into a rally cry.

"The theater is in foreclosure. I'm sorry. It's over." She stood alone on the stage. This was her starring role, and she'd forgotten her lines. Everyone stared. No one could save her.

She closed her eyes. The sound of feet on the stage steps pounded in her ears.

"Go." She didn't need their pity.

Then Sarah's arms were around her. Then Axel and Tock wrapped them in a group hug. Even Arabella patted her on the back.

"Can you tell them to go?" Izzy mumbled into Sarah's sweater.

Behind them someone said, "This is our community space."

"Where are we going to stage our art exhibits?"

"And hold the queer youth group?"

Izzy pulled away from her friends and turned to the crowd.

"Be your own heroes."

Through the blur of tears she saw the crowd staring up at her.

"How much do you owe?" someone called out.

Someone said, "We'll do a fundraiser."

"We believe in you, Blue."

The crowd echoed with *heck yeah* and *always*.

"It's not Blue. It's Izzy. Izzy Wells from shit-up-a-creek Oregon. Except there's no creek. It's just desert and…" Why was she talking about the topography of Broken Bush? "And I failed."

"You know what Axel always says," Arabella said. "Failure is the cross street of opportunity and proper nutrition."

"I do not say that," Axel protested.

Suddenly Izzy was surrounded. Everyone was onstage, like a laying on of hands at a revival. Finally they released her and she sat down on an overturned crate.

"Do you want to talk about it?" Sarah asked. "You don't have to."

But she wanted to. Her troupe sat around her on the moldy stage and listened. She told them about the mortgage and the double mortgage and the problems the building inspector missed and how she knew that winning *The Great American Talent Show* was too long a long shot, but she didn't know what else to do. And when she was done, everyone started talking at once.

Tock pulled out his phone. "I'm calling consumer protection. Then we're getting you a real estate lawyer."

One of the men with clipboards was a contractor. Another woman worked in corporate fundraising. An older man was part of the historical society. Arabella offered to hack the bank, which Izzy refused as quickly as she could.

"You don't have to do this alone." Sarah sat by her side, patting her back.

"And we're still doing the work party," one of the stage kittens said, waving a paint brush like a wand, "because we're not losing the theater."

The crowd agreed with a cheer.

"Come on," Sarah said. "Let's go backstage. Someone brought a case of Montucky Cold Snack and a pizza. You look like you could use both of those."

Izzy felt like the footage you saw of disaster victims after they'd been rescued. Sarah sat her on an old couch and actually put a blanket around her, then sat beside her. Axel sat on her other side, holding a plate with pizza for her. Actually holding the plate like she might be too weak to hold it herself. Arabella and Tock pulled up some old crates and settled at her feet.

"We know Lillian left," Axel said. "I mean, we don't *know* know."

"But we know you," Sarah said. "It's not just the theater, is it?"

"I'm so sorry," Axel said. "We'll find her, and we'll tell her she left the most amazing woman in the world and she's a total fool."

"I'm sorry you had to go through that and the theater stuff too," Tock added. "But there is a legal remedy to this."

"There is no legal remedy to a broken heart," Axel said.

Arabella nodded approvingly. "That one works."

Izzy tried to swallow a bite of pizza, but her mouth had gone dry. She took a sip of beer and choked it down.

"She didn't leave. I told her to go."

Now that she'd started talking, the whole story poured out.

"She'd never stay," Izzy finally finished miserably. "And I know it's true, but she doesn't know it." Izzy dropped her head.

"I hurt her *so* much. That's the worst part. But I don't want her to give up something that she's worked her whole life for. I saw her dance. Not for the show but really dance. It was like physics changed because she asked it to. It was like she made the world whole because she'd worked so hard to make something exquisite. I don't know. She was…is…the most beautiful…woman, person, being. And she was upset about losing on the show and worried about her dancers, that's the only reason she wanted to stay."

"It's really important to honor *your* feelings," Sarah said, "but you can't go in other people's minds. Their feelings belong to them."

"You have to listen to their words and their actions," Axel said. "What did she say? How did she treat you?"

That she wanted to be together.

Like she loved me.

Izzy put her face in her hands.

"She's in this documentary by Ashlyn Stewart. *The* Ashlyn Stewart. And she didn't want to do it because she felt like she had to say all this stuff about how great ballet is and not talk about how she could never be her full self, how hard it was, what she gave up. She felt like she had to just act happy about it. Now the documentary is premiering at this film festival. And I can't be there with her."

"Why not?" Sarah asked.

"It's not fair to send her mixed messages. *I can't be with you. I want to be with you.*"

"Would it be a mixed message if you said you cared about her?" Sarah asked, sounding dreadfully logical.

"I couldn't see her and not beg her to take me back. She's probably moving on already. She was always clear: No second nights. No cuddling in the morning. No relationships."

"How well did she hold to that?" Axel asked.

"Not at all." Izzy gave a watery laugh. "We don't take our own advice."

"Do you want to be with her at the premiere?" Sarah asked.

"Of course I do. But the premiere is tonight." Izzy glanced at her phone. "Near LA. I could never make it."

"Why don't you text her and ask her if there's anything you can do to support her?" Sarah asked.

"Or call," Axel added. "Be the listening ear on her shoulder."

"No, Ax," Arabella said. "The visual's too weird on that one."

Izzy took her phone out of her pocket carefully. What if she had an out-of-body experience and wrote everything she felt and thought, and begged Lillian to come back because she was so desperately in love? She opened her texts.

"Oh."

"What is it?" Tock asked.

"She texted that she'd still go to the wedding with me if I needed her."

Arabella scooted her overturned crate closer and took Izzy's hands, which obviously meant Izzy was dying. Arabella never took people's hands, never looked at them with the look of concern and affection Izzy saw there now.

"Blue." Arabella corrected herself. "Izzy, they love you—" She gestured toward Sarah, Axel, and Tock. "But they're going to talk this to death. Axel's going to say that the hawk shouldn't land on the dove, and it's going to take us an hour to figure out what that means. You only have six hours. So I'm gonna lay it out. Izzy, I love you, and you massively fucked up."

"Ari!" Axel said. "Babe, no."

Ari? Izzy stepped out of the pit of despair for a second. Were Axel and Arabella...? The strangest couple ever?

"Don't worry about it," Arabella said, glaring at Izzy. "We're talking about you right now. You and Lillian like each other, love each other. You messed up. People do. It's not the end of the world. You just have to get to the premiere and make it right."

"Is there any way I could make it on time?"

"I know people," Arabella said. "I'll get you a flight."

Izzy was scared of the people Arabella knew. But losing Lillian was scarier.

"Do I still text her?" Izzy sniffed.

Arabella rolled her eyes. "Damn. You do need to read Sarah's books. Yes, you still text her. Text her from the car. We'll drive you to the airport."

Soon, Izzy was wedged in the last row of a perfectly normal-seeming—although it had probably been purchased on the dark web—Delta flight to LAX. When the captain authorized Wi-Fi use, Izzy checked her phone to see if Lillian had responded. She hadn't. Izzy took a deep breath. Even if Lillian realized she didn't want to be together, she wouldn't ignore Izzy. She wasn't cruel like that. Lillian was just getting ready for the premiere, staying focused. Maybe she'd left her phone in the car so it wouldn't go off during the film.

Or maybe...Izzy began rereading the single-spaced paragraph—more like an essay—of unpunctuated text she'd written while Arabella broke as many traffic laws as possible on the way to the airport. Maybe Lillian was still trying to figure out what Izzy had meant. What exactly had Izzy typed that autocorrect had interpreted as *your are the most postage Evenfall I messed up.* And, perhaps the worst declaration of love ever, *I've want more then just* and then a GIF of a cat vomiting Froot Loops. And then a long explanation of how she'd meant to select a dog-in-sunglasses meme, but she'd touched the wrong one.

And she desperately wanted Lillian to know that's what happened after they were voted off. She'd been overwhelmed and rushing, and she'd made the wrong choice, but she'd never meant to hurt Lillian, and if Lillian believed they had a chance, Izzy would take it a hundred times over. Or, as her phone understood it, Izzy would *say yes a herded tines.*

chapter 47

The Summit Film Festival filled the Oscar Micheaux Conference Center in Hidden Hills, California. Lillian had downloaded the program, but she was only going to one premiere. She was going because Eleanor loved her, because Eleanor hadn't left her alone in a trailer in the middle of nowhere, because Eleanor had given up time and money and peace of mind to fight for Lillian so she could have the career she wanted. This documentary was Eleanor Jackson's legacy, and Lillian owed it to her to be there and to thank Ashlyn Stewart for dedicating herself to telling this story. To thank them both for changing the world. And if Lillian felt like she'd sacrificed too much, that was on her.

Blessedly, Kia had grabbed their seats in the back.

"How you doing?" she asked.

"This place is packed." The room must have held two hundred people.

"Ashlyn Stewart is a star."

The whole festival was epic. Famous directors and actors flitting from one showing to another. Hundreds of fans, reviewers, tech crews. Social media feeds glowing with praise and cutting with criticism. Kia said the organizers had briefly suggested Lillian and Eleanor perform a short dance after the screening, but Uncle Carl sailed with one of the organizers, and he'd shot the idea down hard.

The lights dimmed. Stewart documented the early history of Black ballet beautifully, but the sequences dragged on for Lillian. She wanted it to speed up, skip the second half, and be over. Her stomach tightened as the chronology of the film got closer to her own story. About an hour in, Ashlyn had included a clip of Lillian that she had never seen of herself. She was probably six, dancing across a lawn, laughing and spinning out of control. She'd watched hours of her own performance videos to look for flaws. She'd never gone back and looked at the joy.

Over the footage of her dance, someone read the courtroom testimony.

"Do you concur that Lillian Jackson is notably superior to other students at the school?"

"The school maintains a traditional ballet image."

"Is she better than other students at the school? Please answer the question."

"Quality is a matter of judgment."

"You said you were qualified to judge. Is she superior to other students at the school?"

A pause.

"Please answer the question."

Lillian remembered that day. She could feel her high-collared dress pressing against her throat. She could stand in first position for hours, but sitting in the courtroom made every bone in her body ache.

The film cut to Eleanor sitting in the same room where Ashlyn had interviewed Lillian.

"Lillian was a prodigy," Eleanor said. "She deserved a world that recognized her talent."

"Are you glad you brought the lawsuit?" Ashlyn asked from off camera.

Eleanor nodded gracefully. "The case changed the way schools and companies cast dancers of color."

"Were you glad you brought the lawsuit?" Ashlyn asked again.

"Professional dancers sacrifice a lot." Eleanor turned toward a window. "I thought that fighting the institution was how to love her. But there must have been a moment when a good mother would have said, *You don't have to do this.* I don't know when that moment was. I know I missed it."

"Have you told her this?" Ashlyn asked.

"She's so talented. And I'm so proud. I don't want to take anything away from her success. Lillian sacrificed everything. I don't want her to question that."

"Do you think she questions it?"

"I don't know."

"Do you think she's happy?" Ashlyn asked.

"That's all I ever wanted for her."

"Do you think she is?"

For a moment, it seemed like Eleanor couldn't speak. Then she stilled her body with a breath.

"No."

And just as Izzy had fled from the greenroom, Lillian stood up and half walked, half ran out of the theater. The bustle of the hallway startled her. So many people. Tears blurred her eyes. Was it relief? Happiness? Rage? Lillian didn't have to be an icon. Her mother saw what Lillian had given up, and she cared, and she wanted Lillian to be happy. And the betrayal of it all! All these years. *Relaxation is failure. Rest is the land of mediocrity. Never be distracted.* Lillian had believed Eleanor. And she'd missed her chance with Izzy. But Izzy hadn't given her a chance. How could Izzy have seen her so clearly and not seen that all of this was new to her? Liking a woman. Loving a woman. Having fun. Wanting more. Of course she wouldn't get it perfect the first time. Obviously, because when it counted she hadn't said the right things, or she'd said them at the wrong time or in the wrong way. And she'd reminded Izzy of every woman who'd hurt her. And shame on those women because Izzy was amazing, and they should have appreciated her. And just a little bit *shame on Izzy* for not seeing that Lillian was different.

Lillian rushed past a celebrity-spotting tour group. She half heard the tour guide say, "And wait, hold on! That's Lillian Jackson from *The Great American Talent Show.*"

After everything she'd given up for ballet and the fact that Stewart's documentary was playing right now, some fame chaser spotted her because *The Great American Talent Show* had released its preshow social media feed.

She walked faster.

A man with a reporter badge (which he might have printed at home like Kia) stepped in her way. The tour guide had caught up. Their attention drew some curious spectators.

"Can we get a picture?" one of the reporters said. "Over there, in front of the Summit banner. Just one shot."

One photo. That'd be easier than being hounded. If Izzy were here in her Blue Lenox persona, she'd sign some breasts.

"Get her with her sapphic sweetheart," one of the reporters said.

"The gays are going crazy for them."

Lillian backed up against the Summit banner.

She'd avoided the social media feed. She couldn't look at the pictures of Izzy. If she did, she'd never stop looking, studying every detail and remembering how Izzy stood, how she laughed, how she winked, and how she bowed her head when she felt shy.

"There is no sapphic sweetheart." No one was listening to her.

"Great, right there." One of the reporters turned her shoulder slightly, then looked away. "There she is. Over here." That's how fast their attention turned elsewhere. Before Lillian knew it, America would forget this year's *Great American Talent Show*. She would be the only one watching and rewatching the footage on YouTube.

Then before Lillian could blink away enough tears to see who the new source of interest was, someone had shoved someone else into the frame beside her. Someone had shoved...Izzy? She was dreaming. This wasn't real. Izzy wore a tuxedo over a bejeweled corset. She looked as shocked as Lillian felt.

"What?"

Izzy stumbled over a cord on the floor. Lillian caught her as easily as if they were waltzing, one hand on Izzy's waist, the other on her arm.

"I'm sorry," Izzy gasped.

She didn't mean bumping into Lillian, and Lillian could tell by the way Izzy stood that Izzy thought she should back away, and she didn't want to, so Lillian put her arm around Izzy's waist and turned them to the cameras. How was Izzy here? Could there be any explanation besides Izzy had come for her?

They stood for a few pictures, dazed. The reporters seemed satisfied. The Summit Film Festival was a banquet of celebrities. Two reality TV stars warranted only a moment.

"Can we go somewhere quiet?" Izzy asked, her face pleading.

Lillian's bedroom was quiet. She shouldn't jump to that conclusion. Izzy could still be here by coincidence or to discuss the logistics of…but no. There could be only one reason she was here, right? If Lillian was wrong, she'd never recover.

"Let's go outside."

They didn't speak as they navigated the crowd, eventually emerging on a balcony set with bistro tables overlooking the city. They made their way to the corner, as far away from the minglers as possible.

When they stopped, Izzy blurted, "I want to be with you," as though they might be pulled apart at any moment. She reached out to clasp Lillian's hands, then stopped herself and twisted her own hands in front of her.

Then she opened her arms and Lillian stepped into her embrace.

"Did you get my text?" Izzy asked.

"I let my battery die."

"I said…well, I said a lot of things. And I think autocorrect changed them all, so it probably doesn't make sense, but what I meant to say was you are so worth it." Izzy spoke quietly, but her words poured out as though she had only seconds to say everything. "That's what I should have said when we got voted off. If you only have a day to spend with me or a week or a month…if we're together and you leave, I'll die, but it'll be worth it, Lillian. If you want a second-night stand, I'm yours. And it's okay if ballet is your first priority. I can be your second or your third."

"I don't want you to be my second—"

"Sarah says I shouldn't have tried to make your decisions for you."

Lillian sank into Izzy's embrace.

"It wasn't fair to think I knew what you wanted better than you do. And Axel said I should pay attention to what you did and what you said. And everything you did was kind, and you've been honest with me from the beginning. And then Arabella just kind of pushed them aside and was, like, *Look, Izzy, you fucked up.*"

Kia was right. Lillian didn't know how to do relationships. This was the part where she should cross her arms and spit her words at Izzy. But she'd fallen into Izzy's arms, and Izzy was cradling her, and Lillian felt too fragile to pull away. And, yes, Izzy had hurt her. And Izzy's voice was teary because she was hurting too. And there was a script for this; Lillian was supposed to make Izzy suffer for a while even though there was no world in which Lillian didn't take her back. But Izzy was stroking her hair, and Lillian loved her. So simple. So real. She just couldn't muster up all the angry things she probably should say.

"If we're going to be together, Izzy, you can't run away. I was trying to tell you how I felt."

Izzy held her tighter.

"I know."

In that moment, no one could have comforted her except Izzy, even though beautiful, tender, mischievous, outrageous, wounded Izzy Wells was the cause of all her swirling emotions. Or maybe Izzy wasn't the cause of *all* of them. Lillian needed to tell Izzy about the documentary, about Eleanor saying she wanted her to be happy after all those years of *rest is failure*. How did Lillian understand her life without Eleanor's legacy looming over her? Did she want to keep dancing? Did she love it? Hate it? Love it and want out?

She needed Izzy to make love to her gently and then hold her while she poured out the whole confusing story. Because she knew one thing: she wanted Izzy Wells.

"I thought you saw me," Lillian said. She could feel Izzy's heart beating against her.

"I did. I do. I want to, and I want you to tell me when I don't."

"I don't want a second-night stand. And I don't want you to say you'll be my third choice. I want you to be my first. I want you to fight for that."

"I will."

They rested there for a moment, Izzy stroking her back, Lillian listening to Izzy's heartbeat as it slowly matched her own.

"Did you see the documentary yet?" Izzy asked quietly.

"Most of it."

"Was it...okay?"

"My mom said she wanted me to be happy." Lillian pulled back so she could look at Izzy, as though Izzy might make sense of it.

"She adores you."

"She thinks she pushed me too hard. Maybe."

"You talked?"

"She said it in the documentary." She leaned her forehead against Izzy's shoulder.

"How did you feel about it?"

"I don't know." *I don't know. I don't know.* "I love her. I'm mad at her for not saying it sooner, not saying it to *me.* I get how much she did for me, and I'm so grateful, and I don't know what I want next." She felt Izzy stiffen. "The only thing I know is that I want to be with you. I love you, Izzy. In case you didn't get that."

"I love you." Izzy placed her lips on Lillian's as gently as if she were kissing an orchid petal.

Izzy kissed her again, and the balcony disappeared, along with the film festival. There were just stars and sky and sun and her and Izzy...until she heard someone say, "It's the sapphic sweethearts from that show."

Their kiss turned into a laugh, their smiles mingling.

"Sapphic sweethearts. How did that even happen?" Izzy asked.

"The joys of reality TV," Lillian said, her arms still looped around Izzy's back. "Or maybe just because...we are?"

"For real?" Izzy sounded tremulous.

Lillian wanted to squeeze her and never let go.

"Yes. And now all I want to do is go home, but I think I should go to the reception, thank Ashlyn Stewart, at least tell my mom we're heading out. Am I doing it again? Not taking my good advice and saying no to what I don't want?"

"I took our advice. I'm not going to the wedding," Izzy said. "I told Bella. But it was really nice of you to say you'd go. It was more than nice."

"I knew it'd be hard for you."

"She said my mother did it all for me, to get me back in their lives." Izzy sounded incredulous. "Bella doesn't even want a big wedding. She wants to get married on the beach. She wasn't going to invite me. That was Megan's idea. It wasn't that Bella didn't want me there. Bella just thought it'd be weird if she asked me out of the blue." Izzy leaned against her. "It doesn't make sense. I don't know what to think."

"Makes two of us." Lillian breathed in Izzy's perfume. "Families." She sighed. "Should I go to the reception?"

"What's easiest?"

"Go for a minute. With you."

"Then let's do that."

Izzy rested her hand on Lillian's lower back as they stepped into the reception hall. There was some Blue Lenox in the strong, protective touch. Eleanor spotted Lillian as soon as they came in.

"I should go talk to her," Lillian said.

"I'll wait here." Izzy stopped at a bistro table. "Unless you want me to go with you."

"I should talk to her myself."

Eleanor met her halfway across the room, looked at her, pulled her into a hug, and then held her shoulders and studied her. An image emerged from the fog of childhood memory: Eleanor kneeling in front of her and asking her what was wrong as the other dance moms collected their giggling children and headed out. Lillian couldn't remember what had upset her, just that even at three or four, she'd run to the bathroom to cry. When she came back, no one could tell. Maybe her dark complexion hid the flush of tears; maybe she was simply composed. Only Eleanor could tell she'd been crying.

Now Eleanor said, "I didn't know the documentary would upset you. You know I worry about whether you're happy, right?"

"No."

Eleanor looked so stricken, Lillian almost wished she could take the word back, but Eleanor had to know.

"What happened to *rest is failure*? *Distraction is failure*? Isn't happiness the path to mediocrity?"

Izzy was yards away, but Lillian could still feel her presence: the ultimate distraction.

"I was your coach," Eleanor said. "You were the best. I had to push you." Were those tears welling in Eleanor's eyes? Eleanor had never cried. She had exited the womb stoic. She pulled Lillian into another hug. "And I was wrong. Happiness isn't failure. Ever."

When they stepped apart, Lillian saw Eleanor's tears recede, her back straighten, her neck arch like a swan's, and Lillian knew she was doing the same thing. She was certain Eleanor saw it too. And they both laughed. They would always be who they were. But things would change too.

"We should talk more," Eleanor said. "I should have always talked to you more."

Lillian nodded. Eleanor looked over her shoulder.

"I like her," Eleanor said. "I'm glad she came."

Maybe later Lillian would tell Eleanor the whole story.

Lillian returned to Izzy. They circled the room, saying goodbye to her father, to Ashlyn Stewart and her wife, and to Kia, who grinned shamelessly.

"I knew you'd come through, Blue. See, lil' puffin? Didn't I tell you she'd make it right?"

Lillian drove Izzy back to her house with a stop at Walgreens because Izzy had arrived without a toothbrush, cell phone charger, or extra underwear. Back at Lillian's, they ordered food and sat on the sofa, the lights of LA spread out beneath them. Part of Lillian wanted to go straight to the bedroom, to burn off the stress and sadness and confusion of the day with fast, hard sex. But more than that, she wanted to share all her swirling thoughts with Izzy, and she wanted to hear how Izzy turned Bella down and how Izzy felt. They talked and talked, their fingers interlaced, pausing to kiss occasionally. Sometimes the kiss was lustful. Sometimes comforting.

They'd dissected the past days and hypothesized about every aspect of their families. Lillian described every emotion she might be having about Eleanor and her career, then rested her head on Izzy's shoulder.

"Is it weird to feel so many things at once?" Lillian asked.

"I think it's human."

"The offer still stands if you want to go to Bella's wedding," Lillian said.

Izzy slid down so she was lying on the sofa, her head in Lillian's lap, her body curled in a little C. Lillian put an arm around Izzy's hip and stroked her temple.

"I thought about it. I do want them in my life, but not with a big show. Bella deserves to have her wedding be about *her*. I'll visit her and Ace once everything's settled down." Izzy sighed happily under Lillian's touch. "And I'll call Megan." She didn't sound upset, although she stayed curled up like a child. "If Bella's right and she planned that whole thing for me, I'm touched. It was sweet. I think. In a messed-up way. She was always like that. Go big. I've blown her off since she left Broken Bush. I want to talk to her again but on my terms."

"No wedding dresses unless they're burlesque?"

"Exactly."

Then Izzy said Tock had an idea for moving the theater from her ownership to a co-op model where the whole troupe owned a share.

"He said he loves me, and he wants to show that the way he does best. Solving my legal problems."

Lillian leaned over and hugged Izzy, as grateful as though she herself had been released from the burden of a decrepit theater. Actually, more grateful.

"And I want to back off from Velveteen Crush for a while. Not be Blue Lenox until everyone remembers that *I'm not* Blue Lenox. If the troupe owns the co-op, then it's really their space. And maybe I'll do a different stage persona."

They brainstormed ideas, moving from serious to ridiculous, then inventing burlesque personas for Eleanor, Kia, and Bryant. Then they moved on to funny moments from the show and marveled at Kia's ability to go anywhere she wanted with a counterfeit badge. They talked until the sky began to lighten. Their voices trailed off. Izzy stretched out on the sofa, and Lillian lay in her arms.

"Maybe we should get to bed?" Izzy asked.

They fell asleep instantly, but Lillian woke, late, to Izzy's soft caress on her thigh.

"Give me a moment." Lillian ruffled Izzy's hair, then hurried to the bathroom to brush her teeth and sip a glass of water. When she returned, Izzy was lying naked on the sheets, the covers pulled back.

chapter 48

Izzy pinned Lillian's hands above her head.

"Is this okay?"

It was more than okay.

"I want to do everything for you."

Lillian was exquisitely aware of the pulse between her legs as Izzy kissed down her neck, at the hollow of her throat, then released her hands and lingered a long time on her breasts.

"Like this?" Izzy sucked gently. "Or like this?" She pinched Lillian's nipple with her lips.

"Both." Lillian arched toward her.

"I want to learn everything about you," Izzy said, her tone both sultry and friendly. She was Blue Lenox seducing Lillian, and adorable Izzy Wells making plans.

"Like this? Or harder?" Izzy asked.

Lillian couldn't stop smiling.

"A little harder."

A slight zing of pain as Izzy bit gently on her nipple made her hips buck. The sensation cascaded over her chest and between her legs.

"You wrecked me from the first time I saw you." Izzy kissed

Lillian's stomach. "So beautiful. I saw you at the bar. I couldn't stop looking at you."

Then Izzy pressed her breast against Lillian's vulva, rocking slowly up and down. Lillian gasped. It was like being touched by the most beautiful cloud. Erotic and achingly insufficient.

"I loved how you were sexy in a Comic-Con sweatshirt." Lillian's words came out on separate exhales as her body tightened and relaxed and tightened as Izzy teased her with her gorgeous body.

"So you weren't disappointed that I wasn't really Blue Lenox?" Izzy rested her cheek on Lillian's belly.

The answer was important even though her tone was teasing. Lillian could tell. She moved from where Izzy had pinned her hands and stroked Izzy's hair.

"Sweetie, I never liked you because you were Blue Lenox. I liked you because you knew it was an act. You knew it was sexy and over-the-top, and you always had this little smile that said, *Are you falling for it?* That first night you said your friends called you Blue, I wanted to know your real name."

She'd wanted to comfort Izzy when the shadow passed behind her eyes as she'd given Lillian her stage name.

"Thank you," Izzy said. "I have a present for you when we're done here."

Then Izzy's lips were on her clit for one long delicious pull before she moved to Lillian's opening and teased her there until Lillian tightened her hand in Izzy's hair and let herself enjoy the luscious, undignified, utterly distracted pleasure of begging. And Izzy gave her everything she asked for and more.

When Lillian had recovered, she rolled Izzy on her back and explored her body slowly, asking her questions as she touched every inch of her until Izzy gasped, "Yes. Any of it. All of it. Just *now.*" As soon as Izzy stopped gasping, Lillian pulled Izzy into her arms, holding her tight.

"No one's ever asked me that many questions." It sounded like Izzy teared up a little as she said it, but mostly she sounded delighted. "God, that was good."

Several hours later, they were finally somewhat dressed. They sat at the kitchen table with mugs of coffee. Izzy set her phone on the table and opened an app.

"This is just a prototype." She looked down. "And it's yours. I don't want to steal your idea, but I want you to see what's possible." She didn't let go of the phone. "It's really rough. You need a professional animator for this. It's way beyond my skill set."

"What is it?"

"It's a present." Slowly, Izzy handed Lillian the phone.

The screen showed a dancer in fifth position and a drop-down menu. Lillian touched the menu to reveal a list of poses and moves. She touched *demi-plié*, and the figure performed the motion.

"The movements are really jerky," Izzy said.

A button at the bottom read *company*. It shifted the screen to a map with numbered circles and a plus sign, which added another circle when she touched it.

"These are the dancers." When she held one of the circles, the screen switched back to the dancer in fifth position. "It's the choreography app."

She looked up. Izzy looked proud and shy, lightly tapping the binary code tattoo on her chest in an unconscious gesture.

"It's amazing." It was. The choreographer could animate each dancer and then put them all together on the stage. "It's exactly what I was thinking of. When did you start this?"

"After we lost."

"You've only been working on it for a few days?"

Izzy shrugged, beaming with pride.

"And you started it after you left. I thought you didn't want to…be with me."

Izzy looked up. "I always wanted to be with you. I wanted to be with you since we woke up at the coast. Maybe since the first minute I saw you. I made this so I could show you how much I cared about you, and whatever you want to do with dance, we can make it work. We can make us work. I don't want you to give up what you love. I just want to be a part of it."

"I said yes to the fellowship, but I'm going to call them and tell them I don't want it."

It'd be a hard call to make. A door closing.

"Do you want to do it?"

"It'd be fun," Lillian said honestly. "It'd be a chance to inspire new dancers, and maybe do it without being as tough as my mom was. I'd do a faculty showcase, but I wouldn't have to train for a running show. I could dance without wrecking my body. Dance isn't forever. I'll age out soon, no matter what I want to do. I think I might like to teach."

"This would be a way to find out."

"I don't want to do long distance, even for six months. I'm tired of putting my heart last. I love you. I don't want to sleep alone. I don't want to text you instead of kiss you. I hope I'm not too much of a lesbian stereotype. I want a life with you. With scones."

Maybe she should clarify that they didn't have to move in together tomorrow. She didn't have a U-Haul packed and ready to go. They didn't have to go that fast. Izzy held out her hands and clasped Lillian's.

"Yes," she said emphatically. "Please be a lesbian stereotype. Ask me to go to Paris with you."

epilogue

Izzy said goodbye to her mother and hung up the phone. Lillian had discreetly stepped out onto the little fire escape balcony of their Paris apartment to give her privacy. Now Lillian climbed back in through the window, as graceful as a breeze.

"How'd it go?" Lillian sat down across the kitchen table from Izzy, pressing the power button on the Nespresso machine, nestled between a vase of flowers and a box holding silverware. The apartment was the perfect size for new lovers, and not an inch larger.

"Okay." It was the third time she'd talked to Megan since she and Lillian had squeezed as much as they could into four suitcases and boarded a flight to Charles de Gaulle Airport. "She's still apologizing."

"For the wedding thing?"

"For everything."

The first conversation had been a tearful lament on Megan's side. She was sorry she drank in her third trimester. (At least she skipped the first two, Izzy acknowledged.) She was sorry she left Izzy alone when she was too young. She hadn't left Bella alone until she was fourteen. (Poor Bella!) She should have come to Izzy's school performances. (She remembered the names of most of them, which was sweet, and also proof that Megan had known about them and chosen to be elsewhere.) She should have fed Izzy better. Was Izzy vitamin D deficient? (Everyone in Oregon was, and it had nothing to do with eating Kraft mac and cheese as a child.)

Megan even had one reason for leaving Izzy that made a bit of sense, although it certainly didn't return her to responsible-parent status. *You'd gotten into college*, Megan had said. *And you had money to go, and if you left the state, they'd take that away*. Megan understood now. That wasn't how in-state tuition worked, and Izzy wasn't going to a public university. She'd gotten a scholarship to a private college. But no one in the Wells family had even visited a college, let alone attended. *I didn't know*, Megan had said, which didn't negate the fact she should have *said* something about it and maybe called her daughter's college to find out if she'd actually lose her scholarship by moving to California for a few months. Maybe when you abandoned your teenage daughter, you ought to have left her with more than a rusty trailer in the middle of nowhere and a hundred dollars in ones and fives.

But oddly, after all the years Izzy had pined to hear *I'm sorry*, Broken Bush felt like a distant memory. Outside the sun shone. The street bustled. The smell of bread and coffee swirled up to their apartment. Through the trees, she glimpsed some glittering gold buildings. And in the other direction was the Eiffel Tower. If she and Lillian weren't out in the evening, they sat side by side on the fire escape and watched it light up at dusk.

"Do you want to talk about it?" Lillian asked.

"I don't mind talking about it, but I feel fine." There was so much else to do in Paris.

Four months into their stay, the thrill of Paris had not worn off. Lillian sparkled as an instructor. The students flourished under her strict but loving instruction. They'd be doing the summer showcase soon, the students performing alongside their instructors, each student provided the opportunity to do a short solo. Lillian could renew for another six months as a teacher if she wanted. Izzy was working and taking classes at the École de Burlesque Moderne. In between teaching and studying and programming and exploring Paris, Izzy and Lillian had been working on the app. Several tech investment companies had expressed interest in the beta version.

Izzy had sent Bella and Ace money for a honeymoon in France with the caveat that they were not staying in Izzy and Lillian's minuscule apartment. That was too much closeness too soon. In the background of the FaceTime call, Ace had popped into the screen and said something about Izzy not wanting to hear her sister. Bella slapped them playfully. Izzy laughed, and it felt like chatting with friends. And Izzy had been talking to Megan, taking the first tentative steps toward a relationship.

Back in Portland, Sarah, Axel, Arabella, Tock, and twenty-two other members of Velveteen Crush were in the process of buying the theater, guided by Tock's legal expertise. They'd invited Izzy to buy in, but she had declined. To Izzy's dismay, a unanimous vote by the company had renamed the venue Theater Blue.

Imani was starting work as dance master for a Hiplet company. Malik was working with one of the Prime Minister's fashion lines, designing inclusive shapewear. Pascale's social media feed overflowed with pictures of her children. Elijah's suggested he was dating. Jonathan had an audition with the Dance Theater of Harlem. As expected, Effectz won *The Great American Talent Show*.

Imani and the other former Reed-Whitmer dancers were planning a reunion party at the Mimosa Resort in the fall. Sarah, Arabella, Axel, and Tock were coming. And Imani had sternly admonished Lillian, *If you say you can't make it, we will come get you and Izzy and drag you there.* After the call, Lillian stared at her phone with a look of happy confusion. *Do they really want me there?* Izzy had wrapped her arms around Lillian. *Yes, they do. Y'all were a team. You care about each other. They know how hard you worked for them, and they like you. Only* you *think you shouldn't be invited to the party.* Pascale, Elijah, Malik, and Jonathan backed Izzy up with a week's worth of texts threatening Lillian with everything from an embassy intervention to a search and rescue team if she didn't send proof that she'd bought flights for her and Izzy.

Everything was wide open, all the possibilities laid out like a banquet. Truth: except for frolicking at the Mimosa Resort, Izzy and Lillian had no idea what they were going to do. In the evening, as they waited for the Eiffel Tower to light up, they tried to figure it out. They loved Paris. They missed home. Lillian loved teaching. Izzy could try to make burlesque her full-time job, or she could throw herself into designing the app. Or maybe they wanted to move into Izzy's house in Portland. It hadn't been too hard to pay off the second mortgage now that she wasn't trying to salvage the theater. They could grow an herb garden and get a dog. Then the Eiffel Tower would light up. The sounds of the city would soften. And it didn't matter if they had a perfect plan. They had each other.

Izzy pocketed her phone, the conversation with Megan rapidly fading from her thoughts. Lillian was here, holding space for her to say more. Welcoming any side of Izzy she wanted to share. Welcoming her tears or a rant or a memory. But today, Izzy wanted to talk about the list of sights they wanted to see.

"Sacré-Cœur de Montmartre?" she asked. "Or the catacombs?"

"Quite some variety there." Lillian put a demitasse under the Nespresso maker and pulled a cup of coffee and then another. She passed one to Izzy.

"You wanted to see some of the Degas ballerinas and that museum of modern furniture." Izzy clinked her demitasse against Lillian's and smiled. "Because we came to Paris to see chairs."

"I do want to see modern furniture," Lillian said. Love and desire twinkled in Lillian's eyes. "But first." She held out her hand. "I worked all week, and it's been too long."

Izzy's body woke immediately. She let Lillian lead her to the bed. They closed the filmy curtains, but they left the windows open. It was a sweet, almost-impossible challenge to be quiet as Lillian worshiped every inch of her body, occasionally whispering, "Shhh."

"How—" Izzy held back a cry of pleasure. "Can you expect me to—"

Lillian held Izzy's legs apart and kissed her.

"I don't," Lillian said, drawing another stifled cry from Izzy's lips as pleasure washed over her in waves.

Izzy returned the favor. Then they dozed, the sounds of the city singing through the window. Lillian was already awake and scanning her phone when Izzy woke up.

"Whatcha looking at?"

Lillian cocked her head pensively.

"The modern furniture museum. You can buy their stuff. Whenever we go back home, I think I'll get these. What do you think?" She held out the phone. "One for you. One for me."

The browser showed a picture of two very small dressers in elegant shades of gray and midcentury-modern orange. You couldn't get much in them.

"Sure." If Lillian wanted to replace all their furniture with beanbag chairs, Izzy didn't mind. Izzy moved closer so her head rested on Lillian's chest. "But what are they for?"

Lillian gave her a little shake even as she pulled Izzy closer.

"They're nightstands. Obviously." Lillian kissed the top of Izzy's head. "A first nightstand and a second nightstand. A set. To go together always."

acknowledgments

Fay and I remember where we were when we decided to write together. We were at a coffee shop, sitting by the window. I was struggling with some plot point, and she was helping me brainstorm. If you look back at my work, many of the best ideas came from her.

Fay said, "We've always wanted to write a book. What if we work on this together?"

For years we wanted to write a book on healthy relationships. When *Second Night Stand* is published, we will have been together twenty-five years. We think we have a marvelous relationship and wanted to share the secrets with the world. Friends have said things like, "I would've given up on love if it weren't for seeing you two together" and "We try to treat each other like you do." A few have rolled their eyes. "There's Fay and Karelia being all cute on Instagram. Again." But we couldn't write a self-help book. We have no platform. We're not therapists. We're just a nice couple who doesn't fight, especially about stupid things like did we go to Vancouver, BC, in 2009 or 2010 and can bears open car doors. (Dude, just google it.) You know that couple, don't you?

But we realized we could share our vision of a happy relationship through romance. We could write characters who talked to each other, who said *I love you*, who were kind even when things weren't going well. We could show people how sexy it is to communicate during sex. We could also provide a happy ending for an interracial lesbian couple—a demographic that hasn't historically gotten the happy ending, a demographic that, along with other people of color and others in the LGBTQ+ community, faces discrimination.

We often praise ourselves (behind closed doors where we're not too obnoxious). Gosh, our yard looks beautiful. What a brilliant placement of the sofa. Aren't we great at planning a road trip. And, most importantly, don't we have a fabulous marriage. We joke that you have to praise yourself because you can't count on people to do it for you. In the case of the couch, I'm pretty sure that's one hundred percent true.

So we start our acknowledgments with praise and appreciation for each other. Fay is incredibly creative. She can produce a hundred ideas an hour. If we're stuck, she sees a hundred ways forward. And she's attuned to the subtleties of human experience and dedicated to clarity of language. And she's just plain fun to work with. I love you, honey!

From Fay: Karelia, I want to thank you for saying yes and sharing this life with me. Thanks, for your daring and sharing. You are so organized and disciplined. Thanks for tolerating my wild and unorthodox note-taking. Your creative energy is contagious and I am hooked. Oh, the laughs we've shared. I absolutely love our collaboration. You are so much fun. You are my heart, my everything.

Next I want to thank my readers, who I hope will become *our* readers the second this book is published. It goes without saying that we couldn't do this without you, dear reader. We wouldn't want to. Sometimes people will write to share how much one of my books spoke to them—how a book helped them come into their true self, learn about sex, or spark more romance in their relationship—and they'll add something like *I know you probably get tons of messages like this. You're probably sick of it.* I promise, if I write for another hundred years, I will never be sick of hearing from readers. You honor me with your praise and the stories you share with me. Please join me and Fay as we share our story with you. And extra special love to Jennifer @dejeneratereads. Can't wait for our next Disney day!

We wouldn't be able to reach our readers without the podcasters, reviewers, and influencers who help the world find its next favorite read. I hesitate to start naming people for fear of leaving someone out because you are all so awesome!!! But here are just a few. Know that all y'all are in my heart and in my DMs! Thank you @flippin_and_sippin_mn, @reesesbookclub, @booksnblazers, @themisscongeniality, @mackinstyle, @amitymalcomwrites, @sapphic_book_club, @book.ishjulie, @LGBTQreads, and so, so, so many more. Also a shout-out to new book ambassador, creator of the mobile bookstore @thesecondhandlibrarian.

Thank you to Sarah Wendell and everyone at Smart Bitches, Trashy Books; the Lesbian Review; Liz Donatelli from Reader Seeks Romance; the Bad Bitch Book Club; Cara Tanamachi and PJ Benoit at Skip to the Good Part.

Thank you to Mel Saavedra, CEO and founder of Steamy Lit, the Steam Box, and the AMAZING Steamy Lit Con. Thank you to Cookie Navarro, organizer extraordinaire! Can't wait to see you next year! And thank you to all the amazing readers and writers we met at Steamy Lit Con 2023.

Thank you to the librarians across the country who are fighting censorship and standing up for the freedom to read and learn.

Thank you to the Barnes and Nobles across the country for featuring diverse books right up front. And thank you to the hundreds of independent bookstores doing the same. A special thanks to the teams at Grass Roots Books and Music, Jan's Paperbacks, Elliott Bay Book Company, and, of course, the Camelot of bookstores, Powell's. A special shout-out to booksellers @foreverabookseller and @lyttlebyrd. We're also sending love to two places we've never been. To the Ripped Bodice, visiting your store is an absolute bucket-list item. And thank you to Betty's Books in Baker City, Oregon, for putting up a Pride display. Courage like yours changes the world.

Thank you to Starlin Moran for sharing your reality TV experiences with us. We can't wait to see you on another season of *Forged in Fire*.

Thank you to our fabulous editor, Madeleine Colavita, and the whole Forever team! Thank you to all the Forever authors. You write amazing books!

Thank you to all the authors whose books inspire, entertain, and teach us!

Thank you to our agent, Jane Dystel at Dystel, Goderich & Bourret. I've talked about you for years, and Fay is so excited to now be your client.

Thank you to Venessa Kelley for designing the gorgeous cover of *Second Night Stand*. I couldn't stop smiling when I learned you'd be the cover artist. I had your art framed in my office long before I dreamed that you would bring our characters to life.

And of course, a huge thank you to our friends! Mitzi, John,

Terrance, Ramycia, Tristan, Dio, Will, Shannon, the dynamic duo Liz and Liz, Maria, Scott, Keith, Jered, Anne and Amit, and so many more.

Thank you to Lucielle S. Ballz and King Kween and the Dam Right Drag Night team for bringing inclusive drag and burlesque to the Willamette Valley.

Thank you to everyone at the Golden Crown Literary Society, especially my students in the Writing Academy. I see you winning awards, making top-ten lists, and popping up in the *New York Times*. I'm so proud of you.

Thank you to our dear father/father-in-law Al Stetz, who loves and supports us, inspires and guides us, who has bailed us out of scrapes and been our safety net throughout the years. Thank you to Elin Stetz (1940–2022) for loving us and loving the world, a woman who never said a mean word or shared a catty thought in her life. Thank you to Fay's twin sister, Cheryl Dory Paules, for sharing the womb with Fay, supporting her through thick and thin, and showing her the courageous way.

And thank you to all the people who make our comfortable life possible. Thank you to our nice neighbors, to the people who make sure our drinking water is clean, to the trash collectors, to the lesbian police chief and the officers who work to keep our town safe, to the people who kept our country running during COVID, to the people who stock our grocery stores and grow our food and fix the power lines and pave the roads, and all the millions of others who make the world run.

about the authors

Ambassadors of real-life happily-ever-after, **Fay** and **Karelia Stetz-Waters** have been together for twenty-five years. They live in Albany, Oregon, with their pug mix Willa Cather and a garden full of dragonflies and hummingbirds. Their writing process involves many afternoons spent at local coffee shops and brewpubs outlining scenes, going over drafts, and high-fiving each other. The process works beautifully. *Second Night Stand* is their first novel together but definitely not their last.